Dirty Laundry

Dirty Laundry

A Novel

DISHA BOSE

Ballantine Books
New York

Dirty Laundry is a work of fiction. Names, characters, places, and incidents are either the products of the author's imagination or are used fictitiously. Any resemblance to actual persons, living or dead, events, or locales is entirely coincidental.

Published in the United States by Ballantine Books, an imprint of Random House, a division of Penguin Random House LLC, New York.

BALLANTINE is a registered trademark and the colophon is a trademark of Penguin Random House LLC.

LIBRARY OF CONGRESS CATALOGING-IN-PUBLICATION DATA

Names: Bose, Disha, author.
Title: Dirty laundry: a novel / Disha Bose.
Description: First edition. | New York: Ballantine Books, [2023]
Identifiers: LCCN 2022022019 (print) | LCCN 2022022020 (ebook) | ISBN
9780593497388 (hardcover; acid-free paper) | ISBN 9780593497395 (ebook)
Subjects: LCGFT: Detective and mystery fiction. | Domestic fiction. | Novels.
Classification: LCC PR6102.O86 D57 2023 (print) | LCC PR6102.O86
(ebook) | DDC 823/.92—dc23/eng/20220509
LC record available at https://lccn.loc.gov/2022022019
LC ebook record available at https://lccn.loc.gov/2022022020

Printed in the United States of America on acid-free paper

randomhousebooks.com

2 4 6 8 9 7 5 3 1

First Edition

Book design by Virginia Norey
Watercolor stains art by Claudia Balasoiu/stock.adobe.com

For Richard

Dirty Laundry

September 29

T HE HOUSE SMELLED OF PORRIDGE, DETERGENT, AND soiled nappies. A few years ago, it smelled of patchouli, filtered coffee, and Black Opium by Yves Saint Laurent.

"I hate him. I hate you, and Daddy, and Granny. And I hate him the most."

"Bella, you don't mean that." Reasoning with a four-year-old was a losing game, so Ciara tried only half-heartedly.

She had Finn, the baby, on her hip, swinging him gently. When he was even smaller and cried all the time, this was the only way she could stop him from turning purple. She preferred not holding him often and creating bad habits, but she found herself needing to hold him like a comforter against Bella.

"I do, I mean it. I hate him the most." Bella pointed at her brother's unperturbed face.

"So what do you want me to do about it?" Ciara was staring at the hillock of congealed tea bags, where they'd stained and discolored the marble countertop. It was a few days since she'd bothered using a dish to discard them or giving the counter a wipe.

"I'm going to cut off his hair."

Ciara turned to her daughter. She felt an itching desire to drag her out of the house and leave her in the front yard.

However, she couldn't be seen dragging her daughter, kicking and screaming. She was in an entirely acceptable pair of leggings and a sweatshirt—they suited her brand—but publicly reprimanding her daughter was not. Her children were not known to make scenes.

A year ago, she'd video-blogged about her six-step skin-care regimen, not expecting much, but it had gone viral. She'd turned into an overnight Instagram sensation. She promoted self-care and researched interesting ways of looking after skin health: for instance, freezing a jade roller to rub over her face to tighten the pores.

Now she had everything a woman could desire—children and skin-care expertise.

Her most recent video, posted a week ago, was different. She had given her followers a peek into her personal life. Some of her followers had applauded her for her honesty and the rawness of the video. It was imperative now, more than ever, that people in the village didn't notice anything amiss. She needed to show she was in control, even though she wasn't anymore.

It was apparent in the rips and tears in her voice when she spoke to Bella. Ciara was almost certain that her brain was physically bulging out of her skull. She couldn't allow anyone to see her like this. That could discredit what she had said in her video.

"Go on, do it, then. The scissors are right here. Cut your brother's hair. See what happens," she hissed at her daughter. Her heart thumped as she half-expected Bella to do it, just to prove a point. She saw herself in her daughter in moments like these. They looked so alike, with the same golden hair and oval faces, their chins dropping low when they smiled.

In her house today, there were toys everywhere. The kitchen sink was piled high with dishes she hadn't loaded in the machine. A laundry basket full of clothes was lying outside the utility room. If she couldn't have the house looking spotlessly clean, then she didn't want to bother cleaning it at all.

Bella's nostrils flared. The tops of her cheeks were beginning to turn a distinct shade of plum. Ciara was exhausted. They needed to leave her alone. Every last fucking one of them.

Finn remained silent. He was watching his sister with big eyes, as though he was committing this scene to memory. It was impossible to tell how much he actually absorbed at this age. He was only a year and a half; Ciara still had a few years to go before she needed to worry about what he was going to turn into. At four, Bella was already out of her hands. Of all the things Ciara wished she could have done differently, her daughter topped the list. It was the one she'd never admit to anyone.

When Bella finally conceded, spluttering and blubbering in a hot mess of tears, Ciara turned and walked to the stairs. It was time for Finn's nap. Once left alone, Bella was going to stop crying in a few minutes, and she would have learned an important lesson in life. Unlike some mothers who petted and soothed every teardrop, Ciara wasn't going to reward her daughter for acting like a bitch.

BY THE TIME Ciara returned downstairs, Bella had helped herself to the TV in the sitting room. Finn was going to nap for two hours. This would give Ciara enough time to herself, but she wasn't going to clean up.

Instead, she was feeling like a fight.

Her phone had been pinging with notifications from the local WhatsApp group, where all the local mammies congregated to form one large, busy hive mind. One of the women had brought up the subject of treating stuffy noses, and everyone had an opinion.

A nice hot bath before bed does the trick.

You should invest in a diffuser. Eucalyptus oil really opens up the airways.

Have you tried rubbing some Baby Vicks on the soles of his feet?

Do you have one of those nose-suction things?

Ciara scrolled through the responses and rolled her eyes as she tapped out of the chat. She had a feeling they were waiting for her to respond, but she wasn't going to give them her time today. She was going to ring Gerry instead.

These days, they rarely spoke on the phone. Communication took place primarily through text messages. They stuck to the point.

> Dinner?
>
> Yes
>
> Finn needs nappies
>
> Okay
>
> ———
>
> Out of eggs
>
> Okay
>
> When will you be home?
>
> I don't know

When she rang him now, Gerry answered quickly, and she heard the urgency in his voice. She nearly didn't recognize it.

"Ciara, what's wrong?"

Yes, something was wrong. When she considered it, a lot of things had gone wrong. She'd expected more from everybody, especially from him.

"What do you mean?" she asked.

"Are the kids okay?"

"Of course the kids are okay. It's my job to make sure they're okay. I wake up every morning and see to it that they're okay. Then I repeat the process the next day."

"All right, Ciara, why are you ringing me?"

"When was the last time you asked if *I* was okay?" It was something she had to say, because wasn't that how all the scripts were written?

Gerry sighed, but his voice didn't sound rushed anymore, now that he knew the kids were fine. "Is there something wrong?"

"It's been a shitshow here today. Finn's been refusing to eat. He won't even eat oranges, which, I don't know if you know, he normally devours. No clue what's going on with him. Bella has declared she hates you, me, and your mother, but she hates Finn the most. Lucky him."

"She's four years old, Ciara, she doesn't mean any of it."

"Exactly. She's four years old and she wants her ears pierced. That's what this is about. She threatened to cut off Finn's hair."

Gerry said nothing, which was just what she expected of him. She could picture him sitting at the desk in his office, which was essentially a cube made of glass. He would be leaning on his desk, on his elbows. A hand covering half his face, while he held the phone to his ear.

"And the house is a fucking mess."

"Maybe we should give Ruby more hours, so you don't have to worry about keeping the house clean."

"Her name is Rita, and no, I don't need any more help keeping the house clean." She hadn't told him that she'd been refusing to answer the door when Rita called to the house because she didn't want anyone inside or to see her like this. She was certain she'd scream if she saw Rita digging out the empty bottles of wine she'd stashed under the bed.

"I know you didn't want to talk about it the last time, but maybe we should discuss hiring a nanny."

"I'm not having someone else raise our kids." Ciara slashed a hand through the air. "Do you really want our kids to start emulating some stranger's bad habits? Picking up slang? I've heard enough horror stories about nannies bribing kids with junk food, just to shut them up."

"Then tell me what I can do. I want to find a way to help you, Ciara."

"There's nothing you can tell me that'll solve the problem. You are part of the problem." She was hopeful in the silence, trying to push him as far to the edge as she could. No matter how far she pushed him, Gerry never lunged at her, never tried to fight her off. Sometimes she wondered if she did physically attack him, would they even find her DNA under his fingernails? Any signs of self-defense? Or would he just lie there, taking her punches and blows?

"Sometimes I lie awake at night, fantasizing about being alone. Without the kids, without this house, without you." Still, silence. "But you will never know that feeling because you have never had a day like mine."

"I want to help you, Ciara. Tell me what to do." He was boring her by repeating himself.

"You've never been any help to me, so why should that change now? I don't even know why I rang."

She hung up before he could answer. It wasn't as though he had anything surprising to say. He'd stopped blowing her mind a long time ago.

She eyed the wine rack greedily. She wouldn't let them see her drinking in the day, not the kids, and certainly not Gerry. Her phone pinged with more notifications from the group.

"Ah, go fuck yourselves, wouldja?" she shouted, bringing the phone right up to her face. She wished they all heard her. She wished she could tell them to their faces how deplorable they all were, with their million insecurities about raising their children. Ciara didn't ask questions; she didn't need anyone's help. She just got on with it.

She hadn't completely abandoned the idea of pouring herself a glass of wine when the doorbell rang. It left her with no time to consider cleaning up the mess. She hoped it was only the postman.

It was Mishti, with her daughter, Maya. They were staring up at her with their big brown eyes.

"Oh!" She hadn't expected Mishti to turn up. Not since their last conversation eight days ago, when she was certain that Mishti was taking a stand against her. She experienced a thrill of victory; Mishti hadn't been able to stay away for long! They needed each other.

"It's okay, we can come back later. Or tomorrow?" Mishti apologized. She was always apologizing for something, even now, when Ciara was the one who had some explaining to do.

On any other day, she would have been embarrassed by the state of the house. She wouldn't even have let Mishti in. Today, she couldn't care less.

"No. No, come inside. I'm glad you came, we need to talk. I'm sorry about the mess—well, you'll see. But you won't judge me, will you? I know you'll understand. You know what's been going on." Anybody else would promptly go elsewhere to gossip about perfect Ciara's imperfect state of affairs. Mishti had no one else to go to.

Ciara was Mishti's only friend, and if she was being honest with herself, Mishti was her only real one too. Now their friendship was dangerously on the brink of collapse, and it was all because of Lauren.

"OF COURSE, YOU can have as many as you like, baby, but you'll have to share them with Maya." Ciara made an effort to speak sweetly to Bella. She left the tray of wheat crackers and cheese cubes on the coffee table for the girls. They were watching *Frozen,* again. Ciara hadn't resisted her daughter's new obsession so far, expecting it to die a natural death. Now it looked like she was going to have to pull the plug on it herself. But not today.

In the kitchen, Mishti was pouring water from the kettle into two large porcelain mugs.

"I haven't been keeping track of the group. Have they been discussing anything significant? Apart from runny noses and nappies?" Ciara tried to begin on a lighter note, as she walked in.

"Are you asking if they've been discussing your last video?" Mishti spoke without looking up.

"Have they mentioned it?"

"What do you mean by *it*? The bullying you brought up?"

Ciara tilted her head to one side. "It's obvious why I said what I said, Mishti. Someone needs to put a stop to Lauren. You should hear some of the stories these women have from when they were in school with her. I mean, some of the things she did were just awful. Someone needs to stand up to her."

Mishti looked away.

"If there's anything you want to say, Mishti, now is the time."

"I think *bullying* is the wrong word. What's going on between you and Lauren should have been kept private. That is all."

Ciara rarely felt threatened, by men or women, and she despised Lauren even more because it sounded like Mishti was taking her side.

"I'm using my resources to put Lauren back in her place. She's gotten away with mistreating people all her life, but I'm not going to let her do that to me."

Mishti's silence softened Ciara. She had to try a different approach.

"Things have been a little complicated around here lately, and I needed some time off my socials. Frankly, I couldn't focus on my work at all. Then I was inundated with messages and emails, just because I hadn't posted anything in a few days. I felt like I owed my followers an explanation, which was why I made that video."

Mishti held her mug close to her chest, trying to keep warm. Even though it was only September and the weather was still mild, Mishti was always cold. They'd known each other a few years, and Ciara expected Mishti to start layering up soon.

They could hear the voices of the girls in the sitting room, singing along to a song on TV. Bella sounded happy when she was around other people.

"Bella's been acting up; maybe it's because she hasn't been seeing much of Maya lately."

Mishti hadn't looked up from her mug yet. "I'm glad they're close. I'm happy Maya has a good friend. A good childhood friend to grow up with."

"Yeah, I never had one of those." She wanted Mishti to look at her, so they could really talk. "Sometimes I feel like I don't know what to do with my kids."

"You always know everything, Ciara." When Mishti finally did meet her eyes, it wasn't with empathy.

"Is that what you think? You don't see I'm just as afraid as everyone else?"

"Are you afraid, Ciara?"

"I don't know what I'm doing. With the children, with my life. That's what's got me here." She wanted Mishti to see her vulnerability, but Mishti was already looking away.

"I should go check on the girls," Mishti said.

"They're fine. They're watching a film and they have snacks. You and I need to talk," Ciara said.

Mishti walked away to the sitting room, pretending not to have heard.

Ciara had never felt more lonely in her own kitchen. When Mishti turned up at the door today, she had hoped they could move on, but this felt like a rejection all over again. Mishti had never questioned Ciara's actions before. It had to be something else. *Someone* else.

In her peripheral vision through the window, she was alerted to a scene unfolding in Lauren Doyle's garden.

Lauren's three children were chasing one another. Freya, the oldest, who was six, was making bubbles using a giant bubble wand. Harry, four, was entirely in the nude, streaking after his sister, screeching. The youngest, Willow, was a toddler, and she too was bare from the waist down. Lauren was trying to get ahold of her while waving a nappy in the air.

At first Ciara was filled with rage as she watched them. Just the sight of Lauren angered her, the very idea that Lauren could have something to do with the turn Mishti had taken against her. Soon, a smile grew on Ciara's face, as she knew things were about to explode any moment now. Lauren had managed to grab Willow, but there was no holding her down. She had little to no chance of getting that nappy on.

Ciara's spirits were lifted. She itched to record the scene and show it to Mishti. She snapped a few photographs, hazy and from a distance—shots of Lauren's unruly children, the look of exasperation on their mother's face. Proof of how scattered Lauren's life was. It would be many massive rungs down for Mishti to align herself with Lauren.

Ciara had been desperate for a reaction from Mishti, anything that would confirm they could be friends again. She couldn't be honest with anyone besides Mishti. It would be social suicide to tell anyone else around her what she had gotten herself tangled in. This demure wife of an immigrant, a woman separated from her family and the world she grew up in, was Ciara's only hope for baring her soul. It was all she had ever needed: complete and inescapable loyalty.

However, lately something had shifted between them. Mishti had never been much of a talker, but she was speaking even less now. Ciara had noticed her warming toward Lauren, and she knew the strength of female solidarity. How quickly public opinion could turn against her. Especially, how easily malleable Mishti was. If Lauren was able to present Mishti with options, would her loyalty waver? It made Ciara prickle with envy.

Outside, Lauren had managed to get the nappy on Willow, but she'd had no luck with Harry yet. Then Lauren looked up, squinting against the sun but looking directly at Ciara's kitchen. She may have sensed she was being watched, even though she couldn't see inside.

Ciara decided that she and everyone else needed a reminder of why Lauren would never win. Without budging from the window, she scrolled through photos on her phone. Photos she'd taken of her kids on better days. She found a series at the beach in Inchydoney from a few months ago. White sand sparkled like precious minerals in Bella's metallic hair. Finn was learning to walk, finding his footing in the sand. She'd taken multiple photos of that moment, hoping to capture the perfect one: in which the children were smiling, looking at the camera together, their hair disheveled by the sea breeze but their clothes perfect.

Mishti's soft nervous laughter accompanied the girls' louder high-pitched cackle from the sitting room. Ciara selected a photograph and got working. She expertly went through the motions with a rapid series of drags and taps. This was her job, whether or not anyone else looked at it that way. It earned her a serious income, most of which Gerry didn't know about.

She took care to not over-edit the photograph, referring to the

resource of hashtags she'd built in a separate document, then thinking up a quick and clever caption. She knew Lauren followed her on
Instagram, as did all the other women in the village. She was sure
Lauren was going to see it the next time she looked at her phone, in
exasperation, to steal a few moments of peace away from her unruly
children. By then, Ciara's post would already have amassed several
hundred likes and comments. They usually poured in within minutes, from all over Ireland, and lately from other parts of the world
too. The more collaborations she did with international brands, the
more global traction her profile received.

As for nipping Lauren and Mishti's camaraderie in the bud, she
was going to keep it classy. She would show Mishti the hazy photographs of Lauren's children in the garden if and when she needed to
make her point.

Ciara hoped that when Lauren came across the post of her tran-
quil and sunny children—adored even by complete strangers—it
would slice through Lauren's heart, like a carving knife through a
perfectly cooked piece of meat.

Ciara heard the front door open and was forced to put her phone
away.

"Daddy!" It was Bella's voice in the sitting room.

Gerry was very early, but Bella was already running down the
foyer to the front door. Ciara's husband was slipping off his wing-tip
brogues. Despite arriving almost too early for it to be acceptable, he
was still following protocol: removing his light autumn coat first and
hanging it neatly on the rack. Then he lifted their daughter in his
arms.

But none of that mattered anymore. He could have walked into
the kitchen with his shoes on for all she cared. Everything felt different.

It took Ciara several minutes to drag herself to the sitting room.

Mishti and Maya were huddled together on the sofa, each like the
other's protector. Each as socially awkward as the other. Ciara was
momentarily resentful of their closeness, and then she saw Bella
hanging from Gerry's neck, having apparently forgotten how much

she hated her father just an hour ago. In fact, it seemed that Bella was a lot happier around Gerry these days than she was around Ciara. It wasn't fair or grounded in logic; Gerry's contribution to the raising of their children had been decorative, at best. But now that Bella was attached to him like this, Ciara thought their daughter looked more like him. They had the same plump lower lip, the pinkness smudged in the corners, like crayons gone awry. The same wide forehead, protruding slightly in the middle like they'd bumped their heads on a doorframe recently.

He was nattering on about the weather to Mishti, who, like Bella, was much more responsive with him than she'd been with Ciara. This was unhelpful, since they still had some ironing out to do. Things needed to be squared away soon.

Historically, Mishti had always been on her side. As much as the other women in the village wished it were them, Mishti was the one Ciara trusted. The only one she could rely on to keep her secrets. The only one who wouldn't immediately start a secret group chat to gossip about Ciara's fall from perfection. Once things returned to normal between them, Ciara knew, she would have the motivation to load the dishwasher again.

"I don't think I'll ever get used to the rain," Mishti said. Gerry smiled politely and turned to Ciara, just as she was slipping into the armchair on the other side of the room.

"Can I have a word with you?" He used the same voice he put on for his secretary, a bit too polite. She would have much preferred if he caught her elbow and led her to the kitchen forcibly. Put on a show for Mishti. Earn her some sympathy. She filed that thought in the back of her mind.

She needed to regain Mishti's trust. The last thing Ciara ever wanted was to be pitied—she was never going to be the battered wife—but she might have to tweak things a little for Mishti's sake. Perhaps she needed Mishti to see her as a woman in need of help, protection.

Ciara took especially long to stand up again, while Gerry struggled to peel Bella off him. He had to promise he'd watch the rest of the movie with her later.

"Maybe we should leave," Mishti said.

"No! Don't go anywhere. I doubt Gerry is here to stay. Whatever he has to say won't take long. He won't do . . . He won't make a scene while you're here." Mishti's eyes widened at that. A seed of doubt had been successfully planted.

Gerry was in the kitchen, trying not to stare at the dishes in the sink. In the six years they were married, he had never come home to the house looking like this. It made Ciara smile—no, it made her want to laugh. It was hilarious, what he had come to expect of her.

"Why are you here?" she snapped.

"I came home early because you said you were having a shit day, and I wanted to help. Now I see you're entertaining guests and acting like that phone conversation never happened."

"Do you want me to ask her to leave?"

"That is not what I'm saying, Ciara."

"I don't understand what you're doing here. You think your presence in this house is going to make a shred of a difference to my day?"

"We need to talk about whatever's happening with you. This can't be good for the kids."

"You think you know what's good for them?"

"I *want* what's good for them."

She had to hand it to him. For the first time in a very long time, he was at the very least giving one of their arguments the good old college try.

"Thank you very much for your thoughts and consideration, Gerry. I'm going to channel that energy and your good vibes. They might help me better raise our children single-handedly."

"You don't have to raise them single-handedly."

"And what is my other option?"

"Let me help."

It sounded so simple now, coming from him. He had never made this offer before. Ciara had always taken the lead; she did up the house after they were married, decorated, planned the pregnancies, found them friends, looked after the children's best interests, made sure they were well respected in the village.

"You've had four years to offer your help. Four years of standing around doing nothing, while I put my career on hold."

She waited for him to say it: He never asked her to give up her job. She *wanted* him to say it. This was bait for him to admit he didn't think much of her social-media career.

He said nothing.

When they first met, Gerry was handsome, and he was even more so at thirty-five. She admired his ability to look after himself. Everything about him was clean. Rich. There was no dirt under his fingernails; the inside of his car was immaculate and smelled nice; he replaced his toothbrush every eight weeks; he had a cleaning lady even as a bachelor, to keep his home looking as polished as he presented himself to the world. And he always had a neat haircut. That was the other thing: He spent time styling his hair every morning. It was the first thing he did, right after he took a piss. He cared about his appearance, about looking after his possessions. Just as she did. And together they were going to make it look effortless. That was the plan.

She looked away when she recalled what her father's hands used to look like. She'd described them to Mishti years ago. The only person she'd painted a picture of her father to: His hands were thick, chunky. Dangerously tanned. The skin around his nails torn and dug up, much like the land lying barren behind the house.

Like with everything else, Mishti hadn't breathed a word of it to anyone.

When Ciara met Gerry, it seemed like she had finally met a man who wanted the same things as she did. To have the perfect family, to leave an impression on the world. Now the only time they were on the same side was when Ciara planned a photo shoot for one of her Instagram posts. He submitted silently to her carefully orchestrated positioning, to testing the light and decluttering the background. He smiled emptily in those photographs, but only she saw through it, because she used to know him once.

"I'll take the kids to Mam's tonight, give you a chance to have some time to yourself. It's Mam's birthday, so I'm sure she'll be happy to spend the evening with them."

"Is this some kind of dig at me for forgetting your mother's birthday?"

"I just want to give you some time off."

Ciara rolled her eyes. "About fuckin' time, Gerry."

"I'm sorry you feel that way, Ciara, like I haven't contributed to our children's lives. Or to yours."

She shrugged. "I don't know what you think you're achieving here. Do you expect me to thank you for taking the kids tonight? Don't even answer that, it's going to sound stupid."

She thought she saw his eyelid twitch. That's all it was. The twitch of an eyelid, then silence. If he wanted to make a difference in her life, he would join her in smashing their porcelain mugs. He'd tear down the curtains with her. He'd laugh while she scream-cried. Maybe they'd do it outside, in the front yard for everyone to see.

"Excuse me while I go be a decent host to our guests. In the meantime, you should return to work. Do the only thing you're good at. Make some money."

September 30

"DADDY, NO!" THE CHILDREN'S VOICES ROSE AS THEY thrashed in bed with their father, breathless with joy. Lauren observed this from her side of the bed, her insides rocking from the jumping. She had come very close to losing this, to losing this man who was a better father to their children than her own had ever been. He was a better father than most. Today, she lay in bed a few extra moments, admiring the happy scene. This had come so close to slipping through her fingers.

Last night, finally, they had made up after their big fight. In the light of the morning, she knew it was the right decision. He promised things were going to be different now, and she believed him. She was going to make a few changes too.

Lauren hadn't been sleeping much. She hadn't got much sleep in the six years since Freya, her oldest, was born. She was convinced that sleep deprivation had something to do with the way things had played out recently. Having three children so close in age made their world very small, where nothing existed outside the bubble. Her relationship with Sean had lasted nearly a decade. Now, more than ever, Lauren was determined to make it work. Their troubles weren't in the past yet, but soon they would be. Once they left this place.

"I'm going to make pancakes for these rug rats; you should have a lie-in. I'll check on Willow," Sean said. He gave her a quick peck on the cheek before he got out of bed. Then he grabbed the kids and tucked one under each arm. They left the bedroom like this, flailing and joyous, their red heads bobbing up and down.

Lauren shut her eyes again, but she knew it wouldn't last. Willow would be awake soon, and she'd bring the house down if Lauren didn't immediately stick her boob in her mouth.

Intoxicated with reassurance and gratitude, she couldn't fall back to sleep. Everything had worked out, just like it always did. No matter what came between them, Sean and Lauren always found their way back to each other.

When they weren't speaking, she felt she was alone, that it was finally over, the stationary turbulence of their relationship. It was strangely peaceful once she had accepted he was gone. But when he came to her last night, practically begging her to take him back, she was relieved.

She had spent almost her whole life loving him.

When they first met, he knew everything, and she hadn't a clue. He was fourteen years her senior, handsome in a scruffy way. He had an easy charm and grace, in ragged leather jackets and no deodorant. He ran a bookshop, and he got all the girls and the women. He would have got the men too, if he was interested.

When she first met him, he had everything, and she, nothing.

Lauren couldn't believe her luck when he hired her as an assistant. She'd moved to the city with big dreams, and finally one of them was coming true. Nobody knew her there, and she had an actual job.

The bookshop was a small space, and it could have been claustrophobic. They were always literally stepping on each other's shoes. It felt like a kind of primal mating dance. She overheard all his phone conversations, and she was self-conscious when she used the matchbox toilet at the back. Hyperaware of the crumpling sound of pages from old books they used as toilet paper. He, on the other hand, barely seemed to register her presence.

Sean's friends were poets who were interviewed by radio stations. The artsy types naturally gravitated to him, perhaps because his home was always open to them. Musicians jammed in his kitchen on mornings after big raves, a full Irish cooking in the oven. There was always someone sleeping on the couch, someone rolling joints on the balcony, leaving teacup rings on the scratched hardwood floors. Lauren wasn't like any of them—she wasn't even much of a reader. It could only have been destiny that had brought them together. He had no other reason for hiring her, when he could have hired any of his friends. Or maybe he just needed someone to keep showing up and on time.

"How many pancakes do you want?" Sean yelled from the kitchen today.

"Four, I don't know, a handful," she shouted back.

She was doubtful he even heard her over the voices of their children. She didn't care about the pancakes anyway; she wasn't hungry. She just wanted to sink into bed and think about all the ways she was luckier than Ciara Dunphy.

WILLOW WOKE UP soon after, and Lauren finally had to get up. She went into Willow's bedroom and lifted her out of the crib, breathing in her sleepy scent. She wasn't so small anymore. Nearly two, growing up fast, and Lauren knew she was her last baby. She fed Willow, changed her, then carried her to the kitchen.

Harry and Freya were sitting around the table, making a mess of the maple syrup and blueberries.

"There she is." Sean pulled Willow into his arms, kissing the top of her head and flipping pancakes simultaneously.

"I'm going to meet with Padder today," he said. He was shouting to make himself heard over the children.

Lauren brought the peanut butter and strawberries to the table. "Have you spoken to him lately? Does he have something for you?"

Sean shrugged. "He will. Eventually. One of the lads is bound to come through. Padder's waiting to hear about the right thing for me. I'm not stacking the crisps aisle at Aldi, Lauren."

He'd had to give up the bookshop six years ago, and he hadn't done much with his days since then. Freya was a newborn when they moved to the village, Lauren's village. This was where she grew up, but it was an adjustment for Sean, who had spent all his life in the city. When she'd left this place, Lauren had thought she got away, but she was back, just a few years later, with a baby and a man in tow. Back to the same place with the same faces. Sean didn't know how to live in a place this small. Then Harry was born and later Willow came along, and Sean said he was more interested in being a father than finding work. The bookshop had never brought in much money anyway.

Lauren had now spent a lifetime with him but couldn't identify his particular skill set.

"Yes, you're right, someone will have something for you," she replied to him. Always encouraging.

They had managed thus far. The house was theirs. Hers. And she had her gran's inheritance, but it would eventually run out. In fact, they didn't have long to go before they would both have to sign on to the dole. Unless Sean did something about it. Lauren tried not to look at her depleted savings account anymore. On the days that she did, she snapped at Sean at the slightest provocation.

The older the kids got, the more their expenses increased. This lifestyle wasn't going to be sustainable for much longer. Sean's friends had hooked him up with a few gigs in the past, but he mustn't have been very good, because they rarely ever called him back. Probably because when he was supposed to be promoting music events, he ended up ordering free pints at the pub with the band all night.

Something had to change so they could move on from what had happened recently, what had led to their big fight. Lauren refused to be in this position again. She never wanted to come so close to losing him, and maybe money would solve everything.

She hadn't told him about her plan to move, but it felt like more than just a passing thought now.

Sean stacked pancakes on a plate. He called Harry over to carry it to the table. Then he leaned toward Lauren because she'd been staring at him.

"I'm going to take care of it, love. Things are going to change around here."

Today she felt optimistic. Something *did* feel different.

SOMETIMES, LAUREN SMOKED a cigarette out in the back garden. She only did this when Sean was inside with the kids. It filled her with the kind of guilt that made her berate herself out loud. Anyone watching her would have thought she was losing her mind. Only she made sure nobody ever was.

Filthy. This is filthy, Lauren. This is your last one. This is it. What if one of the kids sees you?

She didn't even enjoy the damn things anymore. Of all the things she hated about herself, this was on the top of the list, followed by her freckles and her wide ankles, which was why she never wore sandals.

She'd been smoking since she was twelve, stealing cigarettes from her father's coat that hung by the door, knowing he never kept count.

She used to line them up on her palm like soldiers, then hold them up to her nose, breathing in their unfiltered nicotine smell. Her brother smoked too, and her father always had a half-burned cigarette between his fingers: smoking while he put his shoes on, making them hiss when he dropped them in beer cans, lighting up while he drove. Her mother complained about the smell of smoke clinging to his clothes, but she had a secret stash too, hidden under the ball of bras in her wardrobe. It was from her mother's pack that Lauren tried her first one. It was inevitable, like drinking coffee or learning to drive. Even now, every time Lauren sliced open a new box of cigarettes and the trapped smell was freshly released, she was reminded of her childhood. It was the way her father's fingers smelled.

She'd given them up every time she fell pregnant. At least there was that. However, she picked up again soon after. Every time. Cigarettes were her only weakness, other than Sean.

She was usually good at controlling the urge for days, keeping that gnawing feeling at bay for weeks sometimes. Then, all of a sudden, it would take hold of her again. She'd wake one morning and hear the voices in her head, telling her it was okay if she smoked *just one.*

Every time she smoked a cigarette, the guilt tormented her, diminished her in size. She rarely ever finished the whole cigarette before the guilt made her hand shake, and she'd stub it out and run back in the house. She'd wash her hands vigorously, for several minutes. If she could, she'd even take a shower before she touched the children.

"I think I'm going to have a smoke before you leave," she whispered to Sean. They were standing at the sink together, washing up after breakfast.

He'd quit a few years ago, and he was the only one who knew she hadn't. That was the way they were with each other. She'd always been able to tell him anything.

"You can go now; the kids won't notice."

They looked over at their children, who were sitting around the table, poring over a book of stickers.

Go now, the voice inside her head insisted.

THE ONLY PLACE Lauren smoked was in the garden, away from the children and their prying eyes. This, however, put her in plain sight of the Dunphys. Their gardens faced each other.

She was anxious about Ciara Dunphy catching her with a cigarette. Ciara Dunphy with her perfect blond ponytail and airbrushed cheeks. Her angelic children in their wrinkle-free clothes, with no traces of congealed Weetabix in their bangs. In the eyes of every other parent in the village, Ciara was flawless. But Lauren felt sick for Ciara's poor children. She pitied them, just as she was sure Ciara pitied hers.

She'd seen the photograph Ciara posted on Instagram yesterday. She had no idea how Ciara managed to get her children to stay still long enough so the pictures weren't blurry. Or how they always appeared to be cheerful, smiling at the camera, winking at their mother. Lauren wasn't naïve; she knew it was a farce. Especially the photographs of Ciara and her husband, playacting at being the perfect couple. The only thing perfect about them was their teeth.

That knowledge didn't make it easier, though. Just like with cigarettes, Lauren could go several days without looking at Instagram, just to protect her feelings from bristling with *something*. It wasn't envy—she didn't want to be Ciara Dunphy. It was something else, a feeling she remembered from being a teenager. Wishing those girls simply ceased to exist.

This photograph, though, had been particularly frustrating, posted just a few days after Ciara's accusatory video. She knew everyone had watched it, and they all knew who Ciara was talking about. Lauren was expecting something to happen any day now. Ciara didn't know how dangerous this game was, because she didn't know what these women were capable of. Ciara hadn't known them as teenage girls.

Lauren stood at the corner of her garden, holding the burning cigarette behind her back and rocking nervously. Every time she took a drag, she turned her head sideways and quickly blew the smoke out. Lauren was a mother of three. If anyone caught her smoking, a lynch mob would gather outside her door very quickly.

Lauren had spent most of life feeling like an outcast; she was used to it. However, lately it had taken on a different, darker tone.

The women in the village looked to Ciara for advice and validation. She made lists of links to parenting websites and articles for the local WhatsApp group, all of which she claimed to have carefully studied. These mothers trusted her, desperate for the crumbs of approval she dropped along the way. They admired her beautiful home, drooled over her handsome husband, who appeared to have handed Ciara the pants, his holster, and his gun. Most important, Ciara had been validated by the internet, and that was good enough for everyone. So Ciara's very public condemnation of Lauren could have extreme ramifications on her whole family.

As Lauren smoked, she tried to peer into Ciara's kitchen across the gardens. She was almost certain Ciara had been watching her yesterday, when she was chasing the kids. Willow was in the middle of a tantrum, Harry didn't have a stitch of clothing on him, and Freya was running wild. Ciara's children would never have acted that way. They didn't know how.

Then Ciara's photo had gone up, almost on cue. Like a message was being communicated. A comparison was being made.

Today it was the opposite: Lauren was sure she wasn't being watched. The Dunphy household was motionless, noiseless, almost lifeless. Even the baskets of purple pansies hanging around their deck area were entirely still. The house appeared to be shielded from the elements, encased in an invisible bubble.

Lauren finished her smoke and went back inside. Harry and Freya were throwing forks at each other. Willow had climbed up on the kitchen counter using a chair. Sean was nowhere in sight.

"For fuck's sake," she mumbled under her breath, and ran to pull Willow off. She hadn't had the chance to wash her hands after her smoke. The guilt of touching her child with nicotine-laced fingers was going to chip away at her.

"WHERE WERE YOU when I went for a smoke?"

Lauren found Sean in their bedroom, slipping his jacket on. He hadn't noticed her come in, and he'd been staring at himself in the mirror. It was full-length and had been useful in the past. Now it was mostly concealed by scarves, necklaces, tiaras, and Freya's fairy wings.

Lauren had managed to get all three kids in one room and made Freya promise she wouldn't let Willow put her life in danger. Just for ten minutes.

"Oh, yeah, I needed to take a piss."

"You're leaving now?"

"Yeah, Padder's waiting for me. Do you need help getting the kids ready for school?" he asked.

"No, I can do it. I'll be fine."

Sean came over to cradle her cheeks with both hands. He tipped her face up toward him. His smile was still handsome, his beard even more scruffy these days. She'd always liked how cold his rings felt on her skin when he held her face like this.

"We're going to be fine, love, my sweet darling Lauren. Stop worrying."

She pushed his hands away, blushing a little. "Just . . ." she began but couldn't find the words.

"What?"

"I don't know."

"You can tell me what's on your mind," he said.

"Things have been crazy around here lately, and I can't make sense of my own thoughts."

"Everything will find its place. Very soon. We just have to give it some time. We're together, we have our family together, and it's all that matters."

She was surprised to hear him speak this way. Sean had a poet's soul, but he wasn't usually sentimental. He was getting old, and maybe that was a good thing.

"I just need you to keep it together. Don't do anything stupid," he added. It made her step away from him. "I won't be gone long. Just a few hours. We should do something together this afternoon. You, me, and Willow, before the rug rats are back from school."

"Maybe you'll keep Willow busy, while I catch up on sleep."

"Whatever you want, love, but I have to go now. I don't want to keep Padder waiting."

She walked him to the front door, then watched him get on his bike and roar away. The first thing she was going to insist on buying was a family car, once she'd sold this house and had some cash. She wasn't relying on him finding a job.

Standing at the door, she looked in the direction of the Dunphy house. Ciara's Beetle was in the driveway, so someone had to be home.

Freya had dressed herself for school by the time Lauren returned to her children. Harry was sprawled naked on his bed. Willow was crying because nobody was giving her the attention she believed she deserved.

"Harry, come on, you have to put some clothes on."

"But I don't want to go to school."

"Neither did I, and look where that got me," Lauren replied.

IT WAS THE time of year when there were more leaves on the ground than there were on the trees. Lauren had walked Freya to school first, then dropped Harry off at preschool. Willow was strapped to her back in a woven sling, fast asleep. Lauren lifted her phone from time to time and used the selfie mode to check on her. Willow was her only child who hadn't inherited Lauren's red hair and curls. Willow's was a soft chestnut, lighter at the edges, untamable like her spirit. It lay splayed over Lauren's shoulder, covering most of Willow's face too.

Even though Ciara's red Beetle was still in the driveway, Lauren paused in front of the Dunphy house. It was an imposing structure, with gargoyle-like statues atop tall pillars at the entrance. A canopy of trees shaded the gates. The façade of the house was painted a charcoal gray, with accents of exposed stone and glass. It was modern and polished, as effectively formidable as a manor house would've been amidst peasants.

She'd snuck up to Ciara's house before, but only at night, or when Ciara's car wasn't in the driveway.

Before, she'd jump over the wall between their gardens at night, when she was sure they weren't home. It was mostly hedges anyway. She'd walk across the mature, manicured garden, admiring the effort their landscape artist had put into its design. The perfect play of shadow and light, *chiaroscuro*. She'd walk up to the back patio and look through the glass doors into the sunroom. She'd delight at the pile of self-help books left abandoned on the armchair. Toys spilling out of storage compartments. Ciara's espadrilles forgotten on the rug.

Then she'd walk around to where she could look into the kitchen.

This appeared to be the cleanest, most sparkling space in the house. Other than the chrome bowl of carefully stacked fruit, there was no sign of food.

Finally, there was the study, Gerry's home office. It looked lived-in, more than any other room she'd discovered. There were stacks of paper on his desk, whisky that hadn't been cleared away, a tie draped over the back of the swivel chair. There were even crumpled fast-food paper bags on the floor.

Only once had Lauren come close to being caught. It was a few months ago; she'd been standing at Ciara's kitchen window, with her hands stuffed into the pockets of her oversized cardigan. She'd lost track of time, imagining herself perched on one of the mustard bar-stools. The windows were double-glazed, practically soundproof, so she hadn't noticed Bella walk into the kitchen. She registered a flash of pink raincoat, and, just as Bella turned from the open fridge, Lauren ducked. She slid down, her sheepskin boots sinking into the flower bed. She'd buried her head between her knees, shutting her eyes tightly, expecting Ciara to come charging out, making threats. Nothing happened. Bella hadn't seen her. It felt like a narrow escape but hadn't kept her from going again.

Today Lauren noticed that the front door of the house was ajar. She looked at Willow on her phone screen again. Still asleep. She was curious about the house being so still, but, more important, she had something to tell Ciara. Even before she told Sean, she wanted to tell Ciara about her decision to move. She imagined Ciara being just as happy with the decision, just as relieved. This was going to be Lauren's olive branch. This would put an end to it. The years of animosity, the bickering. Once Lauren and her family left, neither of them would have to live with bad neighbors.

She wanted to tell Ciara before she did any more damage.

It made Lauren smile as she walked toward the house, at the prospect of celebrating the good news of her move with the very person who wanted her gone.

She expected Ciara to appear in the doorway any moment now,

demanding to know what Lauren was doing on her property. She was under no delusions; she knew she wasn't welcome here.

There was no sign of Ciara, though, even when Lauren reached the front door. She leaned into the foyer, careful not to step over the threshold.

"Ciara?"

She was met with silence. Ciara's children were always well behaved, but even by their standards it was much too quiet today. Bella might have been at preschool, but there was no evidence of Finn either.

"It's Lauren. Is anyone home?"

She had to be home. Unlike Lauren, who had no choice but to walk everywhere, Ciara wouldn't have left home on foot.

Lauren stepped into the foyer, which looked like the centerfold of a design magazine, with a row of tall pink orchids in chrome pots along one wall, a light fixture tumbling down from the ceiling in a waterfall of bulbs, a gigantic gilded mirror resting against the other wall. Down the hallway was a door, which she knew led to the sitting room. Across was the kitchen, the door to which was left wide open. This felt forbidden and bizarre, like the time she was thirteen and she'd wandered into a sex shop in the city. Her mother was across the street, eyeing jewelry in a display window. Lauren had stood close to the entrance, staring at the posters on the walls, at the strange-looking items she didn't recognize—a spiked leather collar too menacing for a beloved pet. The shop assistants were talking among themselves and hadn't noticed Lauren come in. Her mother's screech had snapped her out of it, as she was roughly pulled out of the shop by both arms.

Still expecting Ciara to appear at any moment, Lauren crept down the hallway, which ended at the grand, winding staircase that led to the bedrooms. If Ciara was asleep upstairs, where were the children? Lauren knew she wasn't supposed to be here, not after the last time she had come to the house, but something—some feeling of wrongness—kept propelling her forward.

Then she saw what looked like a bundle of clothes on the floor. A shock of golden hair. It was Ciara, lying with her face twisted to the side, and motionless. She was just as still as the rest of her house. Lauren had to cover her mouth, to stop herself from screaming and waking Willow. She contorted her arm around, just to touch Willow's dangling foot for reassurance. She could feel her daughter's soft sleepy breaths falling on her neck.

"Ciara! Are you okay?" She rushed toward her, hissing to keep her voice low, then stepped back abruptly, filled with a sickening feeling. There was a pool of congealed blood around Ciara's head, and some had dried trickling down her nostrils. Her arms and legs were at odd angles, like a child's stick-figure drawing.

Ciara was dead, and Lauren knew she had to leave. Someone else would have to bear the burden of finding her and calling the Guards. It couldn't be her. Not after the warning Sean had just given her.

Whether or not this was an accident, Lauren couldn't be the one to find the body.

That was exactly what Ciara would have wanted.

Part One

THEN

Chapter 1

September 2

MISHTI WAS LYING ON HER SIDE OF THE BED, HUD-dled under the duvet pulled up to her chin. No matter what she did, she just couldn't get warm. It was as though the cold had seeped into her bones and settled there, since the first day she arrived in Ireland. Since the first rain soaked into her socks, right through her shoes. She'd tried everything: She wore thick woolly socks, thermals under her clothes, wrapped herself in the Kashmiri shawl she'd received as a wedding present. Nothing worked.

She'd been suffering a perpetual case of the sniffles for the past five years, and it left her feeling constantly hungry.

Mishti was born in Calcutta, to parents who she believed had really just wanted the best for her. The best came in the shape of Dr. Parth Guha. His first words to her, at their arranged meeting, were, "I am a medical doctor, you should know."

He was primarily an academic, with a doctorate in psychology and no inclination for humility. While he lived and worked in Ireland, he was well aware of his value as a groom in India. His parents advertised him to potential brides on the market as *a catch*, and they weren't exaggerating. He was taller than the average Bengali male. He had established himself at a relatively young age in a Western country, where he was paid well. They reported his exact salary like shares on Wall Street. He came from good stock, and the stamps on his passport did most of the talking for him. If he were a house, and his parents the sellers, then he was a property worth millions, in a prime location with unparalleled views. Mishti's parents couldn't believe their luck that they were even in the running along with the other eager bidders. All, with their heads bowed and hands joined in gratitude, presenting their daughters, to be accepted with a shrug or rejected without a second glance.

MISHTI AND PARTH first met at a restaurant in Calcutta that was advertised as an authentic American diner. It had plush leather couches in booths surrounded by Plexiglas and served milkshakes, fries, and hamburgers made with ground chicken. Their parents arranged everything, including the time and the venue.

It was all decided for her, including what she was going to wear (jeans, to show they were progressive, with a more traditional kurta instead of a blouse, to make the right impression of the kind of family she belonged to, that she was capable of maintaining traditional values in his Western setting), what she would order (just a burger and maybe a milkshake if he insisted; too full for dessert, to be polite), and a list of talking points (his academic achievements; the weather in Ireland; what he missed about Calcutta; most important, let him talk about himself).

It wasn't like the old days, when you didn't meet your husband until the final moment, when the veil was lifted and you were bound in marriage forever. Now you were given a chance—several chances, in fact—to meet and get to know this person you were going to spend the rest of your life with.

Mishti didn't think she stood a chance. She had never been abroad, and she wasn't interested in psychology. Her English was good enough to teach class-one children at an English-medium school, but she spoke with an Indian accent and had trouble with prepositions. Unlike a lot of the girls she knew from school and some of her cousins, Mishti never had any interest in settling abroad. She was happy where she was: in Calcutta, with her family and students, in the comfort of familiar company.

Parth had looked her up and down before they were seated. It was the same way her mother had looked at her before she left the house. They were both assessing her proportions, her suitability. How much to charge per kilogram.

She thought he was too handsome for her, in that broad-shouldered, clear tan complexion kind of way some Bengali men have about them. It makes them sort of ageless. Maybe also because they can't grow thick beards and have full, childish cheeks but masculine shoulders. Parth wore his hair swept to one side and had long fingers and quiet hands. She imagined his handwriting to be precise and neat.

Parth was a man of few words. He had a lot to say when he was required to speak: for instance, when he commanded an amphitheater of eager students, she imagined. When he sat across from his clients, though, he must have been excellent at letting them do all the talking.

He was only interested in answering questions when she asked about his work, but when she veered toward his social life, he checked the menu or looked past her.

"I work long hours, I don't have time for fun," he'd said, examining the dessert list.

"Of course. Your work is important." She was pleased with her response, could picture her mother smiling.

"I do important work. Nobody in India cares about mental health. Depression is as much an ailment as having a bad back or being diabetic."

She was surprised by his tone, because he sounded angry.

"That is fascinating. I would love to learn more about what you do." Her mother would have clapped with joy at that.

Parth put the menu away and looked around, trying to catch a waiter's eye. When he wasn't successful, he put his arm up like he was flagging down a taxi.

"When I'm home, I don't like to discuss work. You'll have to do your own research."

Mishti clammed up—she'd run out of good responses; instead, she just stared apologetically at Parth while he complained to the waiter about their slow service.

When Mishti returned home from their first meeting and was informed by her mother that he was interested in the match, she'd laughed. It seemed a ridiculous idea to her. What would they talk about for the rest of their lives? She didn't say this aloud to her mother. Her parents had never spoken much to each other either. Her mother would have taken it as an insult.

They were married quickly, because Parth didn't want to make another trip to India for the wedding. He'd already selected his bride.

Mishti barely had time to consider the proposal, let alone time to reject it. She was intimidated by him and her future with him, but everyone else had already made the important decisions.

"Your father's gone to book the reception hall," her mother told her, the morning after her first meeting with Parth. That evening, she was being measured for blouses and petticoats for the wedding saris. When she had a moment to herself, she tried to make sense of what Parth had seen in her but couldn't come up with anything.

After a weeklong honeymoon in Darjeeling, Parth returned to Ireland. He left Mishti behind to await her spousal visa. He was still a stranger to her but the only man who had seen her naked.

Friends and family congratulated her on the prized groom she'd landed. She spent the next several months in his home, with her new in-laws. She went to sleep in his childhood bed, alone, staring up at the slowly rotating ceiling fan. There were nights when she wanted to sneak back to her parents' home, to sleep in her own bed, to wake up to her grandfather humming in the bathroom while he shaved.

She had been hopeful, pining to begin her new life with her new successful husband. Instead, she was living with his parents in Calcutta, just a bus ride away from her own home, which she couldn't visit because her mother-in-law had decided it was too soon. That she should be immersing herself in her marriage. A marriage where her husband was living in a different country.

When Mishti was allowed to use the landline and call home, her mother lectured her to view it as an opportunity to be initiated into the family and their ways, so she'd be well prepared to make a good home for her husband when the time came. His mother instructed Mishti on how he liked his daal and lamb curry; his father lectured her on Parth's exemplary successes, tracking his progress from when he was in kindergarten. She heard all the stories, but her new husband had called her only twice in their months apart. He rang his mother every Sunday.

It wasn't until she finally arrived in Ireland that she understood why he'd picked her, when he could have married anyone he wanted. A more worthy candidate from an affluent family, with a better education, who had holidayed abroad, with a sense of personal style and the confidence that came along with all that.

Parth had wanted the exact opposite. A blank slate.

MISHTI TURNED OVER to watch him sleeping beside her now. He had fallen asleep with the bedside lamp switched on, and she didn't turn it off. His shoulders rose and fell with every soft snore. She stared at his profile, at the way his fingers sometimes quivered where they lay splayed on his chest. His Adam's apple stuck out of his narrow throat, bobbing up and down like a buoy. She had no idea what her husband was dreaming about. Did anyone?

In the five years they were married, Mishti hadn't built up the courage to ask the big questions. Things she should have asked at their first meeting:

What are your greatest fears?
What were you like as a child when your parents weren't looking?
Why did you choose to study psychology?
What do you think of me?
Would you like to know something about me?

Maya opened the door and walked into their bedroom on tiptoes. She knew she wasn't supposed to wake her father. When Maya was a baby and woke up crying at night, Mishti had to do whatever she could to not interrupt Parth's sleep.

In India, all mothers slept with their newborns by their side. Here, they had a name for it—co-sleeping—and the practice was severely debated in online forums all over the internet. Mishti hadn't known if she was doing the right thing by keeping Maya in her bed as an infant, especially since Ciara insisted against it. Eventually it proved impossible anyway, since every time Maya woke, Parth woke too, jumping out of bed in fury, stomping out of the room to go sleep somewhere else. He said he couldn't stand the crying, making Mishti feel responsible. She felt she wasn't being a good mother, because she couldn't get Maya to sleep through the night.

So, for the first two years of Maya's life, they slept in one of the spare rooms together, as far away from Parth as possible, so he wouldn't be disturbed. Now she wished Maya hadn't grown up and demanded her own room.

"Ma, I can't sleep," Maya whispered, still on tiptoes.

Mishti looked over at her husband, placing a finger over her lips to remind her daughter to be quiet. Then she slipped out of bed and led Maya out of the room and down the stairs to the kitchen.

"Would you like something to eat?"

She was already scooping yogurt into a bowl, to which she added chunks of jaggery. It wasn't until she'd discovered the Asian grocery store in the city that Mishti finally felt settled in this country. Once she got her full license, she drove to the store once a month. Everything tasted better when cooked with ghee. She didn't have to resort to boil-in-the-bag rice anymore and could now stock up on large quantities of basmati. They even had the particular brand of coconut hair oil she'd grown up using. It made all their sheets and pillows smell of her childhood.

Maya devoured the yogurt, while Mishti sucked on a big piece of jaggery she'd broken off for herself.

"Why can't you sleep?"

Maya shrugged, a habit she'd only acquired since starting pre-school.

"It's very late and we should try to get some sleep. You'll be tired for school tomorrow."

"In a bit, Ma."

"What do you want to do?"

"Can we watch some TV?"

"It's too late for that, Maya, no."

"Can we read some books?"

"Maybe."

"Why were you awake?"

"I was thinking."

"What were you thinking about, Ma?"

Bangla sounded different on her daughter's tongue. Maya had only been to India once, and in a few years she was going to forget she ever went. It wasn't that Parth couldn't afford another trip, he just never suggested it again, and she didn't know how to ask. It wasn't her money, and most of the time she felt like a guest in his life.

"I was thinking about home."

"Isn't this your home, Ma?"

"I grew up in Calcutta, you know this. Calcutta will always be home to me."

"But this is my home."

"Yes, it is. Ireland will always be home to you."

The older her daughter got, the less they had in common.

They read a few books together, after which they lay in Maya's bed, talking about her friends. Maya dozed off mid-sentence, but Mishti remained beside her. She was more comfortable here than she ever was beside her husband.

On the bedside table, her phone was vibrating with notifications from WhatsApp, so she reached for it.

The other mothers were discussing the group playdate Ciara had organized for the next evening. Mishti was a lurker but not much of a contributor to these conversations, never quite knowing what to say or how to join in on the jokes. It did make her feel better about herself to see she wasn't the only one awake at this hour.

Even though Ciara was prompt with her replies, it was unlikely that it was her kids keeping her up. She'd trained both her children to sleep through the night by the age of one. Mishti didn't understand it, but she trusted Ciara to know what she was doing. She never confided in Ciara how much she enjoyed it when Maya woke her up. They often ate bowls of yogurt and jaggery together in the middle of the night. Someday, Maya was going to stop coming to her bedroom, and Mishti knew she was going to miss this.

The women were discussing hairdressers, the conversation having quickly steered away from their children. The messages were coming in fast, making it hard for Mishti to keep up. Eventually, Lauren Doyle said something about how she'd been cutting her own hair for years, and nobody responded to that. She was usually ignored. From the way these women sometimes spoke about Lauren behind her back, it was surprising she'd even been added to the group. Perhaps it was their way of keeping tabs on her.

Mishti lived on a different continent now, but the rules of engagement between women were the same here as they were in Calcutta. It hadn't taken her long to deduce that Lauren was the outcast in their little community. She dressed differently from the rest of them, in brashly patterned blouses, bootcut jeans thrifted from charity shops, and long floating skirts. She was almost too thin and often talked at length about her interest in crocheting. The other mothers rolled their eyes at her when she wasn't looking.

Mishti felt fortunate to have been taken under Ciara's wing. She knew that if it wasn't for Ciara and her friendship, this place would be a whole lot colder and wetter. When she'd had nobody else in those lonely days of her pregnancy, far away from her family, Ciara had saved her life.

Chapter 2

September 2

LAUREN AND WILLOW TREKKED TO THE SHOP. TO THE only real shop in the village, which was beside a chipper, wedged between two pubs. The walk to the village center wasn't very long, but they took the shorter route through the woods, so Lauren could point out different trees and flowers to Willow on her back. She knew these woods well, having spent most of her childhood wandering here alone.

They crossed the familiar site of a litter of premixed-vodka-drink cans and cigarette butts, a half-burned old tire hanging from a tree, a trampled-on hoodie. The smell of piss was everywhere. Teenagers in this village had been up to the same extracurriculars for decades. She sang to Willow to keep her distracted as they hurried past.

At the shop, Lauren dawdled in the aisles, trying to avoid two women she'd gone to school with. She hadn't forgotten about the names they'd invented for her when they were children. *Porridge Face. Hairy Laurie. Bo Peep.* Neither had they.

Ciara's arrival in the community had rekindled all those memories and seemed to have spurred these women on. It was as though Ciara had handed them a golden ticket, giving them all permission to behave like teenagers again, just when Lauren thought they were all past it. Ciara and Gerry were blow-ins, but they'd purchased the most coveted property in the village. They set the benchmark for what the rest of them aspired to be. They were following the Dunphy lead.

Lauren had been idling in front of the dried-fruit-and-nuts section, trying to be invisible, as the two women chatted at the dairy fridges. She'd already overheard them mention Ciara, something about a skin-care brand she'd recommended on Instagram. Then one of them looked over and caught sight of Lauren. Their eyes met, and Lauren frantically grabbed at some bags of almonds. The women shuffled away with smug faces.

Lauren finished her shopping quickly and paid at the counter. The women had already left the shop, and Willow was whining on her back in the sling. When Lauren stepped out onto the sidewalk, she was out of breath with anxiety. She saw the women sitting in their cars, parked on opposite sides of the narrow main road, throwing their voices across at each other as they made to leave. When they caught sight of her again, Lauren lifted her hand to wave before she could stop herself. They revved their engines on cue and drove off, leaving her with her hand suspended in midair.

MOTHERHOOD HAD COME naturally to Lauren, just as unexpectedly as her first pregnancy had. When she was young and bright-eyed, following Sean everywhere like a disciple, she did not picture herself carrying children on her back. She didn't know the first thing about raising kids, having grown up with only an older brother. For starters, she certainly didn't know how much they wanted to be held as infants or how soul-crushing their cries could be. The sleep deprivation took some getting used to. Six years on, if she ever managed to sleep longer than four hours straight, she woke up with what felt like a hangover.

Despite the trials, she'd slipped into motherhood as easily as she'd slipped into love with Sean. This was what she was meant to do: to be a mother to these three children and in love with the man who had fathered them.

Fatherhood, however, hadn't come so quickly to Sean. When he first held Freya, Lauren saw hopelessness on his face. He was at once hurtling into a kind of love he'd never experienced before and terrified of the mewling creature in his arms. He'd practically flung Freya back at her.

Lauren was prepared to do it alone. She hadn't expected Sean to want to stick around. So, at the hospital, when he told her he needed some fresh air, she didn't ask when he was coming back. She expected he'd leave this city altogether, that he needed to escape her and the baby. When he returned three hours later smelling of Scotch and cigarettes, she was surprised. He had a bouquet of roses in one arm and a stuffed bear in the other.

"I'm sorry. I didn't know what to do. I shouldn't have just left you here like this." He fumbled with his words, while Lauren held Freya to her breast, stroking her red hair.

She paused her stroking for a moment to look at him. "You're here now," she replied, then kissed their daughter's forehead. "But if you're going to stay, we have to leave the city. We can't raise a child in that tiny flat of yours. She will eventually need her own room, a garden."

Sean kneeled beside the hospital bed, rubbing both hands over his red face. "I'll do whatever you want me to do, love. I just want us to be a family. I don't know where we'd go, but you're right, we can't live here, especially now that the bookshop isn't bringing in any money."

"We could move back home. To my home. Gran's house is just sitting there."

They'd stared at each other until they both had smiles on their faces again. It had made perfect sense then.

Her gran had died in this house. It took Lauren several months to pack away all her things, so it didn't look like an old woman still lived here. The dark corners of the kitchen cupboards still smelled of her gran, though. Rusty biscuit tins and doilies turning beige.

Growing up, she spent most of her time at her gran's house. She snuck custard creams to the cats and sat with her gran in the garden. Her gran may have belonged to a different generation, but she understood what those girls were doing to Lauren. As it appeared, girls had been speaking the same language for centuries.

Everyone preferred her living with her gran, especially her parents. Money was tight, her brother got in trouble a lot, and her parents were better off without the extra mouth to feed. Lauren considered herself lucky that her gran was good to her, loved her.

Her gran died when Lauren was twenty-one, and the house was legally hers. She moved to the city, renting the place out for the cash, and hadn't ever planned on returning.

Now she didn't think about it anymore, how different her life might have been if she'd quit the bookshop the first time she found a woman in a state of undress in the stockroom. Sean had come to the door when she knocked on it and hadn't even tried to block her view. At least the woman looked embarrassed. She was doing up the buttons on her blouse.

"I was going to leave, it's nearly six." Lauren's voice was squeaky. She was surprised she could even get the words out. This was the first time she'd seen Sean shirtless, but these weren't the circumstances she'd pictured in her fantasies.

Sean had already kissed Lauren at the back of the pub a few weeks before this. That kiss was enough for her; her fate was sealed. She thought they belonged to each other after that, but apparently it hadn't been enough for him.

"Yeah, you should go, I'll close up soon. Just make sure to turn the sign on the door," he replied, leaning against the doorframe. He spoke slowly and clearly, like he was in no rush to shut the door or return to the woman cowering behind him.

He eventually did shut the door. She couldn't make sense of him or why he had kissed her, when he had other women to kiss. What did it mean? The floor undulated like a stormy sea as she tried to make her way out of the shop, afraid she'd fall through the glass door, blinded by tears that scorched her face.

By the next morning, however, she'd fixed a bright smile on her face again. Sean arrived late. Dark glasses sat low on the bridge of his nose, and he carried a big mug of coffee. He'd brought it from his flat, which was only a short walk away.

Lauren had spent the previous night wide awake, staring up at the ceiling in the dark, lying on rough cotton sheets at her cramped shared flat. She'd spent the whole night thinking and wishing she could take a sniff of her gran's cold-cream jar, just to feel comforted for a moment.

"Lauren!" Sean shouted her name, as though he had loud music playing in his ears. She was standing right in front of him, behind the till.

"I've already priced and tagged the stock from yesterday."

Maybe he would have said something, tried to explain himself, if she had given him a chance to. If she had made some reference to the woman he was with the previous night. She didn't, because she didn't need an explanation from him. He didn't have to convince her. She wasn't going anywhere.

It didn't matter how many other girls he kissed, as long as he kissed her too.

And then, once Freya was born, they moved to the village together. Things were going to be different, she hoped. For starters, both her parents had passed away and she hadn't heard from her brother in nearly a decade. He was bitter over her inheritance, even though Lauren had never seen him step foot in their gran's house when she was alive. She was now a mother herself, and she had a man. She was a different woman. They were all grown up. Most important, this was the only lifestyle they could afford.

Sean had never lived in a village this small before. He'd spent all his life in the city; the silence and the one shop and the two pubs took some getting used to. He'd always opened his flat to his friends and friends of friends, but he couldn't wrap his head around inviting the postman in for a cup of tea.

Even though Lauren had been to his flat several times, she hadn't realized how much stuff he was going to bring with him. There were books, vinyls, posters, cutlery, chipped mugs, guitars, a banjo, and a bodhrán. For a man who wore the same three outfits on repeat, he sure had a lot of clothes.

She didn't complain, though; she was happy. Sean's streak of infidelity was a thing of the past. He was devoted to the baby. He belonged to them now. Back then it was just the three of them. That was how they'd started in this house. Now they were five.

WILLOW WANTED TO nap when they returned from the shop, and Lauren took the opportunity to prep dinner. The mushrooms, peppers, broccoli, and tomatoes were chopped by the time Willow woke up. She had to drop everything and run to her daughter's room before the crying escalated.

Sean found them a few moments later, and he kissed Willow's forehead and then Lauren's. "I'm going into town, there's something on the bike that needs fixing," he said. It was vague, and Lauren knew there wasn't anything wrong with it. Every so often, he met up with his old pals. They sat around at the pub and smoked some joints and drank a few pints, jammed like the old days. No big deal.

She didn't take offense that he didn't tell her the truth about where he was going. She let him believe he was doing a good job of keeping it under the radar. He deserved to have something to look forward to in the week, something that would take him away from the kids for a few hours. He wasn't their mother, even though he was a good father. He needed his own time more than she did.

"We might eat dinner early tonight, I have it all prepared. You don't have to rush back," she said.

Sean left, and she settled in, with Willow cradled in the crook of her arm. Willow was going to need some time before she was awake enough to get out of bed. This was Lauren's excuse too to lie still and do nothing. In an hour, she was going to have to walk to the preschool to pick up Freya and Harry. It would be a full house again.

She was glad to be finally putting her gran's house to good use. Filling it with her very own family.

Chapter 3

September 2

CIARA WAS SEVENTEEN WHEN SHE DECIDED SHE WAS going to marry for money.

She didn't have to shut her eyes now to be able to hear the rain splattering on the kitchen window of her parents' house. There was an eerie silence in the house that day, just the water pelting against glass. It ran down the windowpane in oily rivulets, while she stared out at the gray gravel driveway. Her father's car wasn't parked there anymore. He was gone.

She was certain her mother was crying into a pillow in her bedroom, the way Ciara had seen her do many times over the years. It was different this time, though, because Ciara hadn't gone in to lie over her mother's body like a weighted blanket. She knew her father wasn't coming back, and the sooner her mother accepted it, the better off they'd be.

Before he left, he had held Ciara hostage in the kitchen for a full hour, determined to make her agree with what he was about to do. He made cups and cups of tea, all of which went cold. She had wanted to get away from him, because she didn't want to hear his explanations, his excuses. He did get to it eventually. He said it was time he lived his life, because she was old enough now. He had only stayed with them so long because of Ciara, because he didn't want to ruin her childhood. He thought he had done the noble thing.

She had listened in silence, while he fumbled and stuttered his words. Years later, when she was sure she'd forgotten what the lines on his face looked like, and the smell of his cigarettes had faded from the walls of their house, she had tried to write to him. An entire notebook was filled with pages of abandoned letters. Eventually, she threw the notebook away.

Several hours after her father left, her mother came to the kitchen, puffy-eyed and with matted hair.

"Is he gone?" she asked in a froggy croak. She sounded like someone who had forgotten how to speak.

"Is he gone, Ciara? Has he gone to his fucking whore?"

And right then Ciara knew she had to marry for money. It was the only way she could protect herself from turning into her mother. A sad woman in a stained satin housecoat, surviving on dry toast and cigarettes, clinging to a story that hadn't been true for years.

At least she had her mother's looks. From her father, she got nothing.

"Yes, he's gone and he's never coming back."

Her mother coughed and touched her neck. "He'll be back, don't you worry, pet. He always comes back."

Ciara stood up to go outside. She wanted to stand in the rain.

Seventeen years later, she wasn't thinking about her parents as she lay in her marital bed. Her phone screen illuminated her face, as she scrolled through the WhatsApp messages. One of the mothers in her group had sent a picture of a rash her two-year-old had developed four days ago. The woman was worried because it wasn't going away. She wanted advice. The responses ranged from wild guesses about what it could be—ringworm or eczema or an allergic reaction to fabric softener—to suggestions for which ointment to use. Had she tried Sudocrem? Of course she had.

When Ciara saw Lauren's response at the bottom, she had to read it twice.

I always try breast milk first. Literally on everything. Most of the time, it works. It has magical powers or something. I have tons of frozen breast milk. You can have some if you want to give it a shot. As long as you're not too squeamish. Haha.

Ciara sat up in bed, and she noticed how her fingers shook. She was maniacally typing a response underneath Lauren's.

Orla, seriously, the last thing you should be doing right now is asking for medical advice from a bunch of medically untrained mothers. Which is what we all are in this group. This is not the time to read through anecdotes. Call your GP first thing in the morning and have Charlie seen. It's most likely nothing. I hope it's just a heat rash, but you need professional advice. Breast milk is not magic. No matter what Lauren will have you believe.

The response lasted barely a few seconds before others were responding with echoes of allegiance to Ciara's wisdom. They were applauding her for her sensible advice, and yet, somehow, none of them had thought of recommending going to the doctor first.

Just as she was about to put the phone away, the notification for a private message popped up on the screen. It was from Lauren. Ciara wished she had the willpower to ignore it until morning, but she didn't. Secretly, she had hoped for this. Something that would tell her exactly how angry she had made Lauren.

The message contained a list of links. Ciara clicked on one, but she already knew what they were. Articles about the healing properties of breast milk—some were research data and official studies; some were opinions and blog posts. Either way, Ciara didn't care to read them. She was tempted to respond with a few links of her own but changed her mind when she heard footsteps coming up the stairs. She slid her phone under the pillow and shut her eyes.

The door opened and Gerry stood there looking in, waiting for his eyes to adjust to the dark. The husband she had chosen to marry. Not for love. Not only for love.

With her phone gone and no lights in the room, he must have assumed she was asleep.

He made the floorboards creak as he walked around the bed, simultaneously undressing. She had her back turned to him, but she pictured his skinny hairless legs in the plaid boxers he liked to wear. He was trying to be as quiet as possible because he didn't want to wake her. If he was a real man, he wouldn't be afraid of waking her up, of tearing off her clothes and taking what he wanted. Instead, he snuck gingerly around the room like a rat.

Then, in the darkness, as he slipped into bed beside her, he started humming. She was certain she'd never heard him hum before. It was a happy tune she couldn't quite place. It could have been from a children's show or a radio jingle. It sounded almost manic in its upbeat tone. He was humming like a man who had every reason to celebrate. Like he didn't care about the state of their marriage or of lying next to a woman he knew detested his presence in her bed. Like it was a soundtrack to something he was planning.

Ciara stared into the dark and tried to remain still.

He continued humming loudly, high and low.

Heat radiated off him when he brushed against her under their Egyptian cotton covers, and she felt a desperate urge to throw the duvet off and run.

Chapter 4

September 3

MISHTI DROVE MAYA TO PRESCHOOL THE NEXT morning, and when she returned, she saw that Parth was awake. He usually left for his lectures midmorning and didn't return until after Maya's dinner. He had clients to meet and consultations to attend to all day. All this, she had mapped out herself. Parth had never shared his schedule with her.

He seemed grumpy as he sat at the table now, sipping a cup of instant coffee.

"Why did it take you so long?" he asked. She hadn't even deposited her keys into the little dish by the kitchen door yet.

"I needed to talk to one of the teachers."

She hoped it would make him curious about how their daughter was getting on at the preschool. He didn't ask. It could have been a compliment; perhaps he trusted her to attend to their daughter's education without interference from him. Maybe he just didn't care. Either way, she was alone on this.

"What would you like for breakfast?"

"An omelet. Two toasts." He gave her his food order as he would at a restaurant.

She knew how he liked his omelets. It was how his mother made them. She began chopping red onions and tomatoes, while he sat looking at his phone.

They didn't speak while she cooked, and the smell of onions slowly soaked into her dark curls. She could never get rid of it from her fingers or hair, even hours after she'd been cooking. Parth liked onion in all his food, and it was too late to tell him how much she despised it.

As she chopped, she wiped her fingers on the sides of her jeans. Her clothes were going to stink too; she was only making it worse for herself. Her fingers slipped and she nicked the tip of her thumb. When Mishti hissed, she sensed Parth look up. She ran the tap over her hand, the cold water making her toes curl in her runners. His eyes were still on her, and she looked over her shoulder apologetically, terrified of Parth catching her slip-up. He tut-tutted, shook his head, and returned to the screen. He blamed her for falling short of perfection.

Mishti daydreamed about driving away, a thought that came to her in moments like this. If she gave him up, if she *could* give him up, she would lose everything. No matter how lonely she was in their marriage, she couldn't leave. She couldn't return to India, disgraced. Her parents would never understand; they couldn't accept it. There were no divorces in her family, and she didn't intend on being the first. It wasn't like she could simply return to her old teaching job, after all this lost time.

He had yet to finish his coffee when she placed the plate of food in front of him. For herself, she had brought over a banana. She wasn't a morning eater, not since she'd arrived in Ireland anyway. Any form of breakfast made her feel too full and sluggish. The pangs of hunger kept her zippy through the day, and then late in the evening she gorged on anything she could lay her hands on. There were rolls of fat on her back, where her bra dug into her flesh. She was afraid her family wouldn't recognize her if they saw her. As teenagers, her cousins made fun of her because she practically had no hips to speak of. Now they defined her silhouette.

Parth looked surprised when she slipped into the chair across from him. He usually ate alone, while she started the housework around him. Today he sensed she had something to say, and he didn't appear too happy about it.

Mishti peeled the banana but left it on the table while her stomach rumbled dully. She didn't want to distract from the speech she'd prepared in the car.

"What?" He didn't snap at her, but she heard the impatience in his voice. She was expecting it and decided to soldier through it.

"I was thinking we could plan a trip to India."

"What's brought this on?"

"Nothing in particular. We haven't been in a long time. It would be nice for Maya to experience it before she grows up. It might be too much of a culture shock for her later."

"It will be a culture shock for her even now. Her upbringing is entirely different to what she'll see there."

"Does it matter?" she asked. Mishti pictured driving with Maya, driving anywhere that wasn't paid for by Parth. That place did not exist.

"You're the one who brought up culture shock."

"I brought it up because you wanted me to explain why we should go to India."

She could feel her heart beating faster than it normally did. It was very seldom she spoke this way, especially to Parth. His brows furrowed, as he watched the expression change on her face.

"I just don't see a reason for us to go," he said. "Ma and Baba will be visiting next summer, so Maya will get to see them then."

"And what about her other set of grandparents? When will she see my ma and baba?"

"She sees them on video calls, doesn't she?"

Mishti felt a momentary surge of bitterness toward her parents. They were the ones who had put her here. Trapped in a foreign country, in the possession of a man who had given her Maya. Maya. This country wasn't foreign to her daughter. This was her home.

Mishti could never leave and uproot Maya from the only place she had ever known.

Mishti picked up the banana and shoved most of it into her mouth. It made her cheeks swell up like a chipmunk's. It was the only way she could stop herself from saying the things she wanted to hurl at him. It would make matters worse. Her cut thumb throbbed and she pressed it into the table, allowing the dull ache to travel down her arm, and hip, and leg.

Forcing herself to finally swallow, she said, "I think it would be a good idea to introduce her to her roots. Show her where we come from."

"It's a waste of time and money. You are aware of how high our mortgage is, what our expenses are like. I'm not made of money. You should have married a lawyer or a businessman, if that is the lifestyle you wanted."

Mishti hung her head. He had shamed her into feeling greedy and selfish, reminding her once again that the money they had wasn't hers. That she was going to spend the rest of her life seeking her husband's permission. Just like she'd spent all her childhood seeking her father's.

"I don't like having to explain this to you over and over again," he added.

She'd never brought it up before. They rarely ever spoke about money, because this was exactly the conversation she wanted to avoid.

"There are some sacrifices we have to make, so we can live in this house. So we can have this life, in this country."

She wished she could allow herself to cry in his presence, but she knew it would only spur him on further.

"Was there anything else?" he demanded in a calmer voice.

Mishti shook her head and stood up. There were dishes that needed washing, laundry that needed folding, sheets that needed changing.

"Make me another cup of coffee before you go, will you? This one's gone cold." He stopped her in her tracks, before she could slip away. She didn't yank the cup off the table, she didn't even stomp her feet as she went to turn the kettle on. He was watching her closely for signs of aggression, for any hint of rebellion.

But he needn't have worried. Mishti didn't know how.

LATER THAT AFTERNOON, Mishti tested the waters with Ciara. They were on their way to the playground to meet the mothers group. In the handful of years they'd been friends, Mishti had rarely spoken about her marriage; she didn't feel that she had to. It was one of the things she appreciated most about Ciara: She didn't ask any uncomfortable questions. Especially the questions she already knew the answers to.

"Do you make your husband another cup of coffee if the first one goes cold?" Mishti asked, before Ciara had finished her previous sentence. Ciara did a double take.

She glanced at Finn asleep in the buggy. Maya and Bella were walking ahead of them, dancing around trees, eyeing up puddles, holding hands. They looked so starkly different as they hopped together, it made Mishti's stomach ache with joy and uncertainty. Dark hair against blond, curls like springs beside Bella's straight hair like dry spaghetti, Maya's smaller rounded hands clasped by pale bony fingers, Maya's slightly knocked knees and Bella's sharp edges. They carried identical backpacks covered in sequins and were wearing the same light-up shoes.

"I can't remember the last time I made Gerry a cup of coffee," Ciara replied, staring straight ahead. "Is that what you do? Is that what Parth expects from you?"

When they turned to look at each other, Mishti felt a jolt in her bones, like Ciara could see right through her. She was embarrassed. There were already a million things that made them unequal.

"Does he expect you to wait on him, Mishti? I hoped he'd have left those expectations behind in India."

Already this felt like a bad idea. Mishti didn't know where to begin, to explain to Ciara the intricacies of the social construct and norms that came with a marriage like theirs.

Ciara reached for her arm, stopping Mishti in her path. "Are you listening to me? It isn't right if he treats you like the hired help."

Mishti's stomach growled with hunger, and she looked in her handbag for a protein bar as an excuse to look away from Ciara.

"No, he doesn't expect it of me. I do it myself sometimes. They go cold so quickly here. It's not something we worry about in India." Mishti forced a giggle, which sounded tinny even to her own ears, and hot tears prickled the backs of her eyelids. Ciara refused to let it go.

"Just microwave it—better still, tell him to microwave it himself."

Mishti giggled again, like this suggestion was ridiculous. She couldn't stop her body from shaking, with cold and hunger. Ciara grabbed her elbow tightly, like she knew how to make it better.

"Don't make him another cup of coffee, Mishti." She sounded determined. It wasn't a suggestion; it sounded like a command.

"It's okay, I don't mind. It's not like that. I was curious, that's all."

Ciara kept staring at her, even though they were nearly at the gate now. The girls had already run in. From the corner of her eye, Mishti could see a group of women walking enthusiastically toward them.

"I'm sure. Parth doesn't seem like the kind of man who would demand such a thing." Ciara sighed and finally gave in.

Mishti was saved by the other women approaching, just in time. They all but pounced on Ciara, as Mishti stepped away to make room. For a moment there, she was afraid she was going to tell Ciara everything. How she hated sleeping in the same room as Parth. How she had never seen their bank account. How she spent all her nights making trips to the kitchen to wolf down leftovers from the fridge.

She knew Ciara would have understood, because Ciara's father had never loved his wife either.

AFTER SOME TIME at the playground, the children began behaving badly, as they usually did when they got together like this. The non-parents, the ones speed-walking or jogging on the looping path around the park, shook their heads and threw looks at the rowdy kids. Even if they were parents, they clearly didn't have small children anymore and seemed to have forgotten what it could be like.

The mothers took turns supervising, peeling off in pairs to keep an eye on the children, while the others chatted and drank their coffees. The number of benches for parents was disproportionate to the number of children the playground could accommodate. The mothers huddled together near the gated entrance where the bikes and scooters were piled, along with discarded coats and hats.

"I like your scarf," Lauren said, joining Mishti on the bench where she sat alone on the periphery of the group, listening but silent. "Is it from India?"

Mishti blushed, because she never knew how to take a compliment. It made her nervous and sheepish.

"Yes, I bought it in India. No, I didn't buy it, someone gave it to me. My sister—she's actually my cousin but like a sister to me. She gave it to me before I left." She knew she was over-explaining and hoped Lauren wouldn't care. Unfortunately, Lauren seemed interested and nodded along.

Over Lauren's shoulder, Mishti could see Ciara looking at them. She stood in a group with some of the other mothers. That steady gaze made her uncomfortable.

"It looks handmade, it's beautiful," Lauren continued.

"Yes."

"And the colors, they're so vibrant."

"Yes."

Lauren was smiling at her now, twisting the loops of her own woolen check scarf. Mishti had nothing to add. In the distance, Ciara had finally turned her attention to someone else, laughing loudly at something.

"There used to be a shop in the city when I was growing up, and the lady who ran it sold beautiful scarves and bags she sourced from India, among other things. But I've never seen anything like this one before."

"Mmm-hmm." Mishti didn't know what to say, so she stared at the chipped green polish on Lauren's bitten nails. This was the first time she was noticing that Lauren had quite the masculine pair of hands, with broad knuckles and square shapeless wrists. A spongy-looking green vein ran all the way up the inside of her right arm, disappearing under the half sleeve of her faded tie-dye top.

"I would love to go to India. It's on my top-five places to visit. Maybe someday."

Mishti's eyes remained on Ciara, who had broken away from the group of women—all dressed almost identically in calf-length puffer coats or vests and Lycra leggings—and was walking toward Mishti with intent. The others gazed after her longingly.

"Think it's our turn to watch the kids, Mishti," Ciara said. Her voice was sweet but held an edge. "We should give Aisling and Nora a break. They're about ready to tear their hair out." Ciara gave only a cursory smile to Lauren, then turned her attention back to Mishti.

"Yes, we should," Mishti said, rising to stand.

"I can take this round with Mishti, if you want to finish your coffee, Ciara," Lauren said, and Mishti winced at that. She wasn't certain if Lauren was goading Ciara or if she was just plain stupid.

Ciara stared into Mishti's eyes; her long lashes fluttered on her pale cheeks twice, as though she were beating a drum. She took painfully long to turn and look down at Lauren, almost like she hadn't even heard her.

"I'm not the one who needs a break from my kids," Ciara replied. Mishti was glad she couldn't see Ciara's face, but she could hear the smile in her voice. The color had drained from Lauren's face. The skin on her forehead seemed to have stretched, making her eyes appear watery and wide. For a moment, she thought Lauren was going to burst into tears.

Ciara looked over in the direction of the children. Lauren's kids were the loudest, wildly chasing one another around, screeching, throwing themselves on the springy playground floor. Harry seemed to have lost his shorts somewhere.

"Maybe you should take a walk or something, take a breather. It won't be a bother, we'll keep an eye on them," Ciara continued. Lauren kept her face turned to her children. She had appeared teary a few moments ago, but now her face was as good as stone.

Mishti took a step back, like she was expecting an explosion.

"Thanks, Ciara, you're almost too kind. I make it a point to not hover around my kids all the time and direct their every move, so I do get time to myself." Lauren surprised them with a smile.

She threw a look at the group of women, who were staring at them from a distance, clearly desperate to know what was being said, then she got up and walked away, resettling herself on one of the abandoned swings.

Ciara breathed out deeply, her chest rising and falling like she was struggling to contain herself. "I hate her."

It was the beginning of autumn and there were gaps between the leaves of the trees now, and light filtered through. Ciara's blue eyes dazzled in the sunshine.

Mishti was just glad she wasn't in Lauren's shoes. By some miracle, Ciara had picked her, when she could have very easily cast her aside too. Then where would she have been? Without Ciara, Mishti would have nothing. She felt no true affinity toward the other women in the village, and besides Maya, she would have nobody to talk to. Nobody to share a cup of tea with. Nobody to text or go to the city with for lunch. Even if Mishti wanted to come to Lauren's defense, she knew she couldn't. She had picked sides the day she let Ciara into her house.

"I could see it was getting awkward for you, so I came to your rescue," Ciara said. "What was she saying?"

"She likes my scarf. She said she wants to go to India."

Ciara rolled her eyes as they started walking toward Aisling and Nora.

"I mean, seriously, there are things to talk to you about other than India. You're practically Irish at this point."

They spoke to Aisling and Nora for a few minutes before they were alone again. Mishti focused on the children, who were still pumped full of energy. There were no queues for the slides and a few of them were hanging off the gym bars. All playground rules were abandoned by now, and it made her anxious.

She eyed Maya, who was sitting with two other girls. They were clapping hands together and singing a rhyme she didn't recognize. She hadn't grown up with these songs.

"Look at her kids, they don't even know how to play with the others. What is she teaching them?" Ciara drew Mishti out of her thoughts again. "And she brags about not keeping an eye on them."

Just like their mother, Freya, Harry, and Willow usually kept to themselves and steered clear of the other children. Fortunately, they didn't seem to notice how they were already cast out.

THEY WERE WALKING home together later. It was a short walk to their own cluster of houses, but the road was narrow and winding, and they had to keep an eye on the girls. A stream of cars inched along beside them, held up behind a red-faced cyclist. On the side of the footpath, there were a few houses, spaced wide. On the other edge was the sea, clear and gushing, marred only by orange bobbing buoys and circling gulls.

"And it's not necessarily about the sugar. That's the common misconception. It's the caffeine in chocolate that makes them hyper." Ciara was speaking as they walked.

Maya and Bella bobbed ahead of them, while Finn sat quietly in the buggy that Ciara was pushing. He was a calm toddler, rarely ever fussing or demanding his mother's attention. Maya at this age would have refused to sit strapped in any contraption.

"Oh, I never thought of that," Mishti replied.

"Yes, exactly. Most people don't. Not that excessive sugar is any better."

Ciara's shiny ponytail swung as she walked along. Her runners didn't have a speck of mud on them.

"I don't let Bella indulge after three. That's her deadline and she knows it. She doesn't even ask for sweets or snacks after three. You have to stand your ground with these kids, you know?"

Mishti didn't want to imagine what Ciara would say about her midnight yogurt-and-jaggery episodes. "You're right. It's a constant power struggle."

"Exactly, and you need to make sure they know who is boss. Anyway," Ciara sighed, "today went well, didn't it?"

"The kids had fun."

"Yes, and all the mammies got a break. How did mothers do it before us? With three, four, five kids stuck to their boobs and hanging off their hips."

"I don't know. It's depressing to think about," Mishti said. She pictured her mother cooking in the kitchen, sweat beading her forehead as she stirred several pots at the same time. The other women in the house watched the kids, saw to the laundry. Not a moment's peace, but never alone. Mishti couldn't decide who had it better, her mother or her.

"And they wouldn't have had help from their husbands either."

Mishti flushed. She didn't see much of a difference between Parth and her own father. Maya was just as anxious around him as Mishti had been around her own.

"And now we have all this information at our fingertips. We can choose to do with it what we like. Really, there's no excuse for making bad parenting decisions anymore."

"Do you and Gerry agree on everything?" Mishti asked.

"He trusts me. I've done my research."

As they approached Mishti's house, they saw Parth in the driveway, stepping out of his car.

"There he is!" Ciara remarked, when they were in his earshot.

Parth turned to them with a half grin. "Ciara, how are you?"

"I'm not sure. We've just spent the past two hours with a bunch of kids and their mothers. We were all hopped up on sugar and caffeine."

"You have my sympathies."

Mishti stood back, starkly aware of not being a part of this conversation.

Their bodies were close together, and there was an ease about the way Ciara and Parth stood in each other's personal spaces. All she could see was Ciara's wide-lipped smirk, Parth's eyes lingering on her hips. He looked away when a car passed them, lifting his hand to wave at a neighbor Mishti had never seen him interact with before.

"It was nice seeing you, Ciara," he said, smiling at her before he headed toward the front door.

Ciara was beaming, flushed, as she turned to Mishti. "Let's have dinner sometime. The two families. It'll be fun."

Mishti nodded, smiling, trying not to blame Ciara for how she must have been feeling. It was all Parth.

If he had looked at Mishti that way, she would have been blushing too.

Chapter 5

September 3

CIARA DIDN'T FEEL GUILTY ABOUT LETTING HER thoughts wander to Parth Guha as she set the table for dinner. She was free to imagine what she wanted, about whomever she wanted.

Bella was glued to the TV again, while Finn was on the rug in the sitting room, surrounded by toys he rarely played with.

Parth made for the picture-perfect immigrant story. Educated, charming, successful, a fitting embellishment to their community. From the day the Guha family moved into the house next door, Ciara decided she was going to take them under her wing.

She knew their marriage was arranged, even though Mishti rarely spoke about her husband. The impression she got was that things were strained between them, that Parth was difficult to live with, but weren't they all? If she had him at her disposal, she would have straightened him right up.

It wasn't very often that Ciara even saw the two of them together, so it was difficult to picture them as a couple. Mishti was her friend, her most trusted confidante. Parth was an attractive neighbor. In her mind, the two existed independent of each other.

She bit her bottom lip while slicing a lemon into wedges. She enjoyed these stolen moments of private thought.

Once she was satisfied, she pulled out her phone to photograph the food. She had to go on tiptoes to position the camera directly above the dishes, and it took several attempts before she was satisfied with the angle and lighting. Her followers loved this sort of thing, a peek into her daily life. She was just like them, the photograph said. A healthier, glowing, more aspirational version of them. Just a little out of reach.

"Mummy, I want some sweets. I'm very hungry." Bella came into the kitchen with her nostrils flared. She didn't seem to notice her mother all but suspended in the air above the dining table.

"You're going to have to wait to eat your dinner if you're hungry." Ciara clicked a few more photographs. She moved the cutlery around for the different shots.

"But I'm *hungry.*"

"Go see if your brother's okay." She stood back and scrolled through the photographs.

"Can I have some Haribos?"

"No, Bella. It's nearly dinnertime."

"But I'm hungry now."

"Go check on Finn."

She posted one of the photos to her Instagram stories, captioning it with a few happy, heart-eyed emojis. There were responses and reactions before she'd even had a chance to put the phone away.

Bella stomped her feet violently. The front door opened just as she was about to explode, and she heard her father.

"Daddy!" She ran to him.

Gerry basked in his daughter's adoration, reaching for Bella and lifting her high overhead, then spinning her around. They dissolved in sugary giggles. Ciara thought about photographing the moment so she could post it online, but she turned away from them. She didn't want Gerry to think she was encouraging this sudden birth of a bond between them.

They sat down at the dinner table shortly after. Bella was narrating the plot of *Frozen*. This wasn't new to them, but they had no choice but to listen. Finn was in the high chair and disinterested in his food. He picked out each square piece of grilled chicken and promptly flung it to the ground. Ciara had snapped a photo of him as soon as she'd put the food down on his tray, so she couldn't care less about the mess now.

"I can take him out of the high chair and hold him while we eat," Gerry said.

"You're not here for most of their meals; this is what he's always like. If you hold him once, he'll want to be held all the time. I can't allow it to turn into a habit."

"Daddy, you're not listening to me!"

"I am, baby."

"He just has to learn to be independent. If he doesn't want his dinner in the high chair, he's not getting it any other way."

Gerry glanced at his son apologetically, infuriating Ciara even more.

"Hold him if you want to."

"I don't want to turn this into a thing."

"You already have."

"Daddy!"

"Yes, baby, okay, tell me your story. I'm listening."

Bella told the *Frozen* story like it was something she had personally lived through. It gave Ciara a chance to sink back into the warm glow of remembering Parth's eyes on her, lingering a moment too long. She shifted in her chair.

"Daddy, can I have dessert?"

Ciara heard Bella, and she glared at Gerry from across the table.

"I don't know if we have any," he replied. He was buying time, hoping his wife would step in. She could see him cracking under the pressure, and she held back.

"Mummy, can I have dessert?"

"May I have some dessert," Ciara corrected her. "And no, there isn't any."

Bella put down her fork and pushed her plate away.

"I didn't get any sweets today. I want chocolate."

"You're not having any at this time of the night, Bella."

"Why don't we discuss the possibility of a treat after you've finished dinner?" Gerry said, fully disintegrating to pieces now.

Ciara and Bella were glaring at each other, and then Bella got out of her chair. "I'm going to watch TV."

"No, you're going to leave the TV alone. There are lots of other things for you to do around the house. You have a box full of jigsaws, for instance."

Bella pretended to not have heard her mother and left the kitchen.

Ciara put down her cutlery, and Gerry took a sip of water in preparation for what was to come.

"You have to stop encouraging her," she snapped at him.

"Encouraging her how?"

"Giving her the idea that dessert is even an option."

"I didn't bring it up, Ciara."

"She's obsessed with sugar."

"Ciara . . ."

"You're not here the rest of the day. You don't know what she's like, and I'm the villain for putting my foot down."

Once again, Gerry fell silent. She wasn't even curious to know what was on his mind. Not these days.

"And it's starting to show," she added.

"Show?"

"Her obsession with sweets."

"What are you trying to say, Ciara?"

"All right, you want me to say the words? I will. I'm not going to be politically correct here, Gerry. Bella is putting on weight. When she's not eating sweets, she's sitting in front of the TV. A lot of the times, she's doing both." She left out the part about how she worried what the other mothers would say if *her* daughter ended up with childhood obesity.

Gerry glanced at his son, and for a moment Ciara thought he was going to curse, save for Finn's presence.

"Bella is a growing child. She is not fat."

"I didn't say she is. I'm pointing out that she's developing un-healthy eating habits."

"Okay, so we'll talk to her."

"And tell her what exactly?"

Gerry pressed his thumbs into his temples and shut his eyes. "I don't know, Ciara, I don't know what we'll say. All I know is we need to talk to her instead of fighting her on this."

Ciara stood up with a jerk. Her chair scraped the floor noisily and nearly tipped over.

"You sit here and think about it while I go drag her away from the TV. Once again, I'll be the one actually doing something around here."

As she left the room, she heard Gerry unbuckling Finn from the high chair.

"Bella, you were told you can't watch TV anymore tonight."

Her daughter's face screwed up as she forced the tears to come. Ciara braced herself for what she knew was going to be a long night.

SHE HAD THE baby monitor clipped to her hip while she loaded the dishwasher later. Bella had eventually gone to sleep, screaming and thrashing. Ciara could still hear phantom echoes of her daughter's cries ringing through the house.

She looked over her shoulder when she heard Gerry uncorking a bottle of wine.

"Would you like some of this?"

"Yes."

They didn't drink together very often, not while they were alone anyway. She was mildly curious about him being home early enough for dinner with the kids, but she decided she didn't want to hear about his day or the effort he'd suddenly decided to make to spend more time with his family.

"It sounded like Bella had a hard time falling asleep," he said. He approached her with the wineglass in an extended hand. The dish-washer was fully stacked, and there was nothing else to attend to in the kitchen. There was an awkwardness between them, now that the children weren't around and their hands were free.

"She doesn't like being told what to do."

"I'm sorry I wasn't much help tonight. I'm sorry if I made things worse."

"She was testing my authority because you were around."

"Okay, yes, but I wasn't trying to take sides."

"You have to be able to fight her."

"Does it have to be a fight?"

"With Bella, it does."

They both sipped their wine, standing on opposite sides of the white marble kitchen island. Her phone was lying on the counter, directly in her line of vision. She could see notifications popping up. Reactions from strangers to her photos of their scrumptious home-cooked meal and the adorable photo of Finn in his high chair.

"I want to be able to help you, Ciara," Gerry continued, raking a hand through his brushed-up hair.

"Well, this is a fairly recent development."

"I've always wanted to help."

"So it's my fault you're never around?"

"You don't want my help; neither do you want me around."

"This again."

He came to stand beside her, and she held her glass to her chest. It was an attempt to discourage him from coming any closer. She couldn't remember the exact date or month or year when she stopped wanting him to touch her. It may have been before Finn was even born.

When he did reach for her shoulder now, Ciara felt herself seize up.

When they first met, they couldn't keep their hands off each other. Even then, in her mid-twenties, Ciara knew they were living on borrowed time. She believed what's said about sexual chemistry running out, that the honeymoon period doesn't last forever. She had been pleasantly surprised she had a sexual appetite for him at all.

This was a man who was good enough to marry. She wasn't expecting to be attracted to him too.

Gerry's fingers traveled up her shoulder and lingered on her neck, and she smiled smugly at him. It wasn't going to work, especially not on a night she'd been imagining Parth's fingers right there on that spot.

"I want us to try a little harder, Ciara. Do you think we can do that?"

"Try harder with the kids?"

"And with us. We don't see each other very often anymore. Maybe it's my fault. Maybe I've been working too hard."

She stepped away from him, allowing his hand to fall from her.

"And what do you plan to do about it? Retire? At this age?"

"I could slow down a little."

She went to pour more wine in her glass. He'd barely touched his.

"You're free to do what you want, Gerry. It's your career."

"Do *you* want to go back to work? Is that what you're saying?"

Finally, he had said something that stung.

"You'll be surprised to know how much work goes into what I do."

"You know I'm not talking about the kids. I know how much work you put into them."

"I'm not talking about the kids either."

Gerry's eyes widened, like he hadn't given it a serious thought before. "Oh. Right. You mean your Instagram thing."

Ciara's nostrils flared and she poured more wine. Her "Instagram thing" had generated more income in the past two years than her desk job at Horizon had in five. The only joy she derived from that job, where she processed insurance applications, was by fabricating intricate details of an applicant's life based on what they filled out on their forms. Sometimes she lost hours poring over the bank statements of someone with a sizable spending account: studying their transactions, piecing together a pattern of where they bought their coffees on weekdays, their shopping sprees on the weekends, a big splurge at the toy shop on Sunday evenings.

Her inbox was currently packed with emails from cosmetics and lifestyle brands, offering her her very own sizable chunks of money for collaborations. Then she remembered that Gerry didn't have a clue about the money, not about any of it. He'd seen the products the companies sent her, and he assumed they were samples and gifts. He didn't know they were often accompanied by PayPal invoices.

"It doesn't matter," she snapped. He looked almost relieved, like he didn't want to have to listen to her, once again, explain that her social media had relevance. "I've been at home with the kids for five years. I can't just go back and pick up where I left off."

"You don't have to return to Horizon; you can look elsewhere. I can help with that," he said.

"Start afresh?"

"Yeah, start afresh."

She smiled at her husband, then poured the remaining wine down her throat. "Wouldn't that be the dream? Starting afresh with a clean slate, with nothing and nobody weighing me down."

Chapter 6

September 5

LAUREN HAD WALKED TO THE VILLAGE THROUGH THE woods again but took the regular route home, because she didn't want to have to explain the ring of broken beer bottles to Willow one more time. There had been some showers that morning, and now it was bright and wet. The triangular patches of green at the corners of the footpaths were waterlogged. Willow, who was tied to Lauren's back, pointed enthusiastically at each of them. She'd recently developed a fascination with puddles and jumping in them. Lauren wished she'd never introduced *Peppa Pig* to the household.

"You don't have your wellies on, Willow, you can't jump in puddles today," she repeated, when Willow pleaded to be let down again.

When they turned the corner, Lauren saw Mishti walking ahead on the footpath.

She was in running clothes: black leggings, fluorescent runners, and an oversized hoodie. Like some women who are self-conscious of their bodies, Mishti seemed to share the proclivity to bury herself in clothing a few sizes too large. She was hunched over, with her arms ramrod straight by her sides, trying to create a protective barrier against the cold. Lauren saw a woman with the delicate features of a toddler, a soft round face, cheeks and chin and neck all mushed together.

Rainbows appeared and disappeared amidst the hills that surrounded the village, their edges smudged by mist. A combine harvester droned not too far away, slowly shaving off a field and leaving a golden stubble in its wake.

When Lauren quickened her pace and caught up to her, Mishti startled.

"Hello there. Is Maya at preschool?"

"Huh. Yes, she is. Hi, Willow."

Willow mumbled a response and then went back to eating dehydrated pieces of mango.

"Did you just go for a run?"

"No, it was more of a jog in the park, but I'm not very good at it. I haven't been doing it very long."

"You'll get there, I'm sure. At least you're making an effort. I can't remember when I last took the time out to exercise."

"You have three children—you have your hands full," Mishti replied kindly.

She *was* kind, Lauren thought. When she wasn't under Ciara's watchful eyes, Mishti was more chatty too. "Some mothers seem to have it all together. They have all the answers and the time. I don't seem to have either," Lauren said.

"I don't know anybody who has all the answers."

They looked at each other, and Lauren tilted her head to one side and smirked. She hoped Mishti had caught her drift. If she did, she chose to ignore it.

"Anyway, I was thinking, we never got to finish our conversation from the other day at the playground. I was telling you how interested I am in India."

"Are you planning a trip?"

"I don't think we can go anywhere until Willow is a little older." They had never been anywhere. The kids hadn't even been to Dublin.

Mishti said nothing, which embarrassed Lauren a little. She was caught out trying to make conversation where one didn't exist.

"We haven't had the chance to get to know each other. We've been neighbors for a few years now," she tried.

"I'm sorry, it's my fault. I'm not a very sociable person."

"It's not your fault at all, Mishti. I should have made more of an effort."

"You've always been very kind to me, and Maya loves playing with Freya and Harry."

"Which is exactly why I think we should have dinner together sometime. I'll cook. The kids will be thrilled."

Mishti nodded in silence but didn't look very enthusiastic. A kind of noncommittal nod, like Sean gave her when she asked him to clean out the shed, which was crammed with his books and vinyls, all gone moldy.

She stopped in her tracks while Mishti continued on, noticing several moments later that Lauren wasn't by her side any longer. She turned back with a look on her face that said, *What?* However, it wasn't something Mishti would say out loud, and certainly not in that tone.

"Is it because of Ciara?" Lauren blurted.

"Ciara? What do you mean?"

"She's the reason why you don't want to bring your family over to my house for dinner."

"I didn't say that."

"But you're not going to, are you?"

"I just have to check with Parth; I'm not sure when he's free. He's always working."

Lauren wasn't certain, but she thought she detected a wince in Mishti's voice. "It would be kinder if you were just honest with me and admitted we can't socialize because your best friend wouldn't approve." It hurt her to even use that phrase, *best friend,* like she was that kid again.

Mishti wrapped her arms around her stomach, like she was feeling sick. Immediately, Lauren regretted pushing her. Mishti wasn't the person who deserved this barrage.

"Ciara hasn't said anything," Mishti mumbled.

"No, I know. I'm sorry, I shouldn't have brought it up. Forget it, okay?" She tried, but Mishti was already backing away, ready to make her escape, reminding Lauren once again what most people in this neighborhood really thought of her.

"You can text me with the dates you think will suit Parth for dinner," she called out, but Mishti was already giving her a small wave, then she turned and bounded away.

From where Lauren was standing, Mishti looked like quite the expert jogger.

SEAN WAS STRETCHED out on the sofa in the sitting room when Lauren returned home. It took her a few moments to get Willow out of the sling and settle her down.

"Didn't expect to find you home," Lauren said. She forced sweetness into her voice. She could still taste how sour her mouth was from her encounter with Mishti.

Sean rarely had anything to do but hang around the house, so she was being sarcastic. He hadn't had a business to run for a while, and now there were no musicians and poets to entertain either. He smiled at her and put his book away.

"What did you get at the shop?" He spoke to Willow, who came running over to climb on top of him.

Lauren got the kettle going.

"Mango," Willow said.

Lauren watched them from the kitchen, smiling. Whatever awkwardness and discomfort she experienced because of Ciara—and she did blame *Ciara* for what happened with Mishti—was gone when she saw Sean with Willow. They were content.

WILLOW'S NAPS WERE the only free time for Lauren all day, and they never lasted very long. She usually spent the time washing leftover dishes, folding the laundry, getting dinner started, sometimes even squeezing in a shower if she could manage it.

While awake, Willow demanded all of her attention; the household would have collapsed around them if it wasn't for Sean. He always stepped in for the other children when Lauren couldn't.

Lauren was chopping peppers and broccoli in the kitchen when Sean emerged from his shower in just a pair of faded black jeans. Sloppy tattoos covered his bare chest and biceps. They used to be brighter when they first met but were faded now. His skin showed some evidence of sagging, but she would never mention this to him.

Sean came over to kiss her, and she pressed her nose to his stubble. Sometimes she missed the way he used to smell of cigarettes and old books, his fingers rough and calloused from playing stringed instruments. Now he smelled of something minty from the shower, and all his callouses had healed a long time ago. He was a responsible father and a reliable partner. The way she saw it: She had to lose some to gain a lot.

"I met Mishti Guha on our way home," she said.

He leaned into the refrigerator and responded with a mumble.

If she told him what had happened, he would tell her she was overthinking it. He understood her conflict with Ciara and her clique, and his advice was always to keep things nonconfrontational. But he wasn't the one who'd grown up with these women.

"And?" he asked, looking over his shoulder at her.

"Nothing. She's nice; we got talking. I invited them to dinner."

Sean raised his brows in surprise. "I hope you're not expecting anything to come of it. You think the good doctor and his family will turn up here for dinner some night?"

Lauren was surprised by his tone.

"Are you suggesting there's something wrong with us?"

He gave her a wink, expecting her to join him in some humorous self-deprecation. This wasn't the first time they'd talked about how different they were from their neighbors. In fact, Sean would never have picked this village, this neighborhood, to settle in if it wasn't for the free house. Usually, Lauren was able to laugh it off like him. Usually, she remembered that she didn't need anything or anyone other than her family. Today, the expression on her face was different, and he saw it.

"There's nothing wrong with us, love. All these people, they're the ones stuck in their sad little lives, in this sad little place."

"This place is beautiful."

"Of course it is, and maybe I'd notice it more often if it wasn't for the people living in it."

Lauren sniffed, placing the damp wooden chopping board on the windowsill to dry.

"Are you okay? Did something happen?" he asked.

She didn't want to confess what she'd said to Mishti. "You don't mind, do you? If we have the Guhas over?" She chose this moment to bend down and take her muddied boots off, just so she wouldn't have to meet his eyes.

Sean shrugged while picking some leftover curried chickpeas out of a bowl. "I don't mind, but maybe don't hold your breath. Maybe you're just trying to be friendly, but you have to remember whose spell she's under."

Lauren reddened, remembering. Was Mishti going to tell Ciara? What kind of public humiliation would that lead to? How would her words be twisted, and what would Sean think of her then? She still cared what Sean thought of her.

"You're right, it's probably for the best if they don't come over. I'm sure we have nothing in common with them anyway," she said.

Chapter 7

September 8

A FEW TIMES EACH MONTH, CIARA DROPPED FINN off at her mother-in-law's while Bella was at preschool. Then she would put on some clothes from her old wardrobe. Clothes that weren't designed for squatting in front of a toddler's potty seat. She'd even labor over her makeup, take some mirror selfies to post online. Then she'd get in her car and drive.

Usually directly into the city. Unless she needed her prescription filled, in which case she would make the customary visit to her GP first. Ciara had had trouble sleeping after her mother died, and then things got a lot worse in college.

Today she didn't have to visit the doctor, so she took the longer, scenic route, rolling the window down to let in the sea breeze, driving at 100 and barely slowing at the bends. Without the kids in the car, she was free to listen to whatever she wanted. Usually, pop songs from the early 2000s. Songs she'd grown up listening to in her room, to drown out her mother's sobs.

Sunlight flashed off her rearview mirror; her scarf billowed in the breeze. The narrow road wound around green rolling hills, and she laughed at mountain goats hopping from one big rock to another. She felt as free as a paper bag caught in the wind over a shingle beach.

Ciara was a teenager when she'd visited the city for the first time. She hadn't grown up doing things as a family with her parents. Even though she loved her father, she belonged to her mother, and her mother rarely left the house.

They drove up in his battered Grand Vitara, just the two of them. Her father hadn't even bothered unhooking the empty trailer, so it rattled behind them the whole way. Ciara was embarrassed when she stepped out of that car in the shiny city, and a group of teenage boys sniggered as they walked past. Her father hadn't noticed. He was pulling the pockets out of his trousers in search of his wallet.

She was suspicious when he told her he wanted to buy her a dress for her fourteenth birthday. There was nowhere to wear a brand-new dress, and there was nothing special about this birthday.

The city surprised her, and she leaned toward her father as they walked together. When they made to cross the road, he reached for her hand. A pair of teenaged girls in low-rise jeans and matching Britney Spears choppy bobs stood on the other side. They were laughing with their heads tilted toward each other conspiratorially, and so Ciara snatched her hand away from him.

"There she is!" her father exclaimed as they crossed over. Ciara didn't know who to look at. A crowd swarmed around her as the traffic lights beeped. For a few moments, she thought she'd lost him. Then she saw him standing next to a woman she didn't recognize.

"Ciara! Get over here." They were both beaming at her, and she stood very still. She'd never seen this woman before, but she knew who it was.

"This is Simone," he said, as though Ciara was expecting to see her. It didn't even sound like a real name.

Simone looked older than him. She wore dark clothes, with a coat that hid her ankles, and a furry scarf. She smelled of incense sticks and had very long pink nails. The glasses she wore had a slight tint to them, so Ciara couldn't tell if they were sunglasses or prescription. The first thing Simone did was reach out to touch Ciara's hair.

"Like spun gold," she said, in a rich voice.

Ciara took a step back and glared at her father.

"Simone is going to help us find you the perfect dress."

"My treat," Simone said. She beamed as though she hadn't noticed Ciara flinching.

"I don't want a new dress," Ciara said. She felt like someone had to stand up for her mother. They had known about Simone—not by name or any of the particulars. So far, Simone had just been an ever-present sensation hanging over them in the house. Now she was a living, breathing person, with Ruby Woo feathering at the corners of her wrinkled mouth.

Her father reached for Ciara's shoulder. "Don't be difficult. We have a whole day planned together, Buttercup. Simone told me about this Chinese restaurant we could go to after we're done shopping."

"I want to go home, Dad." She had stopped looking at the woman.

"Give her a chance, will ya?"

"Pat."

"I'm going home."

"We're here now," he said.

"Pat, you better take the girl home."

The beeping started again, and another throng of people surrounded them, pushing past in all directions, separating them for a few moments. Ciara searched for someone in those strange faces, and she realized she was looking for her mother. The woman who was still asleep when they'd left the house early that morning. The woman who wasn't going to remember her daughter's birthday next week.

"Mind yourself." It was Simone. She'd grabbed Ciara's wrist and pulled her back onto the footpath. Ciara hadn't noticed that she'd drifted toward the street.

This was not how she had pictured herself in the city. Lost and wearing her mother's old turtleneck Aztec sweater.

"Your father's going to take you home now," Simone said.

She nearly threw herself at this woman, nearly begged her to take her to the shops and buy her some new clothes. Then she looked at her father and saw how desperately he wanted that too.

"Don't fucking touch me," she snarled. Simone took a breath and looked at him. He said nothing, just shook his head like he wished he was in a different life. Then they were crossing the street again, to go back to the car, but this time he didn't reach for Ciara's hand.

IT WAS STILL early when Ciara parked in the city today. Then she walked to Margaret's Meadow, stopping only to look at the window of Brown Thomas. Even though Margaret's shop was on the High Street, it wasn't a High Street clothing brand. Here, they pampered her with prosecco in champagne flutes and brought out tiny bowls filled with sugared almonds.

The shop was too exclusive to draw a crowd, and when Ciara walked in, she was the only customer there. Two eager women turned: Margaret, along with her assistant, Maggie. Their matching names always made her smile.

"We were wondering when we might see you again. You have to take a look at these new trousers we have in stock." Margaret was all smiles as she dismissed Maggie, presumably to arrange the bubbly and the treats.

"I can't stop for long, so these better be good."

Ciara made herself comfortable in an ivory armchair. It was placed conveniently in the middle of the shop floor, facing the racks filled with beautiful pieces. Ciara took her phone out to snap a few pictures. Margaret stood back and watched proudly. Every time Ciara posted these photographs online, the shop's social-media pages gained a host of new followers. Ciara couldn't be sure, but she had a feeling she'd generated at least a few thousand euros' worth of sales in the past few months alone.

Margaret pulled out a pair of trousers that were made from what looked like wet leather.

"Do you see the detail?" Margaret held it up, bringing it closer for Ciara to inspect. The detail she was talking about were some asymmetrical pleats around the thigh area. Ciara had seen these before.

"Biker chic, wouldn't you call it? You can wear them with anything. Tunics, tops, blouses, or even oversized tees. Don't you think?"

Margaret's enthusiasm was a nuisance, but Ciara enjoyed the fluttering and coddling.

Maggie appeared with the tray, but Ciara ignored it today. She didn't have the time.

She rubbed the material between her fingers. It was pleather. She had never been on a bike and wondered what her so-called friends would say if they saw her in something like this. She would never want them to think she was trying this hard.

"Yeah, I'll take one."

Margaret visibly shook as she tried not to make eye contact with Maggie. It had to have hurt, her pupils reaching the very corners of her eyes.

It was the quickest sale Margaret had ever made, and she took 50 percent off the price tag.

Chapter 8

September 8

IN CALCUTTA, AS A GIRL, MISHTI SPENT HOURS IN THE sun with her hair soaked in coconut oil. She'd bought a Walkman with birthday money from her grandfather. She'd plug the earphones in and lie on the cemented floor of the terrace, insensible to the sounds of traffic, the yelling in the streets.

Eventually, she'd go down and help her mother with the cooking, by which time the warmth had seeped into her bones. Enough to last her the night.

Mishti shared a room with two cousins, her father's brothers' daughters. They lived together as a joint family. Her grandparents, her two uncles, their families, and them.

Her cousins never found out about the Walkman, because she'd never used it in front of them. If she had, it would either have been taken away from her or she'd have been forced to share.

Over time, she had spent more money on the cassettes than on the Walkman itself. While most other girls obsessed over Bollywood songs and boy bands, Mishti listened to Dylan and Springsteen. When it was decided she and Parth would move to Ireland after the wedding, her cousins were thrilled she may live near one of the Westlifes.

She hadn't shared their taste in boys either. The three of them would lie awake at night, discussing their latest crushes, but Mishti wasn't interested in boys who got their hairstyles from magazines and film stars.

It didn't matter, either way. Mishti knew very well that her parents would never approve of her having a boyfriend. She, like all the other girls in her family, was being raised for the long game: marriage. Yet finding a groom for herself was out of the question. If anyone had ever asked her, finding a groom wouldn't have been one of the questions at all. She longed for a life different from her mother's, even though she couldn't picture it. There had to be something else, something more. Her parents didn't trust her judgment, and neither did she. Mishti had no experience with boys. Theirs was a mostly female household. The only men she had any access to were her father, uncles, and grandfather, and they were all alarmingly alike. They spoke very little; if they weren't talking about cricket, they were arguing over football. They sat together for their meals, the men. The children ate early, and the women ate late. Mishti knew what her father thought of the Congress Party, that he couldn't care less about BJP, and that he always voted for CPM. Other than that, she didn't know him very well.

When she met Parth, she knew she was lucky he had chosen to marry her. Of all the other girls he must have met, just as briefly, he decided she was the one he was going to spend the rest of his life with. In Ireland, she wasn't going to need a Walkman to shut out the street noises. But nothing could have prepared her for how her bones missed the warmth of the terrace sun or how her head was filled with the constant, loud chatter of voices she missed.

IT WAS NEEL'S voice she missed the most. She had known it all her life.

As far back as she could remember, she'd been aware of his existence. Except their families would never have encouraged their friendship. Neel's family home was much like her own but in significant disrepair. Her father and uncles made a decent income, enough to maintain the house and keep them all comfortable. The male members of Neel's family didn't fare as well; his youngest uncle was the local drunk. The man spent most of his days under the old banyan tree at the end of their street. He was usually found either passed out from his previous night's frivolity or playing endless rounds of rummy with other similar neighborhood characters.

Mishti's mother and aunts regarded the men under the banyan tree as wasted youth and shook their heads, gossiping about the shame they brought upon their families. She had once overheard her father pointing out that it wasn't the drunk uncle's fault. He was only a child when their father had passed away, leaving the family in serious debt.

Whatever led the Banerjees to their downfall, the children from Mishti's family were warned against them. As though the simple act of speaking to them could bring ruination upon their own. Which was why she never called out to Neel when she watched him from her balcony.

She'd look down and watch Neel play with stones he had collected, building them up in a tower and then knocking them over from a distance. He always played by himself, talking to himself loudly, and Mishti assumed he had no siblings or friends; it made her sad to think he must be lonely. He used perfectly flat stones with rounded edges. Over time he'd perfected his aim, so he only needed one shot to knock the tower over.

Sometimes, he was out on the street late at night, and it seemed no adults in his house ever noticed. Mishti would step onto the balcony when she'd hear him whistling to the stray cats. He'd bring them bowls of leftover rice, big mounds of it, which he'd place on the footpath. The cats gathered around him adoringly.

In all those years when she silently observed him, Neel never once looked up or caught her staring. If he knew she was there, he chose to ignore her.

It wasn't like she daydreamed about him the rest of the time. She focused on school and homework, helping her mother and aunts in the kitchen, playing Monopoly with her cousins, braiding one an- other's hair, and listening to her Walkman. The years passed, and the cousins stopped playing games together. Hair didn't need braiding any longer. She still saw Neel every day, except he didn't play with stones anymore. He'd stopped feeding the cats too. The only times she saw him now were when he rushed past her balcony with books tucked under his arm. He smoked all the time, and his unacceptably long curls were always disheveled. He was short and plump; the hint of a protruding belly tightened his kurta. "The mother doesn't cook— what else can they expect, eating all that street food all day," Mishti's aunts gossiped about him while they chopped vegetables together.

She didn't tell anybody she adored everything about him.

MISHTI WAS NINETEEN when she spoke to Neel for the first time. She was walking home from the bus stop, listening to music on her earphones, and didn't realize he was just a few steps behind her. He came up to her, matching her stride. When she sensed him, instead of turning to look at who it was, she picked up her pace in an at- tempt to get away from a stranger, a man. It was the reality of life in India, especially for a young woman. Even in broad daylight. Even just a few feet away from the front door of her own home.

She stopped in her tracks with a gasp when he jumped in her path, blocking her. She was fearful at first, and then the hairs on her nape stood up when she realized who it was. She had never been this close to him before.

He was smiling and pointing to his ears, urging her to take the music out. When she removed the earphones, traffic sounds broke through her thoughts. They disoriented her for a moment. A man walked past them. He was pushing a cart of vegetables, shouting to announce his wares, trying to grab the attention of the neighbor- hood's housewives. Mishti clutched the strap of her canvas bag where it fell across her breasts.

"What are you listening to?" Neel asked, and she immediately looked toward her house.

Nobody was at the windows or on the balcony.

"Dylan."

He raised his eyebrows like he was impressed.

"Is that a Walkman?" He tipped his head at the machine clipped to the waistband of her jeans. He was surprised, as he ought to have been. These had gone out of fashion in the late nineties. Mishti never graduated to iPods. She still preferred aligning the cassette with the grooves and hearing it *click*.

"Are you making fun of me?" This was the most she had spoken to any stranger. That was who he was, even though she had seen him almost every day of her life, tracked the maturation of his voice from a lonely boy's to a grown man's.

"No, why would I? If you hold on to that thing for another ten years, you could make a small fortune selling it."

"I don't want to sell it."

"Then you don't have to, but they're going to stop making cassettes soon."

"I don't need to buy new cassettes. I'm happy with the ones I have."

Neel looked up at her balcony for a moment. It was the only indication he ever gave of knowing she used to watch him.

Then he reached over and caught the earplugs looped around her neck. Mishti stood completely still as he tucked them back in place and "Tangled Up in Blue" poured into her ears. His fingers brushed her cheeks accidentally, and it was enough. She knew she had fallen into something with him.

NOW HER MEMORIES of those old years with Neel were jumbled and interspersed with her first memories of meeting Ciara. The timeline was wrong in her head; she'd met Ciara several years after Neel, after all. Mishti was a new bride, married to Parth, at a time when all the street names here were foreign to her and she couldn't read the road signs. Nonetheless, meeting Ciara held the same significance as speaking to Neel for the first time.

Ciara was pregnant with Bella when Mishti and Parth had just moved into the house down the street. Parth was away a lot, working long hours or gone on trips to Dublin, Belfast, Mayo, for conferences. Mishti found herself alone most of the time.

Ciara would appear at her door to make insignificant small talk, stroking her big round belly, reminding Mishti she was yet to conceive. Her mother-in-law had mentioned it a few times when Parth handed her the phone on Sundays. In between asking about the cooking and cleaning, his mother mentioned the box of Parth's childhood clothes she was saving to pass down to her grandson and the Ayurvedic tea Mishti should be drinking for fertility.

Every time she met Ciara at the door like this, Mishti was struck by how different they were, by how sociable Ciara was, how she knew to be polite and welcoming toward a new neighbor. Ciara's body was blossoming in a way only a pregnant woman's does: with cheeks like red shiny apples, skin translucent and shimmering like mother-of-pearl, arms lean but soft. Mishti hadn't begun putting on weight yet, but she was self-conscious even then. Her haircut was basic, just to keep her curls manageable; her knuckles were chapped by the cold, dry air. She was suddenly very aware of the fine dark hairs growing on her fingers.

"Fancy a walk? We could both do with some fresh air," Ciara once said. They had only ever chatted casually at Mishti's doorstep so far.

When Mishti had reached for a thin cardigan hanging by the door, Ciara laughed, but not unkindly.

"We need to get you a good raincoat. In fact, you need a couple of coats. Something practical for our walks, and something lovely for when we go out. Something waterproof, and something in a pure wool blend."

Mishti was too ashamed to tell her she didn't have the money for these clothes. She would have to wait and find the right opportunity to ask Parth, and even then, she didn't know if he'd agree it was money well spent.

A few days later, Ciara had turned up at the house, dressed in a beautiful turquoise coat that wrapped elegantly over her growing belly. Diamonds studded her earlobes. She wasn't dressed for a walk.

"Shall we?"

"Where are we going?"

"Shopping. I know a lovely little place in the city that has everything you need. You'll see." Ciara looped her arm around Mishti before she had a chance to even lock the front door.

She was anxious getting in Ciara's car. It smelled of her perfume, floral and immaculate, and the back seat was already fitted with a baby seat.

It had to be *now*. Mishti knew she needed to say something before they were on the road and it was too late.

"Maybe some other day," she blurted, when Ciara pressed the button that got the engine going.

Ciara checked the mirrors without looking at her, then started reversing.

"We're doing it today, Mishti. You need to stay dry. You need to get out of that house more. It'll be okay."

"I'm sorry, but you don't understand. I need to speak to Parth first."

"I do understand," Ciara said. Then she reached for the dial and turned the music a little higher. "Now, there's a scarf in the compartment there. You might want to tie it around your head if you don't want to mess up your hair." She pressed another button and the roof of the car started to slide open.

Mishti scrambled to get the scarf out, hurriedly tying it without knowing what she was doing or why. She'd never been in a car with the top down. She didn't have a chance to think about it, and they were already roaring down the motorway. The wind whipped Ciara's long silky hair, but she didn't seem to care. She was singing along to Kid Cudi's "Pursuit of Happiness." It wasn't Mishti's kind of music, but she found herself laughing. It may have been her first instance of genuine laughter in Ireland.

They didn't slow down until they hit the city, and Ciara lowered the music with a sigh. When cars pulled up around them at traffic lights, people stared.

"We make an unlikely couple, don't we?" Ciara laughed, tapping her gold ring on the steering wheel lightly. Mishti had been thinking this too, wondering if this was the reason that Ciara had chosen to be friends with her. She'd seen the comments on Ciara's Instagram posts—she already had a small but dedicated band of followers back then, before the stardom. It was plain to see that Ciara had her pick of friends but none with quite the shock value of Mishti. If there was one thing she was learning about her new friend, it was that she loved it when people turned to look.

They were flying again, zipping around this city that was brand-new to Mishti. They parked at the city center, and Ciara slipped her arm over Mishti's once more. Mishti told herself it was all in her head, that she was just imagining people gawking at them. Even though she hadn't seen anyone else who looked like her, there had to be other brown people in the city. Parth had mentioned there were some other Indians, some Pakistanis on the faculty with him. Apparently there were a lot of Indian nurses who worked at the hospitals.

They stopped at the door of a shop Mishti would never have entered on her own. She wasn't a window-shopper, and she didn't go into shops where she knew she wouldn't find anything appropriate.

Ciara turned to her. "Listen to me: We're here to have fun. Don't think about it. Don't think about him."

They hadn't discussed Parth until then, just like Ciara didn't mention Gerry much. With that, they walked into the shop.

Ciara picked out coats she thought Mishti had to have. A pair of practical but still stylish boots. Boot-warmer socks that Mishti didn't even know how to wear. A couple of hats to suit a variety of outfits. Ciara paid for everything, and Mishti couldn't protest. She stood by, a shadow, as Ciara talked and laughed with the women in the shop, as if they were old friends. A very shiny credit card was slipped over the counter, and nobody seemed to acknowledge it. Ciara gathered the bags in her hands and shouldered her way out the shop door, while Mishti trailed behind.

Once they were outside, Ciara pulled one of the coats out and placed it over Mishti's shoulders.

"You see? Better already." She danced around, tucking tags into the collar and sleeves. "Ah, Mishti, this looks lovely on you."

"Ciara, I can't. I'm sorry. This is too much." She knew it was too late, but still she tried to shrug the coat off, as Ciara held on to her elbows gently.

"Okay, Mishti. I know what you're thinking. Maybe we should have talked about it before we came here."

"I know you're trying to be kind."

"Mishti, I'm not trying to be kind. You don't need kindness, you're not a wounded kitten. I'm trying to be a friend."

"Then you have to take these back."

"I'll take them to my house. I'll keep them in my closet until you're ready to have them."

Mishti sighed and looked away. There was a long queue of student types outside a shop that sold only frozen yogurt. There were so many things she didn't understand about this country. Things she couldn't ask Parth, because she could sense he wanted her to remain ignorant.

"Okay, you keep it," Mishti replied.

Ciara smiled and helped her out of the coat, then folded it neatly back in the bag.

"Coffee and a cake? This baby is craving sugar."

Mishti had a ten-euro note in her purse. It was all she had, but it would be enough.

"Yes, that would be nice."

"Good. You can pay," Ciara said with a wink, making Mishti's stomach drop. Ciara's hips swayed in high heels as she stepped ahead. It was bewildering how not-pregnant she looked from the back. She half-turned, still beaming, and grabbed Mishti's hand. "Come on, let's go."

She shouldn't have worried, because Ciara paid for the food too. Mishti wore the coat on the way back to the car.

Chapter 9

September 8

CIARA WAS NEVER GOING TO WEAR THE TROUSERS she'd bought at Margaret's Meadow. Just like she had never worn the plum chiffon gown with the plunging neckline she'd purchased there a few months before.

The dresses and blouses she'd bought at this shop all hung in a designated wardrobe in her bedroom. They remained untouched but not unloved. Most nights before changing into her pajamas, and only when Gerry wasn't home, Ciara stood in front of the enormous collection of clothes she had spent a fortune on. They were arranged in order of occasion. Casual brunch. Cocktail. Red carpet. Tropical holiday. Funeral. Over time, she added shoes and accessories to match. These weren't the clothes she photographed for her Instagram page. To the rest of the world she was a warrior mama, living in stretchy leggings and name-brand sweatshirts.

Sometimes, in her secret wardrobe, she switched a pair of shoes from under a particular outfit to a different one. Then she stood back and visualized the ensemble put together. She never tried them on after she purchased them. They existed in disuse, never fading with washing, never popping buttons or coming away at the seams, never wrinkling.

Gerry had to have known where she was spending the money every time she went into town. She used his credit cards to make the purchases, and he had to have looked at the statements. In the years since Bella's birth that she'd been going to Margaret's Meadow, he hadn't inquired about it once. He'd never opened the wardrobe either.

Ciara carried the trousers in a large shopping bag, on her way from the shop to the café. She was already imagining the blouse she was going to match with today's purchase. She had a midnight-blue net blouse in mind, with small appliquéd flowers. It was the perfect juxtaposition: the tough biker trousers with the soft floral.

The coffee shop, unlike the boutique, was busy. Ciara walked in without expecting to see any familiar faces. Tucked away in their quiet village on an even quieter street, she often forgot how alive Cork City was. The anonymity thrilled her here. While it was never going to be New York, London, or Berlin, it was something close to it.

Over the past months, she had developed a taste for a very particular coffee order: a tall latte, made with hazelnut milk and two pumps of caramel syrup, whipped cream, and a sprinkling of cinnamon sugar. She only ever ordered it on these trips to the city. Around her family and for the purposes of social media, she still drank a cold brew black and herbal teas.

Ciara was about to join the queue when she spied at the other end of the café Parth Guha, sitting by himself at a table, his nose buried in his laptop. His fingers hovered tarantula-like over the keyboard.

She kept her eyes trained on him until he sensed her gaze and looked up. Then she slowly, casually wove her way among the tables until she was standing before him. His eyes swept up and down her body, taking in the change in her appearance.

"These are my non-mummy clothes," she explained, taking the seat opposite him.

Ciara thought it was adorable how he wouldn't let his eyes wander to the skirt that had ridden up her thighs. Mishti didn't know how lucky she was!

"I nearly didn't recognize you."

Ciara arched her brows, and he broke into a laugh. "My apologies, I didn't mean it that way. I just mean that you look really nice today. Not that you don't look nice on other days."

"*You* look like you're about to burst a vein."

"I'm sorry."

"I haven't taken offense. I take it as a compliment. I wear these clothes when I'm in the city, as a reminder of the woman I used to be before the children were born."

"A beautiful woman. I mean, you're still a beautiful woman." He shook his head, disappointed in himself, and they laughed together. Ciara stared openly at those big strong hands she'd been fantasizing about.

"How come I've never seen you in here before?" she asked.

"I come here often, but never at this time. I don't have any classes today, but I wanted to get out of the house. I have to meet with a few clients later."

"It can be difficult as a parent to get some time to yourself. You don't have to tell me."

They stared at each other in silence, with lingering smiles on their faces. His brown eyes were more expressive than anything Gerry had ever said in words. She knew what Parth wanted. Her teeth marks on his shoulder. Her nails digging into his back.

She was beginning to think it was what she wanted too.

"How are the kids?" he asked, clearing his throat.

"Parth, please." She leaned in, brushing a hand on his arm, but only briefly. "Let's not."

"Can I get you anything to eat?"

"I'll have a coffee—not now, though."

"I don't think I've ever asked you this. What did you do, I mean, where did you work before . . ."

"The kids happened? At Horizon."

"Right. That's excellent."

"Insurance. That's where I met Gerry. Technically, he was my boss. We both quit soon after we were married. It didn't look right, I suppose. Gerry got headhunted by P&E, so it all worked out in the end."

Parth nodded but didn't look overly impressed. Given what he had achieved academically, he had every reason to feel superior, Ciara thought. Even to Gerry the Golden Boy.

"But that ship has sailed for me. I will never be able to jump back into that sector. I've lost too much time."

"That's not true."

She shrugged. "I'm not mad about it. It is what it is. I didn't exactly love my job."

"Is there something else you want to do?"

She sank her teeth into her bottom lip and smiled, as though there was something on her mind that could land her in prison. "I've been growing a social-media presence. It's nothing big, but there's some potential there."

Parth blinked like he didn't understand. At first, she thought he didn't know what she was talking about, but she caught the way he glanced down, how his fingers fidgeted with his laptop screen. Then she understood: He'd stalked her online.

"I'm sure you're great at it," he said.

"You're not on social media, are you?"

He laughed and shook his head. "I'm not active on it, no, but I hear enough about it. Spending most of your day around young people will do it."

"Well, then you probably don't take me seriously."

Parth looked into her eyes. "I think it could be a legitimate source of income. I mean, consider the number of people who look up to you for advice and inspiration."

Ciara nearly blurted the figure out. The exact number of people who followed her, and it was growing daily. "Yes, I am lucky."

"I'm sure there is a lot of hard work involved."

As much as she tried to blow this off, she couldn't get away from the feeling that Parth was the only person who was taking her seriously.

"I appreciate the support," she said, and noticed how her voice quaked. More silence and staring ensued.

"You deserve it."

She patted his knee affectionately, before breaking into a cackling laugh. "You're a very smart man."

"I don't know if that's a compliment."

She stood up to leave. This couldn't go on forever. She needed to put an end to it, before they spent any more time alone together. She wasn't even thinking about Mishti; she was thinking about herself.

"Well, it was really lovely bumping into you, outside of our little microcosm. I'm sure you want to get back to your very serious work, and I should go order that coffee."

There was something like disappointment on his face. "I was about to leave."

"Then I've held you up."

"No, of course not."

He stood up too, and she noticed how they were practically the same height.

She leaned in to kiss the air around his cheeks, and he accepted it awkwardly without returning the gesture. It made her wish she could take it back, but it was done now.

Ciara stepped aside, as he gathered his things and made to go.

Parth waved when he walked through the glass doors. He waved again when he was out on the street, and Ciara offered a wiggle of the fingers, turning intentionally toward the queue.

Even though nothing had happened and nothing was said, Ciara was certain she wasn't going to tell Mishti about this.

CIARA DIDN'T THINK she asked for much, except for this one day off every once in a while. So when her mother-in-law rang her only moments after she sat down with her coffee, she considered it an affront and silenced her phone. However, her screen kept blinking, so she relented and picked up.

"Liz, what is it?"

"I was just ringing to say Finn misses his mammy today."

"Why, what did he tell you? It's rude of him to have full-blown conversations with you and then pretend he can't make words when he's with us."

Liz didn't catch her joke, but Ciara smiled to herself.

"I can sense it. He wants me constantly by his side. Even when I'm carrying him, he's not happy. He keeps making this grunting sound, and he won't eat."

"He hasn't been eating at home either, so it's nothing new. Give him some oranges, he'll eat those. And the grunting thing is a phase. Ignore it, don't draw attention to it. He'll stop eventually."

Liz sighed. "I'm only saying, maybe today isn't a good day."

"For me to take a few hours to myself?"

"I know how hard it is, Ciara. I've reared a child of my own."

"Then you know how important this is for my mental health."

"Some days, when they're so little, they just want their mammy. In a few months you'll have your life back."

"I'm in the city already."

"Sure you can come back a few hours early."

"No, I can't, Liz. I have appointments to keep, and really, he'll be fine. He needs some time away from me."

Liz sighed again, just when Ciara saw Sean O'Grady through the window of the coffee shop.

"Anyway, I really must go now."

Ciara quickly pressed END and slipped the phone into her handbag. Sean was crossing the street, his hands thrust into the pockets of his skinny dark jeans. For a man his age—and he had to be at least fifty—he was well able to carry off the look. Disheveled, long hair, vintage Ray-Bans, an assortment of old leather bracelets on his wrists. He was an artist. Or at least he could have been.

Ciara stirred her coffee and watched as he headed straight for the doors. He stood in silence for a few moments, looking around.

Her stomach rumbled with hunger, and she wished she'd ordered some food along with the coffee. Maybe she should have let Parth buy her lunch like he suggested.

Sean dragged the sunglasses off his face and folded them into the front of his V-neck. It had coffee stains and cigarette holes, and it could have easily been a handful of years old. He reminded her of the distinct smell of college. Greasy food on paper plates, knees stained with grass, nauseatingly bitter coffee, and cheap perfume to cover the body odor of unwashed youth.

His strange blue-gray eyes settled on her eventually, and she smiled at him. It was an invitation.

"What did you buy?" Sean asked, brushing a hand through his hair. It was thick and naturally dark, with streaks of silver on his sideburns and temples.

She said nothing when he reached for the spoon on her saucer. He licked off the coffee foam.

"Some clothes I needed."

"Can I see them?"

"No."

He smiled and placed the spoon on the table between them. Then he sat down in the puffy leather chair like this was his own home. He had his legs spread apart in a way that was only appropriate for teenagers to do. Apparently, it didn't matter to him if anyone saw them together.

"Parth Guha was here."

"And . . ."

"And, well, I *suppose* he's harmless," she said, trying not to raise her voice in impatience, "but it could have very well been someone else."

"And what? Someone would see two neighbors sitting together, chatting. Big fucking deal."

He rubbed the garnet ring he wore on his thumb, grinning at her like she was nothing more than one of his foolish children. Ciara despised him so much it made her eyes and throat burn. "All I'm saying is, we need to be more careful," she said.

"Okay, I hear you. This is the place *you* suggested. I'm not fussed about where we go."

"But now I've changed my mind. We can't be seen here together. It's too . . ."

"Out in the open?"

"Yes."

"Whatever you want, Princess."

She stood up, grabbing her bags. Her coffee was barely touched, but she had no patience for it today. They had wasted too much time already.

She didn't have to turn back as she made her way out, knowing he was following her. She could feel his eyes on her arse.

Chapter 10

September 8

SEAN WAS OUT WITH HIS FRIENDS, HAVING MADE UP some excuse about the bike again. Or maybe he had given her a different excuse this time, she hadn't been listening. Lauren was expecting him to come home baked, either way.

The only thing that annoyed her was that the kids asked for him. They were so accustomed to having both their parents at home all the time that they complained when Sean was missing. But this was something Lauren was proud of, that her children loved their father that much; they both had built strong, unshakable relationships with their children, and she wasn't having to do it alone.

Lauren went about the evening as usual, making dinner and serving it at the kitchen table. Sometimes, when she had a moment to think, she noticed the clutter they lived in. She was embarrassed by what her gran would think if she saw her house now—the kitchen corner entirely engulfed by toys, the two clothes horses permanently situated in the sitting room and dripping puddles on the floor, the mold on the bottoms of the curtains.

Willow hated the high chair, so Lauren sat at the table with Willow on her lap while the child picked at her plate with a tiny fork. Summer had ended, but Lauren's freckles were still prominent, and she stared at them all along her arms. She was covered in them, for as long as she could remember, and they weren't isolated to the cute spots like the tip of her nose or the apples of her cheeks. As a child she'd decided they were the reason the other girls picked on her. They might very well have been.

Freya and Harry leaped up, catching her attention, and they ran to the front door as soon as they heard it open. Like a pair of saggy-tongued dogs.

Sean came into the kitchen with Freya dangling off his arm and Harry stuck to his leg. He was forced to drag his foot along the floor, and he laughed as he hobbled.

"It appears as though I have some barnacles stuck to my surface." The only way he was going to get them off was by covering them in slobbery kisses, which sent them shrieking in all directions.

Lauren noticed Sean's good mood. He seemed to have recovered from his crankiness of that morning. She wasn't complaining.

"I've eaten, so I'm going to let you carry on," he said, once the kids were back in their chairs. They groaned.

"Daddy just needs a few hours this evening. It'll be bath time soon anyway," Lauren said.

Sean mouthed "thank you" and pressed his palms together in gratitude. She knew she was going to find him in their bedroom later, stretched under the duvet, book in hand. Or maybe already asleep, and she'd leave a few soft kisses on his chin without waking him. It was comforting to know the predictable pattern of their life together.

This was the same man who'd go missing for days when he still ran the bookshop. He'd turn up eventually, looking like he'd never slept a wink in his life, with fluorescent festival bands on his wrists and a few new tattoos if things had gone really wild. Then he'd wrap his arms around her and sniff her hair and tell her he'd missed her. She'd always believed him. He was thinking about her, wherever he'd been. It was all she'd needed to hear.

But later this evening, Sean was awake when she went to their bedroom. All three children were tucked away in their rooms, and

Willow was already asleep. Lauren had a few hours before Willow was going to wake and cry for her. That kid had never slept through the night.

"I'll be a few minutes," she said, after she'd kissed his chin and taken off her cardigan. He mumbled and didn't look up from his book.

She scrolled through Ciara's Instagram while she sat on the toilet. There were a few pictures from Ciara's day in the city: photos of clothes she'd browsed, Ciara in front of a mirror with her makeup looking fresh and flawless, a selfie of her in the driver's seat of her Beetle with the wind in her hair.

Lauren couldn't remember the last time she'd been anywhere without the kids. The other mothers—the very same ones who snickered about Lauren—fawned over Ciara's manicure, her taste in clothes, her effortless beauty, her brazen day of freedom. They praised her on her posts, for taking the time out for self-care. Ciara became a hero, just for driving herself out of the village for a day.

Lauren forced herself to put the phone away before she was tempted to type a comment. She was incapable of being subtle with her jabs and didn't trust that she wouldn't dig herself into an even deeper hole.

When she came into the bedroom and sat at the dressing table, Sean put his book and glasses away. He didn't like wearing them around other people, even though Lauren wasn't other people.

"Thank you for dealing with the kids alone tonight."

"They weren't a bother, I got lucky. Although they did ask for you."

"I'll go check on them later."

"Mmm-hmm."

She pulled out her gran's old tortoiseshell brush. It was one of the few things she hadn't thrown away. Lauren's long red curls were very fine and frizzed up easily. She found it impossible to wear it down anymore and had long ago embraced the messy-bun look.

She caught Sean staring at her in the mirror's reflection as she brushed.

"You know, you haven't changed at all. Not since the first day you walked into my bookshop."

Lauren smiled, knowing it was an exaggeration. Her cheeks were plumper back then, and now they sagged. Her hairline was thinning from years of tying her hair back. When they first met, she used to leave it free and tumbling around her shoulders.

She had never put on weight easily, but this was the skinniest she had ever been. She didn't bother with bras anymore. Her features used to be softer, and now they were more severe.

"You've gotten grayer," she retorted. Sean wasn't happy with the comment but tried to hide his irritation. "And even more handsome," she added quickly.

"Maybe you should take a few days off from the kids, from us. We could come up with a plan." He'd never suggested such a thing before.

"I don't need any time off." She moved on to moisturizing her shoulders and neck.

"It'll do you good."

"I enjoy parenting them, you know this. Sometimes I may appear frazzled, but it's not very often. I recover quickly from it."

"I know that, love, but everyone needs a break."

"And listen." She rubbed cream on both elbows and then on her feet. "I may not look like I have things under control, but I do. I put a lot of thought into how we're raising the children. I've done my research too."

"Does this have to do with someone in particular?"

She smiled at the mirror, and he grinned.

"Maybe we shouldn't be talking about her on our time off," she said.

Sean drummed his fingers on his chest. "No, maybe we shouldn't."

"Although," Lauren started, "I did do something rather thoughtless the other day. Pretty stupid, when I think about it."

"What did you do?"

"I kind of attacked Mishti Guha."

"You what?"

Lauren turned in the seat to face him.

"I don't mean physically attacked. I told her off. Just a little bit. I wasn't trying to be rude."

Sean's eyes narrowed at her, and he looked a little worried. His reaction seemed strange to her; he was rarely bothered by village politics.

"It was when I invited her to dinner. Her response to the invitation was . . . it seemed like she had Ciara's voice in her ear."

"How do you mean?"

"She was thinking about what Ciara would say if she accepted my invitation, and that ticked me right off. Like, make your own decision for once. You know? But I know, I know I shouldn't have reacted. I shouldn't have lashed out at that poor woman. She's just caught in the crossfire."

"What did you say, Lauren?"

"Nothing too bad."

"Do you remember what you said?"

"Not exactly."

"For fuck's sake, Lauren."

She stood up, annoyed with him because he was making a bigger deal of it than it deserved to be. He was supposed to laugh it off.

"I just made it clear that I'm aware she's worried about Ciara."

"Lauren! For fuck's sake," he said again, and rubbed his forehead with his fingers, like it was made of Play-Doh. "Why do you have to go and complicate things?"

"Excuse me?"

"You know what I'm talking about. You always do this."

"*Always* do this?"

"You get jealous."

"You think I'm jealous of Ciara?"

"I don't know which one of them you're jealous of, but you're letting your emotions run away with you."

"You don't think it's insulting? That a grown woman has to ask another grown-ass woman's permission before accepting a dinner invitation?"

"You don't know if that's the case!"

"Sean, are you being serious? You don't think Ciara is manipulating Mishti? She thrives on this sort of power play." She stood at the end of the bed, making her case.

"I don't know any of that, Lauren. This is your theory. All I see is a pair of women who get on. Who happen to be neighbors, with kids the same age. Big fuckin' deal like."

She covered her face with both hands and took in a few deep breaths. She inhaled the faint lavender scent of her moisturizer. It usually calmed her, but it wasn't doing the trick tonight. "I apologized to her."

"It doesn't matter if you apologized to her," Sean snapped.

"If she tells Ciara, she tells Ciara. It's not like that woman can shun me any more than she already does."

Sean made an effort to sit up straighter in bed, plumping the pillows behind him so they could look at each other squarely. He made it seem like he had something important to say and that he needed her to pay attention.

"Okay, you're going to forget about this, yeah? You're not going to do anything stupid?"

Chapter 11

September 8

MISHTI WASN'T IN THE HABIT OF WATCHING THE clock, but this evening she'd stared at it until the numbers blurred her vision. Parth wasn't home yet, and though it had rarely bothered her before, this time she allowed it to.

It was very late and Maya was already asleep, which was for the best. Mishti didn't want her daughter to worry, to see her mother such a mess, her hair free from its plait and in a tangled mass. Mishti's kajal had smudged, giving her puffy panda eyes.

She knew Parth had no practical reason to be out this late. His classes couldn't possibly go on this long, and it would be unprofessional of him to meet with clients at this hour. She kept picturing a twenty-year-old blonde in a tight dress and platform heels.

Finally, she heard the beep of the car locking. Since the time Maya went to bed, Mishti had been repeatedly washing the same set of dishes and pans. Now she left them dripping in the rack.

Parth came in with his hands stuffed in his coat. He was heading for the staircase in long strides when Mishti stepped into the hallway. She didn't know what she was expecting to find. Lipstick marks on his collar? Perfume in his hair? His breath astringent with the stench of alcohol?

He stopped at the bottom of the stairs when he saw her.

"Oh. I thought you'd be in bed," he said. His usually neat side-swept hair looked a little disheveled, but that could've been because he liked to drive with the window down. He didn't feel cold the way Mishti did.

"Where were you?"

"I had dinner with some colleagues."

"Dinner with colleagues?"

"That's what I said."

"What were you doing before that?"

"Before what?"

"Dinner with your colleagues."

"I was at the college."

"Your classes would have finished a long time ago."

"I don't just go to lectures and do nothing else. I don't want to get into the details with you, Mishti, but I was working."

She didn't want to believe him, and yet she did. She had to trust him. It came from a place of hope.

"Why are you grilling me tonight?"

"I've been waiting for you. I cooked for you. I didn't know you weren't eating at home."

She wasn't impatient about waiting; it was what she was good at. Waiting for Parth to come home, waiting to pick Maya up from pre-school, waiting for some day to look a little different from today. Besides, the food she cooked always tasted better the next day, after the masalas had a chance to properly soak into the meat.

"I thought I told you this morning."

"You did not."

"Okay, well, you can pack me the food for lunch tomorrow. It's not like it'll go to waste."

They stood in silence for a few moments. He was waiting to see if she had more questions, although he had no intention of answering them. His explanation was simple and complete. She was going to have to accept it.

"I'm going to bed," he said, shaking his head like she'd wasted his time.

Mishti went back to the kitchen, took the food out of the fridge, and emptied the contents of the Tupperware into the bin.

SHE WANTED TO cry when she went to their bedroom, half an hour after Parth had gone upstairs. All she'd wanted tonight was the chance to ask him whether he was being unfaithful. In all these years of marriage, she had never wanted to know, at least not with this intensity. Was he entertaining the advances of the pretty young things who sat in his lecture halls? He was a professor of psychology. Was it that difficult for him to intuit what his wife wanted to know?

Mishti was out of her depth. She needed to ask him, because she couldn't read the signs. She didn't know him well enough to know if there was something amiss. Mishti had never figured out what she wanted for herself, who she wanted to be. Now she was in this marriage, with a child. It didn't matter that she had imagined more for herself; this was what she had.

Parth was still awake, but he didn't look up from his phone. She took her time in the bathroom, washing her face and brushing her teeth and gums hard, until specks of blood swirled in the froth in the basin. She'd changed into pajamas before stepping back into the bedroom. She didn't let Parth see her naked, not when there was no reason to.

He looked up from his phone.

"What is going on with you tonight?"

It was a relief that he'd noticed, but now that she had his attention, she struggled with the words. "Nothing."

The bedside lamp cast a bright light on one side of his face; the other side was in darkness. It made him appear as only half a thing. "Mishti, don't play games with me. I'm tired, I need to get to sleep. So if there's anything you want to tell me, you should tell me now."

"I just wanted to know where you've been, that is all. I would have liked to know how you spent your evening. I never know where you go or what you do."

He almost looked amused as he listened to her speak. "And what will you do with that information?"

It was a good question. How would it affect her life if she knew where Parth had been? Nothing would change.

"Isn't a wife entitled to know what her husband does with his time?"

He slid down in the bed, weaving his fingers behind his head. It made his shoulders taut under the thin material of his T-shirt. "And what is a husband entitled to?"

"You know everything there is to know about my day."

Her voice faltered and made her breathless. She was already regretting the words coming out of her mouth. More than that, she regretted her tone. While Parth had looked amused just moments ago, now he was annoyed. He sat up in bed again.

"Where are you getting this from?" he asked.

"I don't know what you mean."

"Yes, you do. You know exactly what I mean. You don't sound like yourself."

Mishti was certain he didn't know what she usually sounded like. "I don't want to fight with you." She tried a different voice, but it ended up sounding childish.

She didn't want to lie down beside him, not since they'd been arguing. Knowing he didn't particularly want her there either. She considered returning to the kitchen, giving the dishes another wash.

"And yet here you are, fighting with me over one plate of food gone cold."

She dug her nails into her palms. Not that it mattered, but it wasn't the first plate of food to have gone cold in the course of their marriage.

Parth swung his legs off the bed and stood up. When he stepped toward her, she flinched like he'd flicked hot oil at her.

"The more time you spend around these people, these *women* . . . the more you start to sound like them."

The irony was lost on her at first, until she realized he was talking about Ciara. He wanted the very woman he was disparaging. She knew he did—she'd seen the way he looked at her.

She tried to get past him, but he grabbed her arm and yanked her back around to face him. "You need to remember where you come from, Mishti. You need to remember who you are. What would your father say if he heard you speaking to your husband this way?"

More hot oil was flicked at her, leaving scorching wounds all over her body. They itched and throbbed. She tugged her arm away and he released her. He had never held her like this before, and she was reminded of his strength. He didn't always look it, but he was a capable man.

"Haven't I given you everything you could ask for? This house. A child. Your life here in Ireland?"

Yes. A car. The clothes on her back. The toothpaste in the bathroom. The two bottles of now-congealed nail polish she'd bought years before but never worn. He'd given her all that, and it all belonged to him. "Yes, you have."

"Then stop complaining."

She knew what he wanted when he looked at her, what he was about to do. She was his wife. She happened to be in his house when he came home from work. She happened to be in his bed when he wanted to empty himself in somebody. That was all.

"I'm sorry," she mumbled, as he pulled down her pajama bottoms.

"You don't have to be sorry." He led her to their bed.

She lay down, and he stretched himself on top of her. "Just remember who you are. You're not like them."

AFTERWARD, SHE LAY awake and waited until she was sure Parth was asleep. Then she got out of bed, put her bottoms back on, and crawled under the covers again. She pulled the duvet all the way up to her chin. Always cold.

Her phone's vibration alarmed her. She saw a text from Ciara and wished she were capable of cursing. It didn't sound right, not even in her thoughts.

Everyone's asleep but me. Are you awake?

She'd thought about Ciara and her shining ponytail the whole time Parth was on top of her. She'd focused so hard on that blond hair that she was confused by the end of it all. Had it brought her pleasure or pain to think about Ciara? She felt the need to go wash the dishes again, or at least clean her hands. Her stomach rumbled with hunger too—she wanted to stuff herself. She replied quickly.

I'm awake

Hi! How was your day? I feel like we haven't had a chance to talk.

We could go for a walk soon

How about tomorrow?

Okay

Are you okay?

Everything is fine

I don't like hearing that. Everything is never fine. It sounds like a lie.

I don't know what to say. I'm not lying to you.

LOL. I'm sorry. I didn't mean to upset you. I'm sure everything is fine. I suppose it's just me then.

What's wrong?

Nothing

Are you sure?

I'm just exhausted all the time

I know. So am I.

I've been fantasizing about going away somewhere. Just disappearing. No kids. No house. No Gerry.

That would be nice

We could disappear together

Maybe

LOL. I wish we could make that happen. Three kids rendered motherless, in one fell swoop.

Our kids need us

God knows they do, because these men would be hopeless at raising them without us. Wouldn't they?

Most likely, yes

Anyway, I should let you go. I know Maya is an early riser. I should have just called!

Good night, Ciara

XXX

Mishti clicked her phone off and slipped it under her pillow. It was always the right temperature of cool there. Beside her, Parth was snoring lightly, lying naked from the waist down under the duvet. She realized he had no idea that their daughter sometimes came into their room at night.

When she shut her eyes, she saw Ciara's face again. She wondered if that's what Parth was seeing too. It seemed like a cruel joke, the two of them lying side by side, imagining the same woman.

And every time Ciara called for her, she answered like Mary's little lamb.

Chapter 12

September 8

LAUREN KNEW WHAT SEAN WAS WORRIED ABOUT with Ciara, although she wasn't going to let on that she did. She knew he was thinking of Roseanne.

Lauren had been working for Sean at the bookshop for over a year, and she was essentially running the place. He didn't pay her very much, even though she opened the shop and closed up most evenings and did everything in between. She had been sleeping with Sean for some months by then, but she didn't allow herself to get carried away with it; she knew he still slept with other women. The longer she stood by him without making a fuss, the stronger she felt and the more she became a persistent, essential presence in his life. Other people began to see them as a couple, although Sean himself refused to give it a name.

Then Roseanne appeared out of the blue.

Roseanne Mulcahy was an old girlfriend from secondary school. She was back in town after many years, and Sean was acting like a teenager again. Lauren half-expected to find a poster of Roseanne in his bedroom, stuck to the wall with pieces of Blu-Tack.

Roseanne had spent a considerable number of years in London, married to an English musician. Once the marriage ended, she re-

turned to her hometown, looking up old friends, as people do. Roseanne and Sean hadn't seen each other in decades. The woman Lauren
saw now was in her forties and exceedingly stylish. The kind of style
you acquire when you've been married to a musician for many years.
When you've had songs written about you. When you've gained access to people who design clothing tailored to your exact taste and
measurements. Roseanne's wrists were weighed down by a dozen
silver bracelets, which she never took off. She boasted about having
recently shaved off all her dreadlocks and sported a Twiggy-esque
pixie cut.

Lauren reckoned she could just sit it out for a few months, until
Sean grew bored with Roseanne too. But a few months went by, and
it didn't seem like Roseanne was going anywhere. Lauren found
them at the bookshop one morning, smoking cigarettes and laughing as they stood behind the counter. She realized it was the first
time since she'd known him that Sean was up this early. Roseanne's
laugh reached a fever pitch as Lauren drew close to them, as though
they were mocking her.

Sean saw it coming, even before Lauren did.

He was too late, however. She had already launched herself over
the counter and shoved Roseanne roughly to the wall.

"Lauren!" Sean jumped over, tackling her to the floor. "What the
fuckin' hell?"

"She was laughing at me."

"Are you crazy? What are you fuckin' talking about? Nobody was
laughing at you."

He pinned her down, straddling her. She knew he was appalled by
her behavior, but she also liked the weight of him on top of her.

"I saw her . . ." She tried to speak.

"I don't believe this, Sean." Roseanne had gathered herself, and
she stood behind them. A hand hovered over her mouth.

"Just give me a minute, Annie. Just go, will ya?" Sean said, ad-
dressing her over his shoulder.

Annie?

A sound like a growl erupted from Lauren's mouth, and she tried to force herself up again. Sean was able to hold her down until she stilled and Roseanne had finally cleared the shop.

"What was that, Lauren? You could have seriously hurt her." He eased up, but Lauren remained where she was.

"I don't know, I'm sorry. I don't know what happened."

"You should take the rest of the day off."

"I'm fine."

"Take the rest of the day off, Lauren."

He eased off her and sprinted out the door to chase after Roseanne. Lauren felt hollow with shame and exhausted by the image of him and her together. Was he comforting her? Agreeing with her that Lauren was some kind of crazy? She would have to put an end to that.

WHEN SHE THOUGHT about it now, so many years later, Lauren couldn't recall how she had spent the rest of that day. Several times over the years, she had tried to remember, but it was a blank—a hole she could fall into if she was too close to the edge, but she'd never reach the bottom.

She must have made her way to Sean's apartment and used the spare key he'd given her, but she couldn't recall how she'd got there. She also couldn't remember taking Sean's kukri. She had known where he stored it, so it wouldn't have been difficult to find.

It hung from a nail on his bedroom wall, above the sole mirror in the flat. She'd lie naked in his bed on nights he told her stories about his trip to Nepal, the months he'd trekked the Annapurna Circuit. He'd spent most of that time talking with the locals, translated by his Sherpa guide, Orjun. Sean brought the kukri down from the wall sometimes, just to hold it in his hands. It was an ancient Nepali dagger, stored in a decadent wooden sheath. He was proud of it, even though he had done nothing to earn it. His only accomplishment was successfully smuggling it into Ireland past airport security.

Even though Lauren couldn't remember pulling the kukri off

Sean's wall that day, she knew she had it in her hand when she went to Roseanne's house. She must have mumbled something to Mrs. Mulcahy when she came to the door—more holes in her memory— but she remembered the old lady stepping back from the door in horror when she saw the unsheathed dagger in Lauren's hand.

Sean and Roseanne came running out of a room down the corridor. He tripped on a rug like a cartoon character, running toward her with his arms outstretched. Lauren couldn't hear him; the only sound was a buzzing in her ears. She did remember the jerk when he pulled the kukri out of her hand. Heard the sharp metal *clank* when he threw it far away and it hit the floor.

"Lauren, come on, what's going on with you? Did you go to my flat?" That was the first thing she heard Sean say, or at least the first thing she remembered.

"Yes."

"Fuck, Lauren, why?"

"Why do you think? She came here to kill me!" Roseanne was screeching now, huddled behind Sean and clinging to Mrs. Mulcahy. Her mother stroked her bony shoulders.

Lauren felt a warm glow spreading up from her stomach and down to her fingertips. Sean chose to ignore Roseanne, taking Lauren's face in his hands instead.

"Will you talk to me?"

"I don't know what to say. I don't know why I'm here."

"You know why you're fuckin' here. You're a jealous little bitch." Roseanne's screams were punctuated with bubbles of sobs. Even then, Sean didn't turn around, his eyes never leaving Lauren's.

"I'm going to take you home, okay?" he whispered.

Lauren fell on his chest, and he embraced her.

"I don't want to be alone, please."

"You won't be. I'm going to take you to my flat, and we can talk about this."

"You can't be serious, Sean." Roseanne's high-pitched voice pierced the air. "You're leaving with her? She physically assaults me, then comes to my home and tries to kill me."

"She wouldn't have hurt you, Roseanne." He was back to calling her that.

"If you walk out of that door now, we're through."

"Are you going to call the Guards?" he growled at her. Lauren still had her face hidden on his chest.

"Yes, of course I am. She's a crazy person. She's dangerous."

"Nothing happened. This will never happen again. She hasn't been doing well, and it's my fault, okay? All this is my fault. Will you please just let it go, Roseanne?"

Without waiting for her to answer, Sean gently turned Lauren around and guided her through the front door. Lauren stole a glance behind them to see Mrs. Mulcahy following Sean with a strange look in her eyes.

Unlike her daughter, she was relieved to see him go.

Chapter 13

September 9

IN THE FIRST MONTHS OF MISHTI'S ARRIVAL IN IRE-
land, she spent a lot of time by herself. Parth was away for a con-
ference one time. He said he was going to be gone for five days. That
was all the information he had given her. Mishti didn't yet drive and
she still needed his help with things like working the oven and sort-
ing out the trash.

Parth had left early in the morning, and Mishti sat at the kitchen
table for hours afterward. They hadn't discovered the Asian store in
the city yet, so there was no good loose-leaf tea to drink. She took
sips of the tea she'd made using a bag. It left her with a strange, sandy
texture in her mouth. She was beginning to feel sick.

Mishti hadn't been eating much, and now there was a dull ache at
the back of her head. She went through the cupboards. Biscuits.
Bread. Tea bags. Blocks of butter. Sugar. Rice cakes. Honey. There
was nothing in there she wanted to eat. In the fridge there were
bananas, pears, and a mango, all in antiseptic packaging. Nothing
tasted right. They bitterly reminded her of how much sweeter fruit
tasted at home, where her mother bought it from the seller pushing
his cart, waving flies away from his offerings.

Somehow, the ache in her head had radiated all the way to her belly. She wrapped her arms around her stomach when she felt a shooting pain. She was leaning against the kitchen counter. There was a knock on the door at the same time as a whimper escaped her lips.

If she'd been in the right frame of mind, she wouldn't have opened the door. She wasn't thinking. The pain was shooting up and down her sides. It seemed to originate between her legs, and her knees weakened as she pulled the door open.

"Hello, Mishti. I thought I'd stop by for a chat." Ciara was beaming. She stood at the door with a hand over her pregnant belly. Seconds later, her smile disappeared. She'd noticed Mishti's face. "Oh my God. Are you okay?"

The cramps were unbearable, and Mishti staggered backward. Ciara came toward her, throwing an arm over her shoulder.

They collapsed to the floor together. One heavily pregnant, and the other losing blood from between her legs.

"What's happening to me? I don't know what's happening to me," Mishti had cried.

Ciara cradled her, pressing her head to her breasts. With her other hand, she reached for her phone. "I'm going to call for an ambulance, okay? Everything is going to be fine. I've got you."

Mishti was grateful Ciara didn't ask where her husband was.

Hours later, Ciara helped her into bed.

They had returned from the hospital, and Ciara turned the heating on in the house. She helped Mishti change into a fresh set of clothes and made her some buttered toast and a cup of tea.

It had taken Mishti hours to pass the fetus. When the midwife dismissively reminded her that she was still young and healthy with many childbearing years ahead of her, Ciara had glared threateningly at the woman.

Back at the house, Ciara had pulled up a chair by the bed and sat down. There was a cup of tea in her hands, and she lifted it to her cheek. "Get some sleep. I'm not going anywhere."

* * *

NOW IT WAS the morning after Mishti had argued with her husband, and it was significant not only because they didn't argue often but because Parth had made himself toast. Mishti smelled the warmth of the bread as soon as she entered the house after dropping Maya off at preschool. It made the home seem briefly welcoming. The same as buttered popcorn would, or warm radiators and fairy lights on bookshelves.

Parth was already dressed for work. It didn't fit the schedule she thought he followed. Lately he'd been full of surprises.

"What would you like for breakfast?" she asked, putting her things away.

"I've eaten already."

"Just toast?"

"Yes, I'm not too hungry. I'll get something at the college later. I checked the fridge for leftovers to pack."

"Yeah, I threw it away."

If he was surprised by that, he didn't show it. Or maybe he hadn't heard her.

Mishti turned the kettle on, while he lingered in the kitchen. He was strewing crumbs everywhere, carrying his toast around.

"Do you remember what I said to you last night?"

She hadn't expected him to bring it up. They rarely ever followed up on their arguments if they happened to have one. They simply drifted around each other as usual, went about their routine.

"Yes, I think so."

"You need to regulate yourself. You can't lose your sense of identity just because you've made some new friends."

All of his education, his degrees, his research, and *this* was the conclusion he came up with? That she needed to be less friendly with the natives?

"I'm going for a walk with Ciara later today."

"I'm not forbidding you to see her."

"Okay."

"Mishti, do you even hear what I'm saying?"

"Yes. You don't want me to turn into one of these women."

"Something like that."

She wanted to laugh at him for how ridiculous he sounded. He was afraid of Ciara rubbing off on her, because he wanted his wife to continue to be pleasing to his family. He had married a good domesticated Bengali woman, handpicked by his parents, and he wanted to keep her that way. "I will keep that in mind," she replied.

Parth's eyebrows crawled up his forehead, and he appeared to be on the verge of saying something. The kettle coming to a boil interrupted his rising fury.

"I'll let you know if I'm going to be late again."

She turned to the sink to tackle the dishes from Maya's breakfast. She'd never used the dishwasher, and she couldn't start now. Not when nobody had ever seen her using the machine before, not when washing them herself kept her hands occupied.

She heard Parth slamming doors behind him as he walked through the house. A few more minutes and she was going to be alone again. Then the waiting would begin.

After Parth had finally left, she went into the sitting room to dust. She saw Lauren walking past with her children. Willow was tied to her back, a permanent fixture. Harry and Freya bounded ahead. She hadn't told Ciara about their chat from a few days ago, Lauren's dinner invitation.

Mishti envied Lauren. How she didn't care about the pulled threads in her cardigan, whether her bag matched her shoes, or if Harry picked up a stone and began sucking on it. If Ciara disappeared, Lauren's life would carry on. She wouldn't even notice.

FOR SEVERAL WEEKS after they first spoke by the bus stop, Mishti waited for Neel to find her again.

Every day she got off the bus on her way back from college and purposely took her time walking to the house, making her way slowly. Sometimes she stopped to readjust the straps on her shoes, or shuffle the contents of her bag, or change the cassette in her Walkman. She gave him every opportunity to make another appearance, but he didn't cross her path.

She waited by the balcony door every night, when most of her family was already in bed. Her cousins were usually asleep by the time she'd finally see Neel walk past their house, on his way home from somewhere. She made note of different things about him now, features she hadn't paid attention to before. The light dusting of dark hair on his forearms, the caked dirt on his leather sandals, the big tear in the front pocket of his kurta. She wondered where he went, with all those books under his arm.

Mishti knew it had been two months, because she was counting the days. She'd nearly given up hope of speaking to him again. Then one day he was standing at the bus stop, smoking a cigarette. She'd just gotten off the bus, back from college. He threw his smoke to the ground and rushed toward her.

"It's funny we've been neighbors all our lives but never spoken before," he said. It was as though they'd never ended their previous conversation. Like two months hadn't gone by.

"My parents are conservative."

"You mean they wouldn't approve of you speaking to me?"

She couldn't lie to him, so she said nothing. He knew the truth, but he didn't seem resentful. "I don't want to get you in any trouble with your family."

"Is that why you haven't spoken to me in two months?"

It pleased him that she'd been keeping track. "I'm speaking to you now."

"What are those books for?" she asked.

"I tutor some kids."

She looked closely at them, recognizing some physics titles from her own school days.

"Is that what you do? You're a tutor?"

"I'm in college too. Engineering."

It distressed her that her mother and aunts didn't gossip about *this*. Unknown to them, Neel Banerjee was making something of himself, despite his circumstances.

"Are you going home now?" he asked. He meant, *Do you want to go somewhere with me?*

Another bus arrived and they were surrounded by a sudden throng of people. Neel held an arm up to shield her from the crowd that inevitably shoved past them.

"They will be expecting me back soon."

"And you wouldn't want to disappoint them," he stated, but it was like a question.

She had never wanted to disappoint her parents. In fact, she had spent her whole life being certain to avoid just that. He was presenting her with an opportunity to live her life differently, for one evening, and she knew she should take it.

"I'm sorry, but I have to go," she replied.

She hurried away from Neel, but it felt like a mistake, like she should have broken the rules just once.

It didn't take long for him to say he was in love with her.

Mishti had been skipping classes and meeting Neel at a street-food shack close to his college. She was always home when she was expected.

It had a makeshift tarp roof and a few benches, and served greasy samosas and chow mein on paper plates. It was all they could afford, and all they really cared for. It was ideal because it was far away from their neighborhood, where they couldn't be recognized together.

Sometimes they just sat together in silence, on the bench that had become *their spot.* They shared Mishti's earplugs, each using one. They listened to Dylan, Springsteen, the Police, and the Beatles. Sometimes she pretended to read her notes, while he studied for a test and smoked cigarettes. Hot ash dropped like sweat on his pages. When she asked about his childhood or his family, he told her what she wanted to know. He suspected his mother suffered from a mental illness—perhaps she was simply depressed. It wasn't something his father understood or wanted to do anything about. All the male members of his family were alcoholics. Only his uncle, Mihir, didn't know how to hide it. Neel had grown up wanting to escape. He said he was going to take her with him when he did.

"I don't know how to tell my family about us," she said, after they'd kissed for the first time. It was a peck on the side of her mouth as they ran to the metro station. He'd stopped her, in the shadow between the streetlights, and asked her if she was ready. She didn't know what he meant by that, but she'd nodded anyway. It was an awkward kiss, almost ticklish, but it had made her smile. The previous week he'd told her he loved her. Mishti struggled to say the words back, but he didn't need to hear it.

"You don't have to tell them. You shouldn't. We could disappear, and once we're married, they won't be able to do anything about it." They had stopped running after the kiss and were walking slowly toward the metro station.

"I can't just leave, not without their blessing."

"Why not, Mishti? If you don't, they will never let you go. They'll never let you marry me."

"And where would we go?"

"I'm going to get a good job when I graduate. Six more months, and we'll be out of here. I'm going to look for work in Delhi or Bombay."

"If I marry you without their blessing, they'll never want to see me again."

"And if you tell them, they'll marry you off to someone else. They won't let you leave the house. They won't let you ever see me again."

JUST LIKE HER images of Neel, Mishti's memories of Lauren were packed in a bag of what-ifs. Mishti couldn't help but wonder if she and Lauren would have been friends if Ciara hadn't been there first.

The beach closest to the village was a twelve-minute drive away. It was Mishti's favorite place to go when she first got her full license. It had taken her three attempts to finally pass the test, spread out over a period of two years. She was a nervous driver, too shy to pull out in front of a car even if she had the right-of-way.

The route to the beach was an easy one, with few cars and almost no hills, so she barely ever had to change gear. The bends were tricky, but she took them slow, muttering prayers that a car wouldn't appear from the opposite direction on that narrow road.

Maya, only a year old then, loved the beach, always digging her small toes deep into the sand. Mishti would spread their towels and they'd sit together pointing at the seagulls, laughing as they swooped toward the water, then, last minute, pulled back up into the sky. She couldn't believe how beautiful this country was, and how lonely she was here.

They rarely saw other people; it wasn't a popular beach. But one day there was Lauren, hobbling on the sand with her big, pregnant belly, holding Harry by the hand. Maya had fallen asleep, and Mishti was braiding strands of damp seaweed into plaits. Mishti watched Harry break away from Lauren and run straight up to the frothy edge of the water.

Lauren shouted something indistinct to Harry, and he stopped in his tracks, then started gathering seashells. Lauren reached Mishti's towel and plonked herself down on the cold sand beside her.

"We had to wait forty minutes for the bus," Lauren said. They had only ever exchanged pleasantries before this. "Did you drive here? We really need to get a car. Sean has his bike, but that doesn't do anything for me."

"Oh, I'm sorry. I can give you a lift home, but there won't be a car seat for Harry, so I'm not sure . . ."

"You're too sweet. Thanks for offering, but it's fine. The truth is that we're used to it. It's just a pain in the arse because I'm pregnant." Lauren's hair had come half undone from her bun, wild and scarlet, tumbling over her shoulders and blowing across her face. Her gray tank top had ridden up over her freckled bulging belly, and she leaned back on her palms. She was wearing a long silky kimono jacket with a hummingbird print, and it had gotten wrapped around and between her legs. Her black joggers looked well loved and worn around the knees. Her skin was so pale Mishti thought she could see right through her. Her mouth was thin and firm, sunken eyes set wide apart. Lauren radiated a certain regality, though. Like a queen who had lost her dominion but still commanded the respect of her people.

"I had to bring Harry somewhere. He's been driving us up the wall at home. Sean is minding Freya." She spoke while she watched Harry build and destroy mounds of sand. "Shit, I'm sorry. Did you want to be left alone?"

"No. Not at all. This is not a problem."

"I'm glad for some adult company, if I'm being honest. I don't think I can praise another one of Harry's sandcastles."

Mishti had to smile at that, and Lauren looked encouraged. "Aww, look at her. Isn't she just gorgeous. She's the spitting image of you, Mishti."

"My husband's family thinks she looks like him."

Lauren rolled her eyes at that. "It's some kind of subconscious effort to lay claim, isn't it? You gave birth to her. She came out of you. Insisting that she looks like him is their way of saying she belongs to him."

Mishti's breath stopped for a moment.

"Not that I'm saying there's a chance she may not be his. Fuck! I'm sorry. I shouldn't be cursing in front of the kids." Lauren glanced down at her belly. "Besides, isn't your husband a psychologist?"

"He is. And it's okay, I'm not offended. I understand what you mean." She was smiling even more now. "But I won't try and run this theory past him."

Lauren laughed and practically threw herself back on the sand. "Come on, try it. It's nice down here." She had her eyes closed against the brightness of the sky.

Mishti stared at Harry, who hadn't moved from his original spot. She couldn't think of an excuse fast enough. She felt Lauren's fingers tugging at her wrist. She lay down beside her. The sand gave way a little, and then her body seemed to settle in, almost weightless. Mishti didn't shut her eyes but stared at the clouds in the sky, and it felt like she was up there with them.

"It's a little funny how we have to get away from the village just to find some peace."

"I don't go out much," Mishti admitted.

"You're a homebody, like me."

"Not exactly. In Calcutta, I hated being at home. I couldn't wait to get away from my family. I wanted to be free, to have my own life."

"Do you still feel like you're new here?"

"A little bit."

"I thought you've made friends."

"Only Ciara, and she has her own life."

"And what a life she has."

Mishti detected a touch of sourness in Lauren's tone, and she was surprised by it. "Are you not friends?"

"It's not up to me." Lauren opened her eyes, then turned her face to Mishti. "Forget about it. Tell me how you're feeling."

"I feel okay," she replied, but couldn't seem to get past the shift of tone in Lauren's voice. "I just need some time. I've only been here a little over two years."

"I would hate for you to feel unwelcome. I know how things can get here if you're different in any way."

"Everyone has been very nice to us."

"I'm glad to hear that. It doesn't always go that way. People here like to stick to their own. Although something must be changing—everyone welcomed Ciara with open arms too."

"She is very outgoing, makes friends easily."

Lauren breathed in deeply. "Yeah, maybe that's what it is. She made me a basket of scones when she first moved in. Did you know that?"

Mishti shook her head, a little surprised herself that Ciara had never mentioned it.

"We could have been friends too. I was having a bad day. A bad year, really." Lauren chuckled half-heartedly. "And then it just never worked out after that."

Lauren sat up with a jerk, like she'd only now remembered her son. "Harry! That's enough. Please come over here," she called out loudly, but not firmly enough.

Mishti sat up too, feeling too silly to lie on the sand by herself. She wanted to ask Lauren what was wrong. Something had to be wrong, she could feel it.

"I'm going to have to go get him," Lauren mumbled when Harry didn't so much as glance in their direction. She was struggling to distribute her weight appropriately in order to stand.

Mishti was about to offer help but stopped. "Do you feel unwelcome here?"

Lauren gave up her struggle and dropped herself back on the sand again. "I've lived here practically my whole life. You could say this is all I know. This feeling. I don't have a name for it. *Unwelcome* could be one way to describe it, but I can't imagine living anywhere else. This is my home."

Mishti felt some relief, knowing Ciara had moved to the village within the past few years; she couldn't be the cause of Lauren's long-time distress. Mishti thought highly of Ciara and wanted to keep it that way. Whatever Lauren was experiencing must have been from before, from her childhood spent here.

"You don't need to feel sorry for me, Mishti. The only thing I care about is my family. My kids and Sean. Everything else is just a bad background score."

Mishti had never wanted to hug anyone as much as she wanted to throw her arms around Lauren then. She knew Lauren was lying. She was only saying this out loud so she could hear it herself.

"Okay."

"But if I were you, I'd be careful with Ciara," Lauren continued. "I don't know what she wants from you, but it can't be good." Then she swung herself up shakily and headed in Harry's direction.

Mishti waited a few beats, until she was certain Lauren wasn't turning to look. Then she reached for Maya to wake her. She wanted to leave.

When she thought about it now, it was clear that it had always been about Ciara, from the very beginning.

Chapter 14

THE FIRST TIME THEY'D MET, CIARA HAD MADE AN effort, a genuine effort, with her. Lauren was the one who chose the course of their relationship. Shortly after she and Gerry had moved into the house, Ciara knocked on Lauren's door with some freshly baked fruit scones in a basket.

They had chosen this house, this village, because it made perfect sense. They decided against the city because she wanted to live in a sprawling space. Ciara said she wanted to see potential in a house, a place she could make her own. She was full of ideas, and Gerry didn't want to hold her back. He didn't complain about his forty-minute commute to work, and she didn't complain about how close they were going to live to his mother.

Ciara had seen flashes of Lauren through the hedge that ran between their two houses, heard the cries of a child on the other side. She was eager to make friends, like she'd always been.

"Hello, neighbor!" Ciara said brightly, when Lauren opened the door.

Lauren's brows were furrowed, and she looked at the woman standing at her doorway with confusion.

"Hello? Can I help you?"

Ciara was taken aback too. Lauren wore a fabric contraption tied around herself in multiple layers, squeezing a small baby to her body. Lauren's eyes were droopy; dark circles exaggerated them and made them appear more dramatic. She smelled sour, like milk gone off. There were fresh wet stains down the front of her tank top; an oversized patchwork shirt hung off her shoulders; her feet were bare and dusty like she'd been working in the fields. Every item of clothing on her person could have done with a wash, and Ciara had to wonder if this woman had showered recently. She cleared her throat while Lauren stared at her.

"Oh. You bought the big house."

They both looked over at the other house, standing tall and proud on elevated ground, much like a castle on a hill. Both their back gardens had several levels and slopes. Ciara was in the process of planning, planting, and sculpting, while Lauren's was untamed. There were patches of severe overgrowth, the tall grass was overrun with daisies and dandelions. There was one section of the hedge between the two houses that was viciously swarmed by bees on Lauren's side. Ciara hoped she could offer some neighborly help and advice, but Lauren was looking at her with judgment.

"I just wanted to come over and introduce myself, as I'm not rushing off to work for once," Ciara continued, trying to remain chirpy. She was still at Horizon, which meant that the weekend was her only opportunity to socialize, amidst working with their landscape artist and meeting with the interior decorator.

"I'm Lauren," the woman said, but didn't invite Ciara in. Instead, she shifted the wrapped child to her other side, impatiently.

"I'm Ciara. And who is this gorgeous little thing? She looks so peaceful and snug in there." She had some inkling of what to say to new parents, even though her ovaries weren't exactly exploding.

"Freya." Lauren smiled then, as she gazed down at her sleeping baby.

"That's a beautiful name. I made scones this morning, and I brought you some." Ciara held out the basket.

"Oh, thanks," Lauren said, looking at the basket but not reaching for it. "But we're gluten-free."

Ciara was so surprised, she took a few steps back and attempted to hide the basket behind her. "I'm sorry, I didn't know."

A banging sound came from somewhere within the house, which made Lauren look over her shoulder. "I'm sorry, we're having quite the morning. Nobody here has slept."

Before Ciara could ask, Freya woke up from the sound. With her eyes still shut, she wriggled in the tight confines of the sling and let out an ear-piercing shriek.

"For fuck's sake," Lauren mumbled. "Sean! Keep it down!" she yelled over her shoulder, and the banging stopped. She turned back to Ciara and began bobbing up and down, sideways, back and forth, apparently in an attempt to lull the child to sleep.

"Is there anything I can do to help?" Ciara asked.

"Not unless you want to go up there and help my partner take down a rotting wardrobe." Lauren shouted the words over her daughter's cries of distress. Ciara wished she would just take the baby out of the thing, just rock her in her arms like a normal mother would do.

"It seems like I've caught you at a bad time."

Lauren patted the baby's bottom, while she transferred her weight from one foot to the other.

"It's always a bad time around here these days." She rolled her eyes upward, and Ciara tried to smile. She couldn't tell if it was a joke.

"Maybe we should have a coffee or something one of these days, some weekend. You could come see the house; I'll give you a tour. We've been working hard on it—I mean the interior designer and I. Gerry doesn't care about all that," Ciara continued. "I'm sure you remember what the place used to look like before."

"Can't. I'm off caffeine too. I'm breastfeeding." Lauren glanced at Ciara's house and then at her again. Her forehead was wrinkled, like she couldn't believe Ciara was even standing in front of her. "And you don't appear to have any kids. Trust me, you wouldn't want to spend any more time around a newborn than absolutely necessary."

"I don't know about that. Freya seems lovely." There was a smile plastered on Ciara's face, but it was fading fast.

Lauren rolled her eyes. "You say that now, but you don't know. I'm trying to do you a favor."

"I'm not sure what I've done to offend you."

Freya's cries had turned to whimpers, while her mother continued to sway.

"I'm not offended. Maybe I'm just tired; we haven't been sleeping much. I don't know."

Ciara stared at her blankly.

"What I mean is . . . with the baby, and Sean trying to make repairs on the house—we're just kind of a mess right now." Lauren waited several beats for Ciara to respond; she had been silent a long time, allowing Lauren to feel like a fish out of water, slapping itself on a rock. "Why would I be offended by you? You're only trying to be friendly, aren't you? Coming here and telling me about your house."

Ciara tipped her head to one side. "So it's my house. It's my house that offends you, isn't it." It was done. This other side of her was slipping into place. It always reminded Ciara of the mornings she'd sit on the steps, watching her mother pull clothes off the line in the garden. There was a certain way she'd snap each piece of clothing in the air before folding it neatly in the basket. That was the sound she heard every time she changed into this other person. The person who didn't want to make friends. The sound of fabric whacking the wind, and then everything around her looked a little grayer.

"Why would your house offend me? Because we're so miserable over here on this side of the fence?" Lauren had one hand on the side of the baby's head, almost like she was forcibly keeping her pressed to her chest.

"Am I wrong?"

"And you are doing us this big favor, feeding us? Bringing us food?" Lauren's eyes scanned Ciara head to toe. Her sixty-euro blow-dry. The dainty gold chain at her neck, with her initial engraved on a pendant. Her pointy red pumps.

"You could, at the very least, be polite. We are going to be neighbors."

"Yes, just neighbors." A collection of voices sounded from some-where down the road. Female voices Ciara didn't recognize but was now grateful for. She caught Lauren trying to catch a glimpse, up on her toes, straining her neck. Then her shoulders relaxed, and she breathed in deeply.

"I suggest you take those scones over to them. They'll be better appreciated over there. In fact, tell them Lauren sent you." With that, she shut the door with a slam.

Ciara stood on the step for a few moments, staring at the door, until the chatter grew louder. She turned around to find a handful of women in Lycra, walking together with Vitaminwaters in their hands. They slowed down when they saw Ciara in front of Lauren's house, like they too couldn't believe she was standing here, of all places.

A few moments, then there was that whack in her mind again, and everything was restored to its natural color. Ciara presented them with her brightest smile.

"Hello, ladies! I made a big batch of scones this morning." These women assessed her too, quickly taking in the flawless foundation, the brand name embossed on the leather of her handbag, the hunk of diamond on her ring finger.

"You must be Ciara Dunphy," one of them said.

And that was that. Ciara was relieved. None of these women were anything like her, and she didn't expect them to understand, but she was glad she'd found her crowd.

Chapter 15

L AUREN WAS SIX WHEN SHE WAS INVITED TO THE
birthday party for the O'Brien twins. They were turning seven,
and all the kids from their class were attending. Still, Lauren couldn't
believe she'd been invited *and* that her parents were considering
letting her go.

At first she thought it was her absurd amount of freckles that set
her apart, then the fact that she was ginger; then it had dawned on
her that maybe it was the way she dressed. Her parents rarely ever
bought her clothes. She wore what her gran picked out or her brother's hand-me-downs. The older she got, the more obsessed she became with the idea that it was her gran's old-fashioned ways. She
went to school in tight pigtails, with her skirt hemmed below the
knees. Her parents didn't buy her nice-smelling erasers and Tama-
gotchis either. Her gran sewed and stuffed handmade dolls for her
instead.

As much as she loved her gran, she also wished she didn't exist.

Her mother was pouring more milk in her brother's bowl of Nes-
quik the morning they discussed the party. Lauren had been staying
with her parents for a few nights because her gran had the flu and
could barely make her own tea. Lauren knew that the moment her
gran was feeling better, her father would drop her off over there
again. At least he had the decency to come up with legitimate-

sounding excuses: that they'd be working late all week and there would be nobody to make Lauren her dinners, or that Evan was having a hard time and needed all their attention, or that Lauren had been asking for her. Her gran never complained, and neither did she.

"I suppose we'll have to send her to the O'Briens' party," her mother said, stirring Evan's cereal.

Her father didn't look up from the newspaper, while Lauren's brother, practically a man now, popped a whole sausage in his mouth.

"If she doesn't go, people will talk," her mother continued.

"We'll have to get those girls something if she goes." It sounded like a complaint, coming from her father.

Evan stood up and stomped out of the kitchen, leaving most of his breakfast behind. Lauren caught the look of longing in her mother's eyes as he left. All she had ever wanted was a son she could mother. Lauren was an afterthought; there were twelve years between the two of them.

"I don't know what these girls would want. Do you know what we could get them as presents?" All of a sudden, both her parents were staring at her, and Lauren was stumped.

"Friendship bracelets," Lauren blurted. It was what she *wanted* to give them, because then they'd have to wear them, sealing the girls in friendship together forever.

Her father folded the newspaper away. "I don't have the first feckin' clue what those are."

Her mother sighed and nodded. "They can't cost much."

Two weeks later, on the afternoon of the party, her mother forced her into the Bo Peep dress. It was Lauren's frilliest frock, and it made her look like she was headed to her own Communion. Evan walked her to the party, chain-smoking the entire way, so that by the time they arrived, Lauren could smell her brother's smoke in her hair.

She had the two gift-wrapped pouches in her hand. Friendship bracelets weren't available at the shop in the village, so her mother had to drive into town for them.

Molly O'Brien opened the door, and party music poured out of the house.

"Oh!" Molly exclaimed, like she wasn't expecting Lauren.

"Go on, Laurie, give them to the girl," Evan said, flicking his cigarette right down in front of the O'Briens' door.

"Happy birthday." Lauren held the pouches out. She heard the cackling laughter of girls from inside the house, but Molly was yet to invite her in.

"Dad will pick you up in an hour," Evan said, before walking away.

Lauren's cheeks flushed. She had a feeling that the other kids were going to spend more time at the party, but she knew she'd have to be home by five. Showered and changed and at the dinner table by six, in bed by seven. When she stayed at her parents' home, she had fewer liberties.

"You can come in if you want," Molly said, stepping aside so Lauren could enter.

She didn't have time to think about the tone of the girl's voice. She was just glad to be there. She went running in, expecting to be filled with wonder.

And she wasn't disappointed. There were balloons everywhere. Pink and silver. Curtains of streamers hung from the ceiling, swishing like skirts as kids walked through them. Out in the garden was a mind-boggling spread of food: multicolored fizzy drinks, tiny triangular sandwiches, gigantic bowls of crisps, vol-au-vents, and sausage rolls. It appeared that they'd already cut the birthday cakes. Two identical ones with glossy chocolate frosting. Big slices had been cut out of them and laid out on paper plates. Lauren didn't recognize the music, because they didn't listen to the radio at her house, just news on the TV. It didn't matter—she was ready to dance.

She turned away from the garden with a smile on her face, which quickly faded as she noticed Molly and Daisy at the other end of the room, flanked by a group of girls Lauren recognized only too well.

They were all looking down at something in Molly's hands. Lauren saw the gift wrapping and knew immediately they were the bracelets. The girls pored over them, dangling the woven beaded things in front of their faces, giggling and whispering in one another's ears. They were laughing at her. At the idea that they could ever be best friends with her. Lauren saw their imperfections clearly in that moment. Molly's eyes were too close together; Daisy had a big splotchy birthmark down the side of her neck; Nora's laugh sounded like a goose squawking; Jane's belly was so big her top rode up and her leggings rolled down. She wanted to leave their house, to lock herself in her own bedroom, where nobody could see her, but she knew she couldn't go home now. Her mother would berate her for behaving badly; her father would force her to listen to his complaints about the hotel where he worked as the night porter. Besides, it wasn't like she had the privacy of her own bedroom, which she shared with a brother who looked at women's fashion magazines all day. It was worse when she pretended to sleep, because that's when she'd have to listen to the zip of his jeans going down, to his groans and curses.

Her gran was sick, Lauren didn't want to be a burden, so she had nowhere to go.

With the sound of the girls' laughter ringing in her ears, she ran out to the garden, where the music was the loudest. She went and stood in front of the big Sony CD player, focusing on the antenna sticking out of it, and began shaking her arms and legs to the unfamiliar song. She built up a rhythm quickly, and even though she knew they were all watching her, she didn't turn to look.

Chapter 16

September 13

MISHTI WASN'T SURPRISED WHEN PARTH AGREED to have dinner with the Dunphys. It was unlike him to want to socialize with their neighbors, but he seemed vaguely interested when she told him about Ciara's invitation, asking about the time they were supposed to show up, if they should take some wine.

She helped Maya dress for the evening and then spent a few minutes on her own makeup. Parth appeared to make an effort at picking out his clothes. She'd rarely seen him mulling over an outfit before.

They walked together to the gates and then up the driveway. Maya was excited to have dinner with Bella, while Parth stepped ahead of them in determined silence, as though prepping himself for a stage performance.

Ciara was at the door before they had a chance to knock. She had a gingham apron tied to her waist, the picture of a good hostess. Mishti already knew what Ciara was wearing tonight: a little black dress, a diamond tennis bracelet, and the perfect shade of nude on her lips. She'd seen the selfie Ciara posted online half an hour before, along with the recipe of what she was cooking.

The smell of a roast dinner wafted through as they entered. It was a smell Mishti would not have recognized before she moved to Ireland.

"It's so good to see you all." Ciara was beaming.

Parth held a bottle of wine, which he presented to her. Bella appeared and reached for Maya, leading her quickly into the house. Gerry stepped out of the sitting room with a TV remote in hand.

"Howya," he said. He pumped Parth's hand and then patted Mishti's arm.

Mishti could see clearly now why Ciara had married him. Gerry was attractive—at least Mishti thought so—well groomed and clean-cut, always dressed sharply and smelling nice. But Ciara had once told her that she didn't care for handsome men. She had married him because of the freedom he granted her, the freedom to be whoever she chose to be.

"Wine for everyone?" Ciara offered. Her voice was cheerful and bright tonight.

Parth and Gerry walked to the sitting room together, quickly falling into a conversation about football.

"I think I'll just have a tea," Mishti said, following Ciara to the kitchen. Finn was in his playpen. He looked like he was about to burst into tears.

"Oh, have a glass of wine tonight, Mishti. You can have tea after dinner."

Ciara poured the wine, and Mishti went to appease Finn, who had started to cry. She knew Ciara wouldn't approve of her picking him up, so she went down on her knees and talked to him soothingly from the other side of the playpen.

Her eyes fell on a box discarded in the corner. It was the Elsa costume they had given to Bella on her fourth birthday a few months ago. Mishti had thought it would make a good present, since Bella was obsessed with the *Frozen* movie, but looking at it now she saw the costume still intact in its package, untouched. It baffled her that Bella didn't want to play with it or that Ciara hadn't encouraged her to even try it on.

"He'll be fine, don't worry about him. He gets grizzly like this before dinner." Ciara came over with the glass of wine Mishti didn't want.

Finn stared at his mother longingly, with big blue eyes. He was practically begging her to lift him, to hold him for a few moments. He'd stopped crying, but his cheeks had accusatory tracks of tears.

"You'll be eating in just a few minutes, kiddo," Ciara cooed at him, ignoring his pleading look.

Mishti stood back up, and Ciara linked an arm with hers. Their hips bumped together like they were schoolgirls.

"This is nice, isn't it? We should have done this sooner."

"Yes, it's nice for the families to spend some time together."

"Yes, exactly. You and I spend too much time together already." Ciara laughed, and then handed Mishti another glass of wine. "Come on, let's take this to the husbands. Someone needs to interrupt their GAA chatter. It's like they have nothing else to talk about."

Mishti threw Finn a look over her shoulder as they walked out of the kitchen. He was watching them in silence, resigned to his fate of being left behind.

In the sitting room, Bella seemed to have won control of the TV remote from Maya; *Frozen* was on. The two girls were playing with a set of beads, making bracelets for each other as they half-watched the screen.

Parth and Gerry were still talking about football, but it looked like Parth was doing most of the talking.

They handed the men their wine. It was then that Ciara remembered Finn and said she was going to bring him to the room. Mishti suppressed a sigh of relief. When Ciara returned, she put Finn down on the carpet and sat beside Parth.

Mishti had to wonder if Gerry was seeing what she saw—the way Ciara arranged herself, crossing her ankles daintily, fixing the neck of her dress, adjusting her proximity so she brushed against Parth ever so slightly. Mishti would never have sat that close to another man, nor a woman. Parth didn't seem to mind.

"Tell us about India, Parth," Ciara said. "I've heard stories from Mishti, but I want to hear your version."

Gerry sat back in his armchair, seeking out his cellphone to scroll through. Instead of noticing their closeness, he seemed almost relieved to not have to contribute to the conversation anymore.

"I wouldn't even know where to begin," Parth replied. He turned to Ciara as though she was the only other person in the room.

"Tell me about your childhood. About your parents. I want to know what made you *you*," Ciara said. She laughed at the absurdity of her own words, but nobody else did.

Parth narrowed his eyes, thinking back to his early years. He was deciding how he wanted to paint the picture of his life's story.

Later, at the dinner table, Ciara still only had eyes and ears for Mishti's husband.

Finn fussed in his high chair. Maya and Bella misbehaved with their food, making little boats out of the mash in the gravy, turning peas into cannonballs.

Gerry ate with one hand and typed into his phone with the other. The ferocity with which his fingers moved made Mishti think he was telling someone off in an email. He made it look like he was working and their dinner party was getting in the way of it.

Ciara served Parth second and third helpings. He didn't refuse any of it. At home, he complained about the bland food the Irish ate.

"I wanted to cook something you don't eat at home every day," Ciara said, while scooping more stuffing onto his plate.

"We certainly don't eat this every day."

"Maybe Mishti can make some authentic Indian curries when we call over." Ciara flashed her a sudden smile. This was one of the only times she'd acknowledged Mishti's presence all night.

They were interrupted by mash flying through the air. Bella was pretending the ships were under attack.

"Bella! The food is for eating, not for playing," Ciara said, though keeping her tone even, determinedly peaceful. There were to be no battles with the children tonight.

Parth was still regaling Ciara with tales of India and the misadventures of his youth. He'd moved on from his childhood and praising his mother to stories about his teenage years, none of which Mishti had heard before.

"I can't picture you with a ponytail," Ciara said, laughing.

"And I was in a band too."

Mishti noticed how Parth looked directly into Ciara's eyes as he spoke, like a diviner searching for a fresh spring.

"Oh my goodness! This gets even better. Which instrument did you play?"

"I played a little bit of guitar, but I was the lead vocalist really."

"And you can sing!"

Ciara looked crimson, from what could have been the wine or her fantasies of Parth the Rock Star.

When Mishti eyed Maya, her daughter was dipping all her fingers in the gravy and then licking them off one by one. "Maya, use your fork, please," she murmured. Maya bit her lower lip sheepishly, then picked up her fork. Bella was still flinging mash around the room.

At the other end of the table, Ciara continued, "You have to sing for us."

Finn's annoyance with his food had reached its crescendo. He was throwing all his peas and carrots to the floor, flailing his arms and flaring his nostrils. Nobody other than Mishti seemed to notice. Ciara and Parth continued, talking over Finn's protests.

"Not tonight, I can't. I have to be mentally prepared for it. I haven't sung in years."

"We all know how modest you are about your achievements," Ciara said.

Parth wasn't aware that Mishti overheard him every weekend when he was on the phone with his mother. He carried on for ages about how his students loved him, how his clients wouldn't make it without him. How he was quite literally saving lives. "I'm not sure I'd call it an achievement, but, yes, we did have fun."

"You must give us a performance sometime."

"Maybe when you come to ours for dinner. This way, you can't refuse the invitation."

"Oh, you don't have to convince me." Ciara brushed Parth's fingers for a moment, before returning her hand to her plate. "It's only this man standing between me and my curry dinner."

They all looked at Gerry, who wasn't listening. Almost a full thirty seconds passed before he noticed their faces were turned to him. He looked up from his phone, a little shifty-eyed.

"Yeah?" he mumbled.

"See what I mean? It doesn't matter, I'll bring the kids over myself. We won't even miss him." Ciara giggled close to Parth's face, like it was an inside joke between them.

Finn's crying got increasingly louder. Bella was standing on her chair. Maya, who never spoke loud enough for her father to hear her, burst into laughter at Bella's impersonation of a pirate. *Ahoy, me hearties!*

"Bella, get down!" Ciara felt the need to finally say something. Uncharacteristically, she had given her kids free rein tonight.

Finn was tugging at the straps of his high chair in an attempt to break free. Bella continued her act with an *aarrrr*. She was climbing onto the table, and this forced Ciara to finally stand up. Finn started bawling.

Mishti went to him. She couldn't sit in her chair and watch while the child turned a different color.

"You don't have to pick him up, Mishti, seriously, I've told you this before. He needs to learn." Ciara's tone had turned to a whine. It wasn't bitter; she wasn't angry. She sounded like a drunk party girl complaining about her high-heeled shoes.

"I think he just needs a break," Mishti said. She snapped the straps to pull him out. It was as much as she could take, and they were both relieved to be in each other's arms.

Ciara was in the process of dragging Bella off the table, while Gerry and Parth watched in silence. It showed on their faces: their complete and utter helplessness. Maybe they were imagining how they'd break into pieces if they were left alone with the kids.

"What are you doing?" Ciara asked Mishti. She'd managed to get Bella down.

"I'm just going to take him outside for a few minutes. Give him some fresh air."

"He doesn't need fresh air right now, Mishti."

"Well, maybe I do."

Finn had calmed and she stroked the back of his head, walking in the direction of the garden. She was grateful nobody tried to stop her, that Ciara didn't come after her with another glass of wine.

She had always felt most alone with her thoughts when she held a baby, and she desperately needed to think.

Mishti breathed in the cold air and paced the patio, her hips finding the natural sway they always did when she was holding a child. Finn pointed at shadows while they waited for their eyes to adjust to the dark.

She rarely ever stepped out into her own garden at this time of the night, but it was better illuminated here. She felt she needed the darkness. She didn't want to be seen. It disturbed her, where her thoughts had gone tonight, what she thought she saw between Ciara and Parth.

Finn babbled and she bounced him in her arms, humming a Bangla lullaby she used to sing to Maya as a baby. Mishti looked over her shoulder at the house, but she couldn't see them anymore. Everyone must have returned to the sitting room. There was only a deserted kitchen, with dishes piled up on the marble island.

Across the grass, she saw the flicker of a dim orange glow. It was in Lauren's garden. Soon, a human form began to take shape in the dark. The orange glow was the end of a cigarette. Mishti recognized Lauren's distinctive tent-like silhouette, the billow of her floaty clothes.

She waited until Lauren's face became clearer, her eyes dark and inquisitive. She was walking toward them, toward the edge of her garden. Mishti didn't know Lauren smoked, but it didn't surprise her.

Gripping Finn a little tighter, she stepped down from the patio and crossed the damp grass to join Lauren at the border of the premises.

"Hello there," Lauren greeted her. She held the cigarette up like a flag, almost as though she wanted to make sure Mishti saw it. They were separated by a hedge.

Mishti held Finn away from the smoke, but the breeze was blowing in the opposite direction anyway. "Hi."

"Fancy seeing you here this time of the night. Babysitting?"

"No, we're here for dinner."

"Right. How is that going?"

"Okay, I think. I don't know."

It wasn't the response Mishti would have normally offered. Tonight she had temporarily lost her ability to put on a polite front.

Lauren breathed in a lungful of smoke, then twisted away to blow it out.

"I'm sorry if this is bothering you. I can put it out."

"No, it's fine."

"Did you ever smoke?"

"I never would have gotten away with it around my family. I did try it once, when I was in college. I didn't see the appeal."

"Good for you. I wish I never took it up."

There was some comfort in not seeing Lauren's face clearly. It allowed Mishti to speak more freely.

"Where's Ciara? Why do you have Finn?" There was something like an accusation in Lauren's voice.

"He needed some fresh air. He was a little overwhelmed by all the excitement in there." She smiled, but from what she could tell, Lauren wasn't returning it.

"The poor pet. He could do with a bit of affection from time to time."

It was only lately that Mishti had noticed the lack of tenderness in Ciara's parenting. All these years, she had considered Ciara to be the authority on motherhood, just as all their friends and her followers did. Tonight she was inclined to agree with Lauren but couldn't admit it. "Lauren, Finn is well looked after and very loved by his parents."

"Maybe you're right. What do I know?" Lauren smoked some

more, and they stood in silence for a bit. Mishti lightly swung Finn, while Lauren seemed to be looking past her at the Dunphy house. Mishti had the feeling that if she invited Lauren in, she would have stubbed out her cigarette and followed her right then.

"Lauren, I'm sorry about the last time we spoke."

"I should be the one apologizing."

"I just wanted to say I'm sorry. I shouldn't have . . . I don't know what I should have done."

"You did nothing wrong."

The two women stared at each other, or at least at what each estimated to be the other's face.

"I would love to have dinner with you sometime," Mishti continued.

Lauren took another drag. It was so quiet around them that Mishti could hear the paper hiss and burn.

"Yeah, well, I think we should keep our families out of it for a while. Maybe just you and me? We could grab lunch somewhere? Sean could watch the children. Maya too, if you like."

Mishti heard the eagerness in Lauren's voice. Was that what Ciara heard in her own?

"Okay."

"Text me?"

"I will." Finn was already wriggling in her arms, and it gave Mishti the excuse to take a few steps back.

"Go. You should return to the party."

"Yes, I should. Good night."

Lauren waved her burning cigarette in the air and then turned to walk across her garden.

Mishti's shoes were damp. The cold was going to seep into her again. No number of hot-water bottles would do the job tonight, not when it got into her like that.

She carried Finn to the house, humming to him. When she brought him into the brightness of the kitchen, they both blinked wildly. Finn thought it was a game and giggled.

Ciara came in moments later.

"There you are. We were wondering where you went. I thought I saw you standing outside, and then you were gone." Ciara had her back to them as she poured more wine.

"We went for a walk around the garden."

She turned to them, both hands occupied by the glasses. She blew a kiss in Finn's direction. "He loves his little garden walkies, don't you, kiddo?"

She was already going away, leaving Mishti to follow.

In the sitting room, Gerry had disappeared somewhere and so had the girls. In Mishti's absence, Ciara and Parth had been left alone.

Parth's eyes were bloodshot and small. When Ciara handed him his wine, he gulped it down like it was going to deliver him. She seated herself beside him like before. Mishti didn't know where her place was. Eventually, she decided to sit in Gerry's empty armchair, with Finn still in her arms. It faced away from Parth and Ciara, which was for the best. She didn't want to look at either of them for the rest of the night.

Chapter 17

September 13

IT ANNOYED CIARA HOW MISHTI HAD TAKEN IT UPON herself to whisk Finn away from the dinner table. Although she supposed it was nicer to have Finn out of the room. So much easier to carry on a conversation.

As soon as they'd left, Ciara began clearing the table. Neither of the men offered to help and sat drinking their wine. The girls chased each other around the kitchen.

"Bella, why don't you take Maya up to your room? You can show her your new teepee," Ciara suggested. She didn't care what the girls got up to in Bella's room, as long as they were out of her sight.

They went screeching and bounding up the stairs. Gerry got up to follow them, to make sure they did end up in Bella's room and didn't get into any trouble along the way.

For the first time that night, she and Parth were alone together.

"Shall we retreat to the couch?" Ciara said, placing an empty salad dish with a shallow puddle of vinaigrette on the kitchen island. "We'll be more comfortable there."

They walked to the sitting room together a little tipsily, holding their drinks. They collapsed on the couch, like kids falling into beanbags. Her leg touched his, and neither of them pulled away.

He sat with his arm thrown over the back of the couch. Just a few inches in the wrong direction, and she would have been in his arms. Ciara was already too warm from the wine, and she slipped her shoes off. She rubbed the toes of her left foot on her right ankle and watched him watching her. Brown eyes traveling over her body, surveying her shape and every movement.

"You know, I feel like I've finally gotten to know you a little bit tonight." She spoke when the silence between them felt explosive.

"I don't think I've examined my life like this before. I hope I haven't bored you to death."

"I am far from bored. I'm fascinated."

He was looking at her mouth. There could have been only one thing on his mind. "Where is Gerry?" he asked, in a deep, gravelly growl.

"I don't think he's coming back down, not right now. He's probably on his phone, writing an email he's told himself could cost him his job."

Parth reached for her, stroking her knee lightly. She allowed his fingers to linger on the inside of her thigh. She leaned in closer to him, breathing in his stuffing-and-wine breath.

"I don't think you know how beautiful you are, Ciara. How absolutely magnetic."

She had to laugh at that—at his assumption that she wasn't aware. Men liked it better when a woman was unwittingly charming. As though the very knowledge of her own desirability would ruin the appeal.

"I have some idea."

"Of course you do. I'm sure every man who has ever met you has wanted you."

He was parroting lines he thought every woman would love to hear. She was disappointed in him. She'd expected more originality from a man like him, an academic. Now that she watched him closely, she saw that there was something distinctively childish about him. The way he thrust his lips out before speaking. How his thumbs swished like windscreen wipers on his knees when he was nervous.

She sipped her wine. He was trying too hard. His touch was clumsy, verging on shaky. She wanted to scold him a little, remind him to get a grip.

"I wish we were free," he said.

"We are not imprisoned, Parth."

"We are married."

"Yet we are not prisoners."

He shut his eyes, struggling with whatever moralistic thought had suddenly entered his brain. "I just wish I had met you a few years ago."

"Before your marriage was arranged?"

"Yes."

"That's really sweet."

"I'm not trying to be sweet," he said.

"I adore Mishti. She's been a good friend to me."

"And I'm sure your husband is a good man."

"It doesn't mean these people are good for us. Right for us."

"No, it does not."

She was only now noticing that they were speaking in whispers. Something she didn't have to do with Sean. They were never together around people they knew. This flirtation with Parth had felt exciting at first, but it was becoming a nuisance. Especially because of the reverence with which he treated her. She wished he would see her the way he probably saw his students: young, fickle, slutty.

"I don't want to do anything to jeopardize your marriage," he continued.

"Or I yours."

It was a lot of talking for something that hadn't happened yet, or never might.

"Then we should stop now," he said. She saw it in his eyes. He wanted her to tell him she couldn't stop. That she had never wanted any man the way she wanted him. He wanted her to make him feel special, but it was too much effort, and she was feeling lazy.

"Yes, we should stop," Ciara agreed.

He leaned toward her again, and just as his lips brushed her neck, she pulled away. She knew what she'd find if she looked between his legs.

They heard quick footsteps. There was a moment of panic. She was afraid of Mishti finding them like this, when it was too late to make excuses. But it wasn't Mishti; it was Gerry.

He appeared at the doorway with his phone in hand. The three of them stared at one another in silence. Then Gerry turned on his heels and disappeared.

Parth sprang away from Ciara.

"Shit," he groaned under his breath.

"It's okay, it's fine. Don't worry about it."

He shook his head. His eyes were wild, like an animal being led to slaughter.

Coward, she thought.

MISHTI RETURNED WITH Finn soon after Gerry had interrupted them. Ciara was grateful that Mishti decided to sit in Gerry's armchair, turned away from them on the sofa. She hadn't wanted to look at either of the Guhas for the rest of the night. Either way, they didn't stay long after that, and Ciara didn't want them to. The dishwasher needed loading, and Finn was already asleep. Bella was a whole other ball game. Rita was going to be here early the next morning, so Ciara left most of the clearing up for her.

She had been drinking steadily all night. When Bella cried, begging for a few minutes of *Frozen* right before bed, she was too exhausted to fight her. So, while Bella watched a video clip, Ciara sat cross-legged on the floor, digging the flesh around her fingernails.

"That's enough, Bella. Mummy needs her phone back, and you need to go to sleep."

Bella grumbled, slipping under her light fleece blanket.

"If you're going to complain, then you're never getting to watch videos before bed again."

Bella turned her back to her, and Ciara switched off the lights. The soft violet glow of the nightlight filled the room. She stared at her daughter's tiny body, lying in the seashell-shaped bed. No amount of research or parenting blogs could have prepared her for this age. When she first had Bella, she thought babies were unpredictable and demanding. Like little wild animals that had been unfairly domesticated. The emotions and rage they felt against each other now were shockingly intense. Ciara much preferred the newborn stage.

She touched Bella's arm but said nothing. The wine was making her sentimental. In the morning, when Bella was going to refuse her every breakfast offering, Ciara was going to forget how much she had wanted to hold her tonight.

"Good night, Bella. I hope you sleep well."

She waited at the door for her daughter to say something. It was a waste of time. Maybe her son would be different. Maybe there was a chance Finn wouldn't come to despise her as quickly.

WITH THE BABY monitor clipped to her waistband, Ciara went downstairs to the kitchen. She'd changed into pajamas, and she poured herself another wine. The night had been a relative success.

She knew where to find Gerry. The door to his study was shut, and she knocked twice before pushing it open. He was at the desk, typing on his computer lazily.

He didn't look up at her. She knew there were things he would have said to her if he was a different kind of person. They hadn't exchanged a word since he walked into the sitting room and found Parth leaning into her. He hadn't seen anything more. None of the lip-grazing or the thigh-touching.

He wasn't daft, though.

"The kids are in bed." She had to open with something.

"Okay."

The ice cubes tinkled in the glass when he picked it up. He swirled it a little before bringing it to his mouth. When he did focus his eyes on her, he scanned her from top to bottom. He was looking for evidence. Paw prints.

"Mind if I sit down for a bit? I never sit in this room."

There was a navy velvet armchair by the window, with a tall back and elaborate wings. It looked like something that belonged in a room filled with books. Gerry rarely ever read a book. If he did, it was on his phone.

She sat in the chair, with her legs tucked underneath her, taking slow sips of her wine. Gerry's fingers hovered over the keyboard, but his thoughts appeared stuck somewhere else.

They both sat in silence for a while. Ciara watched him, challenging him to start typing again. He was slowly cracking under the pressure. He couldn't type, but he couldn't make himself look at her either.

"One of these days, our children are going to grow up. Then we'll well and truly have nothing to say to each other," she said.

"You're right, Ciara. You are absolutely right."

"Shouldn't we start talking?"

"Yes, you're right about that too."

"Is that all you have to say to me? That I'm right about everything?"

"I don't think I'm capable of saying the right things to you, Ciara."

"Do you remember what you used to call me?" She took his silence to mean he didn't. "Cheri. When did you stop calling me that?"

"Does it matter?"

"Not anymore." She stood up. The wine was making her lethargic, and she was certain she'd fall asleep in the armchair if she didn't move now.

Gerry stared at the screen again. She wondered for a moment if he was sleeping with someone else. She hadn't considered it before, but that would explain his attachment to his phone and the late hours he kept. He rarely came to bed at the same time as her anymore.

"Listen, I don't know what you think you saw tonight, but nothing happened. I want you to know that."

"No, nothing happened."

"That's what I'm saying."

"Yes. I'm saying I know nothing happened."

She parted her lips to say more, to tell him exactly how strange she thought he was acting. How he only grew more strange with time. No, he was incapable of keeping up an affair. He didn't have the gumption for it.

Ciara walked out of the room, pulling the door shut behind her, swaying a little as she went. She'd decided she was going to take the bottle of wine to the bedroom. She'd have it polished off before Gerry came up. In fact, she wasn't even sure if he slept in the bed with her anymore.

There was one particular morning during their honeymoon, when they sat on the grass in the garden of the quaint little cottage they'd rented in Annecy. The scent of figs and plums was everywhere, and a variety of cheeses filled their bellies. Ciara had looked over at the sharp-nosed man beside her. His lean body was stretched out. He was balanced on his elbows, as he sunned himself through his clothes. He was too afraid to take his shirt off, in fear of burning to a crisp. She'd just bitten into the juicy flesh of a mirabelle, and as the flavor exploded in her mouth, she thought she really was in love with him. She remembered that day because the thought had occurred to her that she would like for death to come to her first, so she wouldn't have to figure out how to live without him.

Some of the wine sloshed onto her five-hundred-thread-count eggshell sheets.

Ciara had positioned herself half upright against the cushioned bedhead, with half a dozen decorative cushions thrown on the floor beside her. She was practically lying down. It wasn't the ideal position for drinking, but she wanted to be able to slip into sleep without effort.

She had spent some time taking stock of her secret wardrobe, moving pieces around, holding them up to imagine how she'd look in them. The part of her that would have once wanted Gerry to come up to bed and make love to her, fueled by jealous passion, didn't exist anymore.

She picked up her phone to check the chats. Some women from

the group were sending photographs of their kids. It had turned into something of a nightly tradition, sharing pictures they'd taken of their children throughout the day. Pictures nobody besides other mothers would appreciate: the ones of faces smeared with blueberry yogurt, failed attempts at handstands, wobbly bubbles made with gigantic wands.

Ciara wasn't interested in the photos tonight and scrolled instead through her own gallery from earlier that evening. There were some of Bella and Maya making funny faces at the camera. There was one of Gerry with his eyes half shut; he had looked up from his phone at the same moment she clicked. There was one of Mishti sitting by herself, staring into space, as though she hadn't noticed the company.

Then there was a selfie Ciara had forgotten about. It was of Parth and her. It was taken at a close angle, but it showed Parth's arm around her shoulder, his nose grazing hers. She had tapped the button without much precision, mid-pose. Although she was only trying to pout, to give her jawline that perfect shape, in the photo it looked like she was about to kiss him.

It was just a photograph. Mishti wasn't going to care.

It felt like a strange compulsion, a secret testament that she could have any man she wanted.

More notifications from the group appeared on her phone, while Ciara considered the selfie. These women were still talking about their children; she wasn't interested in the group and their pettiness tonight.

It took her less than thirty seconds to upload the photo to her Instagram. The selfie was posted first, and then she edited the caption.

Just what a tired mammy needs

It made her giggle. She imagined a collective gasp ringing out around the village. Women sitting up in their beds, their jaws dropping open, quickly typing under the photo.

Some TLC

Lucky you!

You look beautiful, Ciara

Wine O'Clock!

On a school night!

Looks like fun

Some fire emojis.
Other comments poured in quickly from strangers.

Ok wowwow

Damn she's fierce

We won't tell. Shhhhhh

You look gorgeous! And enjoy!

Have fun. So jealous. Wish I was there.

Live your best life girl

Sexy mama

Ciara put her phone on the bedside table, then tucked the empty bottle under the bed. She slid down, wedging a pillow between her legs. She felt the effects of the wine, a thick heaviness that might finally pull her into sleep. She wouldn't even need her pills tonight, which was ideal since she was running dangerously low. Her phone kept buzzing with notifications, but when she reached to switch it off, a comment on the screen caught her eye. It was from Lauren.

So you get your neighbor to watch your kids while you spend some alone time with her hubby?

"Fucking bitch!" Ciara shouted. She threw the phone to the floor. She didn't care if it woke the children or if Gerry heard.

She turned over and buried her face in the pillow, then screamed into it.

There was nothing she could do about it now. It was too late to delete her post. She shouldn't have posted the photo. If she hadn't, nobody would have known it existed. Least of all, Lauren Doyle.

"Little fucking bitch," she shouted again. This time, her voice was muffled by the pillow.

The door creaked open.

"Are you okay? I thought I heard something." Gerry didn't step in, like their bedroom floor was hot lava.

"I'm fine. I dropped my phone. I'm going to sleep."

He may not have heard her response, but he left anyway.

Ciara dug her nails into the coolness of her wine-stained sheets. Then she flipped over again, resting her hands on her stomach. It had taken her six months to lose the mummy pouch after Finn, but she got there in the end. It was a reassuring reminder of what she could achieve.

And it hadn't always been like this with Gerry either.

"MY MOTHER THINKS you're too pretty for me." Gerry said this to Ciara after the first time she went to his mother's for tea. He'd proposed to her at an exclusive rooftop restaurant in Dublin a month before.

"So you're saying your mother thinks you're ugly?"

They smiled, sitting in his car in the drive-in queue at McDonald's. Gerry played with the radio system, switching between channels. It was the one thing about her new fiancé that niggled at her—his obsession with cheap fast food.

Ciara had sensed Liz's rejection even before she sat down in her sitting room. Liz had looked her up and down, with a smile that didn't reach her eyes. She hadn't even offered a hug to the woman her son was about to marry. By the time the tea and Jaffa Cakes were brought in, Ciara felt too uncomfortable to know how to sit. Crossed legs were too formal; crossed ankles were old-fashioned. Gerry sat in a well-worn armchair across the room, grinning at the two women in his life.

Conversation began with the weather. Liz didn't ask her anything too personal, nothing about her family or upbringing. Everything else she needed to know was right there in front of her. Ciara and Gerry were well matched, how could his mother deny that?

Gerry loved his mother, Ciara knew. Liz was widowed at a young age and had raised him single-handedly. She was a proud mother too, proud of the son she'd brought up on a hairdresser's wages. Gerry had repaid every sacrifice she'd made, though. Liz now lived in a comfortable home with no mortgage, drove a year-old car, and went to Majorca with the girls every year.

Gerry had been hesitant to introduce them, and he looked nervous as he sat with them in his mother's sitting room. He'd left it until the last minute, weeks after the wedding date was set. He already knew his mother would disapprove.

"She thinks I'm punching above my weight," he told Ciara in the car later.

"Why doesn't she like me, Gerry?"

"That is not what I said."

"But that is what she told you, didn't she?"

He had to move the car forward. His knuckles turned white from the pressure he applied to the steering wheel.

"No, those were not her exact words. I suppose she thinks it's all happening too fast. The engagement, the arrangements for the wedding. She hasn't had a chance to get to know you."

"I can't guarantee she will like me once she does."

Gerry turned to her. His smile was replaced by a frown. "I shouldn't have told you, because it doesn't matter."

"Of course it matters what your mother thinks of me. You should have introduced us sooner."

"I didn't want her to think I need her approval."

"So what are you going to do?"

"I'm going to do nothing."

"You're going to marry me even though your mother doesn't want you to?"

"I'm going to marry you because I'm in love with you, Ciara. What my mother thinks doesn't change anything. I love her too, but you're the one I'm going to spend my life with."

He held her by the back of her head, weaving his fingers into her hair and knocking his forehead with hers. They stared into each other's eyes for a long moment, until he had to pull away because the car behind them was honking. The queue was moving again, and Gerry had a smile on his face as he brought the engine to life. He was so happy to be with her that nothing was going to bring him down.

Ciara sometimes thought about that day now. Liz knew she was handing over the reins that had steered her son his whole life. She didn't want to give that kind of power to a woman who knew exactly what she was doing.

Chapter 18

September 14

TWICE A MONTH, LAUREN ATTENDED A MOTHERS-
and-toddlers yoga class at the community center. It was more
an excuse for the mothers to have a chat while stretching a little.
Sean had encouraged her to sign up. She wasn't particularly keen on
going but thought Willow could do with a bit of socializing outside
the family.

She sat cross-legged on her mat today, keeping one eye on Willow,
who had toddled over to silently stare at another child her age. Lauren saw Ciara across the room, sitting with her group. It didn't take
her long to sense the hive gathering against her. The worker bees
hadn't appreciated Lauren's comment on their queen's photograph
the previous night.

Lauren had tried to make conversation with them before the class
began. Ciara hadn't arrived, and she thought it was the best time to
test the waters. The women exchanged glances when she walked up
to them and ignored her when she greeted them, like she was invisible. She had no choice but to eventually walk away.

Mishti was noticeably absent from class. Maybe it had something
to do with the photograph Ciara had posted. Lauren couldn't help

but thrill to the idea that Mishti was finally beginning to see her friend for what she really was.

Now the other women huddled in a protective circle around Ciara. The instructor walked among them, gently correcting their form. Lauren stretched her legs out in front of her, then saw Willow standing alone. The other toddler Willow had tried to interact with had returned to her mother. Or had she been pulled away? Discouraged from mingling with one of Lauren's children? Lauren experienced an urgency to lunge for Willow and pull her into her arms. This was her fault. Perhaps she had taken it too far this time. She didn't even want to think about what Sean would say if he found out about the comment she'd written. The public statement she'd made against Ciara.

Lauren smiled weakly at Willow when their eyes met. She held her arms open, to encourage her to return, and her daughter toddled across the room and collapsed into her lap. Lauren inhaled the familiar scent of Willow's hair and closed her eyes. She wanted to make this right.

After class, Lauren lingered in the reception room, Willow's hand in hers. This wasn't about her anymore. Childhoods were at stake here.

Ciara hadn't emerged from the studio yet, but there were echoes of happy chatter as mothers and children spilled out the door.

"Mammy, outside!" Willow demanded. Lauren reached into her backpack for a bag of veggie crisps and split it open for her.

Ciara finally materialized, surrounded by her usual gang. They were all dressed in matching leggings and tank tops, in varying shades of gray and blue. Ciara was the tallest, or at least she appeared to be, with her back straight and her shoulders lean but muscular. For such a sharp body, she had an exceptionally delicate face. Her thick bangs and full lips made her look younger than she was.

Lauren stepped toward them, tugging Willow along.

Ciara had Finn on her hip, and she whispered something in his ear. Some of the other women saw Lauren approaching and seemed to lean into one another to raise the alarm.

"I should get him home for his nap before he has a complete melt-down," Ciara spoke loudly, rolling her eyes. It was for the sole bene-fit of Lauren. A preemptive barrier against whatever she was about to say.

"Ciara, I was hoping to have a word with you." Lauren knew she had to say something before this slipped through her fingers.

"What about?"

"Didn't you say Finn needs his nap?" Daisy O'Brien came to Ciara's rescue, taking the bait exactly where it was left.

"Is there something you want to say to me?" Ciara spoke directly to Lauren, making it clear that she didn't need Daisy's rescuing.

"Yes. I thought we could talk privately."

"You usually don't have a problem expressing yourself publicly, so why not now?"

Willow tugged on Lauren's hand, and it was the reminder she needed. "I don't want to bore these lads."

"You don't have to worry about us, Lauren," Molly said. The O'Brien sisters were proving themselves as Ciara's biggest champi-ons.

Ciara smiled at Molly and then sighed, squaring her slender shoulders like she was carrying the weight of the world upon them. "Fine, we can talk, but you can do it right here. I'm not going any-where with you."

It looked like Lauren didn't have a choice. She should have walked away, but this could be her only chance to do right by her children.

"I'm sure you know why I want to speak with you," Lauren said slowly, making herself breathe evenly to keep her voice from break-ing. She kept her eyes on Ciara, willing herself to ignore the rest of the pack.

"No, actually, I don't. Enlighten me."

"You want to hear me say it, don't you?" When Ciara said noth-ing, Lauren continued. "It's about what I wrote on your post last night."

"You mean the vile comment you left for everyone to see?"

"My comment was uncalled for, and I regret it."

Ciara was half smirking as she held Lauren's gaze. The kind of smirk you put on when you don't know how to arrange your face. Willow was tugging at Lauren's hand, bored by the adult conversation. None of them wanted to be here. Except perhaps for Molly and Daisy O'Brien, who were standing on either side of Ciara, ready to throw their punches.

"You know, it is none of your business where my kids are at any given time. If you had nothing nice or supportive to say, you should have simply kept scrolling."

"You're right. I should have kept my thoughts to myself."

"Instead, you chose to say something nasty on a public platform."

"I apologize that it came across like that. I didn't mean for it to be nasty."

"Are you serious? You didn't leave any room for it to be misconstrued." Ciara threw a quick glance around her and met approving eyes.

"I saw Mishti in your garden. She was carrying Finn, trying to calm him. I thought it was ironic you were in there taking pictures with her husband."

That made Ciara whip right back around. She obviously didn't know Lauren had seen Mishti. It frazzled her for a moment. "It was just a silly picture."

"Silly?"

"Excuse me? Are you implying something?"

"No, I'm not. Forget it."

"I thought you wanted to apologize, and now you're making more accusations."

"I didn't accuse you of anything!"

"What are you trying to say about that photograph?"

"Okay, I'll say it since you're asking. Maybe nobody else is mentioning this, but have you spoken to Mishti? Have you asked her how she feels about it?"

"I don't think you understand what it means to have a friend. A good friend." Ciara stepped closer to Lauren, and for a moment she was convinced Ciara was going to take a swing at her. Maybe the only thing preventing her from doing so was Finn being in her arms.

Instead, Ciara broke into a bright smile.

"Mishti was there when the photo was taken. Parth is my friend, just like Mishti is. You don't understand it, because you don't have friends. You wouldn't know how that dynamic works."

Lauren looked down at Willow, who had stopped tugging at her hand.

"So, thank you for your concern, but I don't need your advice," Ciara went on. "As a mother, you should be supportive. We should all be pulling each other up, instead of judging a woman for being friends with a man. I mean, which century do you live in?"

Molly O'Brien looked like she was going to applaud.

"You're judging me for not having friends," Lauren managed to say.

Ciara rolled her eyes. She held her car fob up.

"I'm going to leave now, because you are ridiculous. I would offer you a lift, but I have to . . . No, I don't think I would ever offer you one."

"It's fine. I'm used to it."

"And you should think hard about why."

Lauren might have done something more, if she didn't have Willow with her. She may have put up more of a fight. That comment she posted wasn't about their personal animosity, she wanted Ciara to understand; it was about Mishti and how she was being treated.

Ciara left hurriedly, and Lauren stood there for a few moments, lost and speechless. The other women walked past her too, throwing caustic looks over their shoulders. Lauren pulled a fabric sling out of her pack, and her hands shook as she tried to quickly wrap Willow into it on her back. She kept her head down as she heard the cars backing out of the parking spaces outside.

Lauren didn't want to go home. Sean was going to be there, and if he saw her like this, he would immediately sense something had happened; he always saw through her ruptures. She planned to tell him eventually but not while it was still this fresh. She needed to calm down first.

At school, when she was bullied by the O'Brien sisters, she was glad she didn't have to go home to her parents. She didn't want them to see her with her neck all blotchy, give them any more reason to curse her existence. She'd spend hours in her gran's garden, by herself. She made mud castles from the sticky earth in the shadowy corner, where the raked leaves lived. All those years of relentless humiliation, and Lauren's mother had no idea what brought on those bouts of hives. Her gran did, but she couldn't do much either.

"Mammy. Mammy. Mammy!" Willow shrieked for attention when they were walking again.

"Please, Willow, not right now. Mammy's just trying to figure out what we'll do next, okay?"

"Mammy. Mammy. Mammy."

Lauren shut her eyes and tried to imagine what a visually impaired person would do. How would they make their way along this road? The experiment didn't last long. Since she didn't have a white cane, she nearly tripped over the edge of the footpath.

There was only one thing she could think of doing. One thing that could make this all go away.

An idea had taken hold of her a few months ago, but she'd been rationing her fantasies. She didn't want to get carried away too quickly. She only allowed herself to think about it when she was in desperate need of a distraction.

Lauren walked to the bus stop with Willow. It was going to take them over an hour to get to the city, but she knew it was time for the next step. She was finally going to try on some wedding dresses.

She needed a solid plan before she asked Sean to marry her.

Chapter 19

September 14

NEEL GOT A JOB, JUST AS HE PROMISED, AT A COMpany in Delhi that manufactured fans. Ceiling fans, table fans, extractor fans, pedestal fans. He was going to start at the bottom, but he believed there was great potential for growth.

"We'll have to rent a flat at first, maybe in one of the new complexes they're building around Gurgaon. In a few years, we'll be able to buy a flat of our own."

When she remained silent, he continued speaking. "And I don't want you to stop studying. You can go to a college there; you'll eventually find work too. Things are different in Delhi. Nobody will know us there."

When he reached for her hand, she let him hold it. She had noticed this about him, even when they were children and he played out on the street by himself; he was rarely ever still. While he held her hand, he restlessly tapped his feet. "What do you think, Mishti?"

"I am very happy for you."

"And for you?"

"You want me to elope with you?"

"If you want to put it that way."

"That is what everyone will say. Ronjit's daughter ran away with the Banerjee boy."

"Yes, that Banerjee boy whisked Ronjit's only daughter away." Neel was smiling at her. He even lifted her hand up so he could kiss her fingers. "And in a few years, by the time we have our own flat, they will have forgotten about it."

When they had kissed for the first time a few months ago, he was clean-shaven. Now he was growing a beard. She liked the way his stubble felt around her mouth when she kissed him, but he wouldn't do it in the restaurant, not out in the open. They would most certainly get kicked out for obscenity, or, worse still, an angry mob of self-appointed moral police would force them to ring their parents and confess what they'd been up to.

She wished he would kiss her here. It would solve a lot of their problems.

"We'll be free, Mishti. We'll be free of everyone. My family and yours, and all our neighbors. Maybe we won't have to return to Calcutta again."

She had never been anywhere outside the state. She'd only ever been to the beach in Digha and to Darjeeling in the summers. She barely even spoke Hindi, and the little she knew was from the Bollywood films her cousins watched.

She didn't attempt to draw her hand away, because she didn't want to hurt him. He was waiting for her to say something. "When will we go?"

"I start in three weeks. I haven't told my family, I haven't told anyone, so nobody will suspect a thing. All you have to do is pack a bag and meet me at Howrah station."

"And where will we get married?"

"I'll make all the arrangements; I'll find a temple we can go to. We can get married as soon as we arrive in Delhi. Mishti, we'll be all right."

She wanted to say something so he knew how much she wanted this. It had seemed like a fantasy at first, but now she was picturing a small, pristine flat with yellow curtains. A four-poster bed like the one in her grandmother's room. The sound of an extractor fan in a kitchen that smelled of mustard fish curry. His favorite.

She hadn't planned on telling anybody. She was able to keep it a secret for four days. Every day, she packed a few things away in a bag she was hiding under her bed.

Then she was in the kitchen helping her mother peel the potatoes for dinner one evening. Ma had been complaining about her sister-in-law in hushed tones. Something about gossiping with the maid. "And does she think the woman doesn't go to other houses, spreading this around the whole neighborhood? Why would you talk to the maid about your family and the household?"

Mishti's eyes usually watered when she cut onions, but there were none this evening. She still had tears, but her mother hadn't noticed. She was too busy plunging the potatoes in the wok of spluttering oil. Mishti stared at her mother, who was dabbing her sweaty forehead with the loose end of her sari.

"Ma." She spoke up in a small voice.

"What's the matter, Mishti?"

"I have made up my mind, but I don't want you to be upset."

Her mother narrowed her eyes against the rising smoke from the wok. "What are you talking about?"

"I'm going to Delhi."

"What for? What is this?"

"Ma, I'm going to Delhi with Neel Banerjee."

Her mother stood motionless for a few moments, staring at the discolored tiles on the kitchen wall. The potatoes were going to burn if they weren't fished out soon.

"Neel Banerjee," her mother repeated his name.

"Ma—"

"How long has this been going on?"

"A few months. Less than a year. I never spoke to him before that."

Mishti wasn't crying anymore. She saw the white rage in her mother's eyes.

"And he wants to take you to Delhi and keep you as his little whore?"

"We are going to get married. You have never spoken to him; you don't know what he's like."

"I know exactly what all the Banerjees are like. Druggies. Drunks. Have you seen the state of his mother?"

"She needs help."

"You are not going anywhere with him."

"I'm telling you because I want to say goodbye. I could have left without a word."

"And your father would have gone after you and brought you right back."

"Ma—"

"Mishti, listen to me, you are too young to understand, a boy like him is—"

"I know what you're about to say."

"Then I won't have to say it."

Mishti looked over at the wok, the potatoes had all turned black. They were inedible. Her mother sighed and took the wok off the stove. "We'll have to start over. Get more potatoes, will you?" she said.

SHE TEXTED NEEL to meet her at their spot. When she got there, he was already waiting for her at their bench. He had a paper plate of pakoras in his hand, and he dipped one in some spicy green chutney.

Mishti sat down beside him, noticing how he smelled of soap. The pink ones, like what her mother used in the kitchen to wash her hands after cooking.

"I'm going to miss the food. Calcutta has the best street food—ask anybody," he said.

She sat close to him, so their legs touched. It was comforting to think about how familiar they had become. They didn't even notice when their bodies aligned now. She had known him all her life, even if it wasn't always like this.

He was chewing when he turned to look at her. She didn't have to say a word, and he knew. "What did you do, Mishti? Who did you tell?"

"Please, Neel. Listen to me."

"Let's go to the station now. Did anybody come with you? You don't need anything. You have your Walkman in your bag, don't you? I have enough money to buy the tickets."

He stood up, throwing the plate and the pakoras to the ground. Mishti stayed where she was. She watched as he considered physically pulling her up. He wouldn't have actually done it.

Exasperated, he sat back down. "Who did you tell?"

"Ma."

"And she let you come and see me?"

"She hasn't told anybody in the family, and she had to take Didu to the doctor for her eyes. She doesn't know I'm here." Her grandmother was going to have cataracts removed. It still wasn't going to help her see that her daughters-in-law despised one another.

"Why have you come to see me if you don't intend on leaving with me?"

"Because I wanted to tell you myself, Neel. I had to say goodbye."

"Mishti, I can't just let you go home to those people."

"They are my family."

"And what about me?"

"You will be fine, won't you? You have a nice new job, with prospects. You have always wanted to live in Delhi. In a few years you'll buy a flat."

She wished he'd take her hands, but he didn't. "Yes, I'll be fine."

"Neel, please. We have to say goodbye."

He stood up again, and this time he had no intention of sitting down. "Goodbye, Mishti. I hope they find a good husband for you."

"I don't want someone else. I want you to believe me."

"You should go home before your ma gets back, or she'll have your father and uncles breaking down our doors."

"Please."

He reached in his pocket to pull out a box of smokes. He stuck one between his lips and lit a matchstick. He'd lit the wrong end of the cigarette and he threw it away in anger.

"I should have listened to my mother. She warned me about you," he said, before he left.

MORE THAN A decade later, Mishti still remembered everything about Neel Banerjee.

A few years ago she had sent him a friend request on Facebook. Enough time had passed; they were both married.

It took him a few weeks to accept the request. She thought he never would.

Even after they did become virtual friends, they didn't speak to each other, not even through private messages. It was for the best. The only thing she could give him was some form of an apology, but he didn't need to hear it again.

Mishti regularly scrolled through his photographs while Parth slept beside her. Every night she hoped Maya would wake up, come to their room, and keep Mishti from falling down this black hole. Everyone's photographs on Facebook were happy, beautiful, celebratory. She hoped Neel's weren't an exaggeration, that he was as content as he appeared to be. Though he was married, he didn't seem to have any children yet. From the narrative she pieced together, it appeared he had brought his mother over from Calcutta to live with them. His beard was thick now, and he wore thin-rimmed Gandhi glasses, which suited him well. His wife was clearly North Indian. She had none of those rounded Bengali features or big eyes. Sometimes, Mishti snooped through his wife's profile, just to see photographs of him from her perspective. Neel blowing out candles on a birthday cake; Neel with his arm around her; them standing in front of a mirror together and taking a selfie; Neel's mother cooking in the kitchen, smiling and timidly covering her face.

She had to force herself to put the phone away every time, with her heart racing and aching.

Her marriage to Parth had been arranged four years after she had planned to run away with Neel. It was four years of waiting to see who her parents found for her. Four years of hoping it would be a man who would make her family proud, who she might one day grow to love. A man who was promised to be infinitely better than Neel. In those four years, she had trained as a primary school teacher and had secured a decent job at a decent local school. She had to give that up for Parth too.

Every time she looked at Neel's profile online, she felt an urge to kick Parth awake and tell him what she really thought. That there once was a day when she could have begun a different life with another man.

Chapter 20

September 14

CIARA HAD BOUGHT THE COTTAGE NEARLY A YEAR ago, when she wanted a quiet place to go on the days Liz watched Finn. Some days she didn't want to go into the city and buy more clothes. Some days she just wanted to take her pills and sleep for a few hours in a bed Gerry hadn't paid for.

He didn't know about the cottage. She'd been saving all the money she got from her brand collaborations on Instagram. It didn't cost her much, given the significant disrepair the place was in. Not much land came with it either. The previous owner, a man who had reminded her disturbingly of her father, appeared to be surprised that anyone even wanted it.

There was no need to babyproof the place or even replace the nonfunctional washing machine. The kids were never going to visit. There was no need for a dishwasher here. She could do without heating. There were major cracks on the walls that needed plastering. The bathroom floor was in need of fresh tiles. It was never warm enough, but Ciara liked it just the way it was, with its blackened grease stains around the cooker and sheets that were always musty and cold.

"There's a well out the back," Sean remarked. He was sitting up in the bed, looking through the grubby window, which barely illuminated the room. Ciara was already putting on her shoes. Only a few hours had passed since Lauren confronted her after their yoga class, and the memory of it was fresh in Ciara's mind. She could still see Lauren's smug face as she brought up Mishti's feelings. The sheer audacity of it had made Ciara want to do something physical to the woman. She who had lived in this village all her life and had somehow managed to make no friends.

"A well? I hadn't noticed," Ciara replied.

"Where are you going?"

Sean grabbed her by the waist and pulled her back into bed. He pushed the hair off her neck and kissed her nape. Wrapping his arms around her torso, with her back pressed to his abdomen, he rocked her gently.

She didn't like it when they cuddled, but he needed it. Just like she needed him to push her up against the wall and take her from behind. She didn't want to be the one in control when they were having sex. It was the opposite of what she wanted when she had her clothes on.

He kissed her shoulders and made his fingers dance along her arm. Dust particles swirled in the shard of light coming in through the window. She felt like she'd given him enough time to recuperate.

"Are you going to make those eggs you made the last time?" It was her excuse to pull away from him.

"Depends. If the eggs haven't gone bad."

"Well, they've been in the fridge this whole time."

"But that damn fridge may have stopped working."

Sean was smiling as he swung his legs over the side of the bed. He was always coming up with suggestions to improve the cottage, almost as though he had designs on moving in here himself.

He padded off to the kitchen in his boxers, and she remained sitting on the edge of the bed. Her watch said she still had two hours before she had to pick up the kids. She didn't want to spend that long with Sean. They'd already done what they came here to do.

"Coffee?" he asked from the kitchen. It was the only other room in the cottage.

"Sure."

The kettle was flipped on. He was talking, but she wasn't paying attention. He spoke about the drip in the ceiling and cobwebs in the corners. Ciara didn't intend on cleaning up around here.

He returned a few minutes later, carrying a big bowl of scrambled eggs with chorizo and two mugs of coffee, carefully balanced on an Easter-themed tray. All the utensils and cutlery had been left behind by the man who'd practically shoved this place into Ciara's hands. She couldn't remember if she'd ever washed them. There was certainly no washing-up liquid around.

The coffee tasted bitter and sugary at the same time, but she drank it anyway.

"And maybe we could rent a lawnmower, and I'll bring some tools from our shed. Clear up all the overgrowth," he continued.

She pushed her fork into a big chunk of egg. "Did Lauren tell you what she's been up to?"

Sean clamped his mouth shut like he'd been slapped.

"Looks like she hasn't," she continued with a smile.

"What are you talking about?"

"She's been harassing me online. Like a dirty little troll." It gave her some pleasure to see him flinch, but he composed himself quickly.

"Ciara, I know this thing . . . what we have going . . . it's complicated, but I'd appreciate if you didn't . . ."

"Didn't what? Call your wife out on her horrible behavior? Oh, sorry, she's not even your wife."

"She is the mother of my children."

"Which is exactly why you need to keep an eye on what she does. The example she's setting for those kids. *Your* kids. You should be concerned."

"What did she do exactly? What do you mean, she's been harassing you?"

"She makes it a point to comment on all my social-media posts.

For all the world to see. These are not kind comments. Snarky. Everyone's noticed. Everyone's been talking about it."

"What has she said?"

Ciara put down her mug and started tying her hair back in a ponytail. Sean watched her carefully as she stretched her arms up. It encouraged her breasts to hike up. His eyes seemed to soften, as though he was remembering how they felt in his hands.

"She's said enough, and she knows it too. She came to speak to me today. I thought she was going to break down in tears."

"So she wanted to apologize?"

"She didn't actually say she was sorry. I don't know what she was trying to say. I reckon she thinks we could be friends."

"And would that be such a bad thing?"

"You can't seriously expect me to be friends with her. After the shit she's pulled over the years."

"Are you saying you can't be friends with her because of us?"

"No, it has nothing to do with us. You know what she's like."

"What is she like? I don't understand."

"Maybe you should ask someone else to explain it to you, if you don't already know."

"Ciara, I'm asking you, so tell me. What shit has she pulled?"

"She's just strange. I mean, you've gotta know."

Sean put down his fork and drew closer to her. "Okay, yeah, she can be a little aloof. She does things differently, maybe she's even a bit naïve, but she's not a bad person."

"She wouldn't be attacking me if she wasn't. I don't know what she has against me personally, but I really do hope she doesn't push it any further."

Sean was agitated, she could tell. It made her wonder if this was it. If this was how it would end between them. Maybe Sean wasn't going to accept Ciara's abhorrence of Lauren, despite being the one cheating on her.

"I know you don't have to, but if you could just be patient with her. Give me some time to talk to her. I'll make her come around."

"I don't expect you to make her like me. I don't care what she thinks of me. All I'm saying is, for her sake, it would be wise if she didn't pick a fight with me."

"I know that, and she won't."

Ciara ate some more of the eggs and then stood up. She needed to use the toilet. Sean stared at her longingly as she left the room.

She sat on the toilet with her knees knocked together, wondering if Sean was out there listening for the flush.

It had been more than eight months, and she couldn't work out why she was still seeing him. She knew why it began. He looked really good in a leather jacket. That, and he reminded her of one of her college professors.

When Ciara came out of the bathroom, she thought Sean was going to ask her how it went. He had a curious look in his eyes. She walked past him to examine herself in the mirror. It was surprisingly clean and shiny, compared to the shabbiness of the rest of the cottage. Sean had clearly given it a wipe so he could look at himself. The thought made her smirk. He cared about appearances too, just like Gerry did, but in a different way.

He came to stand behind her. She was rubbing the edges of her mouth lightly. Her lipstick had smudged, but she wasn't going to bother reapplying it.

"Okay, I've had a little think about it. I'd say you're better off not striking up a friendship with Lauren."

"You think?"

"Keeping your distance is probably the wiser decision."

She arched an eyebrow. "I have no intention of getting close to your . . . partner. I have friends."

"Yes, I'm aware, Ciara."

She turned to face him, hooking her hands on her hips. He placed his hands on her arms, stroking the fabric of her blouse with his thumbs.

"I don't want to argue with you, love."

"Don't call me that, please. It reminds me of how old you are."

"I'm not that old." He laughed.

"You're much older than me."

"Yes, I suppose I am."

He leaned in for a kiss and she let him have it. He pulled her in by her hips. She thought about a second round on the bed, or perhaps in the kitchen, except the table was too rickety.

"Maybe we shouldn't talk about our partners when we're together," he said, pulling away.

"I thought you would want to know what people are saying about the mother of your children."

"And thank you for that."

"You're welcome."

They smiled at each other. Maybe this was one of the reasons she was still doing this with him. He was able to make her smile sometimes, just by not taking himself too seriously.

"I like this," he continued, tucking stray strands of hair behind her ears. And just like that, he ruined it.

"That's nice of you to say."

"No, Ciara, I do mean it. I like this time we have together. I look forward to it when we're apart."

"It's nice to get away."

"Like a holiday? Am I a holiday to you?"

They were still smiling at each other, almost warmly.

"Maybe."

"We could go on an actual holiday together."

Ciara sighed and pulled away. He'd already tucked too much hair behind her ears. Her ponytail was ruined and she'd have to do it again. "We can't go on a holiday together, Sean. That would be ridiculous."

"Really? Ridiculous?"

"I have kids I spend all day with. You have kids you spend all day with." He didn't notice her taking a dig at him.

"But we're both entitled to some time away from them, aren't we? I'm sure you can convince Gerry. Lauren wouldn't mind if I took some time to myself. We can come up with something."

Ciara went to the kitchen to reexamine the table. She was still wondering if they could pull it off. He followed her.

"I'm serious, Ciara, we should consider it. We don't even have to go anywhere. We could just come here and spend a few days together in peace. They won't find us."

Ciara stood in front of the table, placing a hand on one end to see how much it wobbled. She tried blocking out his voice, but the room was too small—his voice was everywhere.

"Or we could go abroad, if that's what you prefer. I would love to see Greece with you."

"Greece?" She couldn't help but laugh. "Where did you come up with that?"

"I've always wanted to go to Greece. Have you been?"

"Sean, why would I go to Greece with you?"

He was stumped by her question, staring at her with his jaw dropped. She noticed how his two front teeth stuck out like a beaver's. It may have lent a certain delightfulness to his face as a child, but it did him no favors as an adult. It felt like she was looking at him for the first time. There was so much she didn't like of what she saw.

"I'm not sure if you want me to answer that question." He sighed, like he was tired of all this. As was she.

"No, I don't. I can't see why you think we should go anywhere. Honestly, Sean, I'd hoped you would know better than that."

"That this means nothing to you?"

"I'm just blowing off some steam."

"I don't believe you're happy in your marriage, Ciara. You can't be happy with that lad."

"And what are you going to do, Sean? Rescue me?"

She picked up her handbag, which she'd left on the kitchen counter earlier, wanting to get as far away from her phone as possible. "I will never leave my children, Sean, and I won't ask Gerry to give them up either. They are happy where they are. I hate to break it to you, but I actually like my life."

"I love my children too, Ciara. I don't have any intention of giving them up either, but I don't want to subject them to a lifetime of feeling burdened by my expectations of happiness from them."

A wave of nausea rose in Ciara's throat. She was suddenly re-minded of what her father had said when he was leaving.

"You won't find happiness with me," she retorted quickly.

"Self-deprecation doesn't suit you."

She shrugged. "You've misunderstood. You won't find happiness with me, because I have no intention of making a happy life with you."

Ciara positioned her handbag in the crook of her arm and walked to the front door. There was too much on his mind. He wasn't going to try to stop her from leaving.

"There's a key under the pot outside. Just make sure you've locked the door when you leave. You can stay here a little longer if you want, but don't spend the night."

She was going to collect Finn from Liz's sooner than she'd planned. For one moment back there, she'd allowed herself to imagine what life with Sean might look like. It made her want to hold her children in her arms.

CIARA THOUGHT IT ironic that an innocent picture of Sean cook-ing eggs in a dilapidated cottage could have done more real damage than the picture she'd posted of Parth. What she found even more ironic was that she saw Lauren with the kids when she drove back to the village, after having spent the whole afternoon shagging her man.

Despite the dregs of her conversation with Sean leaving a bitter taste in her mouth, Ciara found herself smiling as she pulled up alongside the footpath, where Lauren and her kids were walking. Lauren looked over and sighed when Ciara slid the window down. They were close enough that she didn't need to get out of the car, and Lauren had stopped walking by now.

"Let me guess, you're not here to offer us a lift," Lauren said.

Ciara pouted, looking at the two curly-haired children as she spoke. "I don't have enough car seats for all of you." She made it a point to always be polite to the children.

Lauren turned to her oldest. "Watch your brother. Don't let him jump in front of any cars."

Once Freya and Harry had walked a little ahead, Ciara spoke again, knowing her own children weren't paying attention from the back seat. The temptation to talk about Sean had never itched like this before.

"Look, Ciara—"

"I just wanted to tell you that I plan on blocking you from my socials if you don't stop what you're doing."

"And what is it you think I'm doing?"

"You have some kind of personal vendetta against me. You have had from the moment we first met."

"You haven't made things easy for me around here."

"You practically commanded me to join the other camp."

"It was inevitable, Ciara. You and I were never going to be friends."

"That day, when I went to your house to introduce myself, you took one look at me and I saw your expression change. *You* made the decision, Lauren."

"Why are you even warning me? Why don't you just block me already?"

"I want to give you a chance to make a change."

"You think I need to change who I am?"

"You're making me regret this conversation."

"Have you convinced yourself that this is some sort of kindness?" As Lauren spoke, Willow peered at Ciara over her mother's shoulder. It disconcerted Ciara for a moment; she'd forgotten about the third child on Lauren's back.

"Can you be honest with yourself? What would you do if you didn't have me to stalk online?" Ciara lowered her voice, not wanting Willow to hear.

Lauren clenched her jaws. "Are you listening to yourself?"

"You thrive on it, Lauren. Admit it. You can't keep away from me."

"If only your thousands of followers heard you talk like this."

"There are a lot of things about me that my followers don't know about. You don't either."

"I know enough."

"You're pathetic." They were an echo of the words she'd spat at someone else, also triggered by a man. Ciara wished she could just come out and say it, why she really thought Lauren was so pathetic. She thought it pitiful that Lauren had stuck around with Sean for this long, had three kids with him, let him live in her house.

"Am I really the one who's pathetic here? The one who has to make up a face every day to be validated by a bunch of strangers?" Lauren interrupted Ciara's thoughts.

"If you didn't care what these people on the internet think, you wouldn't keep bringing them up all the time."

Lauren looked stumped for a moment, but she spoke quickly before she began to walk away. "As much as I shouldn't give a flying fuck, I wish you'd be more careful about all this social-media stuff. You're dreamin' if you think these people won't cancel you if you slip up once."

Ciara was only now beginning to realize that she might have even grown to like Lauren if she wasn't such a fool for Sean, if she could see through him the way Ciara did. A man who didn't deserve either of them. She drove away.

Chapter 21

September 14

LAUREN WANTED TO SPEAK TO HIM ALONE, BUT THE kids kept interrupting them all evening. Sean had spent most of the day in town, helping a friend clear out his shed. When he did come home, he was aloof and uninterested in conversation. Freya and Harry were particularly destructive this evening. Willow refused to go to sleep. She was up way past her bedtime, demanding to be carried around and then sung to. Lauren was exhausted and desperately needed a shower. She knew she stank of armpits when Ciara stopped in her car to talk earlier.

It was midnight by the time all the kids were finally asleep. Lauren left the TV on in the sitting room, since it drowned out their voices and helped Willow sleep better.

"You calling it a night?" She had found Sean in the kitchen. He'd already poured himself a glass of wine and was digging through a plate of leftovers in the fridge, in his frayed boxers and a Manu Chao T-shirt.

"I'm going to read for a bit in bed." He had his back to her. From his voice, she sensed he didn't want to talk.

"I was thinking we could sit together for a while. Talk a little."

"I'm knackered, Lauren. I'm going to bed. We can talk tomorrow."

"You were barely home today."

"I told you I was helping Jim take his shit to the storage."

"Yes, I know. I'm just saying we didn't get a chance to talk today."

"Is there something on your mind?" He was sighing as he spoke, like he was having trouble catching his breath.

"Yes, as a matter of fact, there is. Shall we sit on the couch for a bit?"

Sean looked at his glass of wine and shrugged. When she smiled at him, he didn't return it. She didn't know what she'd done wrong—he couldn't know about what had transpired with Ciara. She considered changing into fresh clothes first, for the sake of this conversation, but there was no time for that.

He followed her to the sitting room. Like Harry, he too had the habit of dragging his feet listlessly, with his shoulders hunched, when he didn't want to do what he was being asked. They sat in front of the TV. A cooking competition was on, and Sean seemed completely taken by it.

She was worried that if she didn't tell him now what she wanted to say, she'd explode and make a mess. "Sean, I've been thinking about everything."

She was vague on purpose, to pique his interest, but he continued staring at the screen. He appeared riveted by an egg being expertly poached onscreen.

"Please, you need to pay attention to what I'm saying. This is important to me."

In all the years they had known each other, Lauren had never asked anything of this man. Whatever he gave her, he had offered without solicitation. So she didn't know how exactly to go about it.

When the ads finally came on, he turned to her. His wine-stained tongue swept over thin lips. "I'm here, I'm listening. What's happened, Lauren?"

"Nothing's happened. I just have something to ask you. I've been thinking about it for a few weeks—well, maybe a few months. I've lost track."

Now he seemed concerned. His brows crinkled. She noticed the crow's-feet around his eyes and mouth all of a sudden, startling her.

She cleared her throat and continued, before she could change her mind. "Will you marry me?" Her voice was shaky, but she was smiling.

Sean stared blankly at first, holding his breath. Then he dabbed his forehead with the back of his wrist. "Is this a serious question?"

"Why would I joke about something like this?"

"I don't know why you do the things you do, Lauren. For instance, why would you pick a fight with Ciara Dunphy?"

"What? Where is this coming from?"

"Is it untrue?"

"Yes, it is. I never set out to pick a fight with her."

"Right. She's just a raging lunatic who imagined it all."

"She told you this?"

"She didn't have to. Everyone in the village is talking about it, aren't they."

Lauren dug her nails into her knees. She tried to remain sitting on the couch, when all she wanted to do was hurl herself at him. "And since when do you believe everything you hear from our beloved neighbors?"

"So they're all lying?"

"Maybe. Depends on what they told you, who you've been speaking to."

"You've been harassing Ciara online. Taking digs at her. Trying to make her look bad." It was a pretty accurate account of what had happened. "Well? Lauren? Are you going to deny it?"

"Are you going to reprimand me for being naughty?"

"For fuck's sake, Lauren. Do you see the problem? This is your fault."

"Are you afraid she's not going to invite us to her dinner parties?"

"So this is all about Mishti Guha?"

"It's about the person Ciara is," Lauren replied. Very seldom had she felt the need to defend herself to him. Usually, Sean was the only one who stuck up for her.

"Why? What kind of person do you think she is?" he asked.

Lauren saw genuine curiosity shining in his eyes. It was as though he wanted her honest opinion of Ciara. Like he was doing a credit check on someone he was about to go into business with.

He'd already forgotten that she'd proposed.

The show came back on, and when Lauren hadn't replied, Sean's gaze drifted to the TV again. "Okay, let's talk about this some other time. You need to have a good long think about what you're doing. How you want people around us to treat you and, by extension, the rest of your family."

"Sean, seriously, you're going to ignore the other thing? You're going to leave me hanging here?"

He dragged his eyes away from the screen, like it was physically painful to do so.

"What other thing? Oh. Right. You want us to get married."

Lauren didn't know what to do with her hands. She twisted them around in her lap until the joints ached from the pulling and tugging. She had never been very good at masking her nerves. "I asked you to marry me. Maybe I should have asked you differently. Maybe you don't realize how serious I am. Should I have gone down on one knee? Baked a cake with a ring in it? I've been thinking about this for a while, Sean. Don't you think it's time?"

He stared at her, with his mouth slightly parted and his eyes glazed over. He hadn't had nearly enough of that wine to be drunk already. It was something else. "Time for what? If there ever was a time to get married, we have long since passed it."

"It doesn't have to be a big deal. I mean, I don't want it to be a big deal. Just something small, with the kids. Your sister could come, and some of our old friends."

She tried smiling, but it didn't sit right on her face. This conversation wasn't unfolding the way she'd been imagining it. Sean wasn't tearing up or falling on his knees with joy and relief. She'd hoped he would confess he was thinking about it too. Then they would embrace and set a date. In the summer, a small celebration in their garden, exactly where her gran would have wanted it. She'd get started on cutting out patterns for the children's clothes as soon as possible.

"It's not about the ceremony, Lauren. It's about the principle of the thing."

"The principle of marriage?"

"You can't tell me now, after all these years, that you've been harboring hopes of one day changing my mind."

They'd never discussed it before, not once. It hadn't even come up in a passing conversation or as a joke. She'd avoided it because she didn't want to hear what he had to say.

"I didn't know your thoughts on marriage. I didn't realize you were so fundamentally against it."

"It's just a piece of paper, Lauren."

"And yet people have been signing this piece of paper for centuries. It has brought joy and stability to millions."

"And it has been the downfall and death of millions more."

"So you're saying that if we were married tomorrow, our relationship would somehow suddenly deteriorate? I thought you didn't believe in curses."

Sean leaned his head back on the couch and shut his eyes. She hoped he was thinking, not falling asleep. "I don't want our relationship to deteriorate," he finally said.

"It doesn't have to. It won't. But I think a wedding could be sweet. The vows and the rings, sealing ourselves to each other. Symbolically. We could get one of the lads to officiate. Padder could easily acquire a certificate online, I've looked it up. It doesn't have to be frumpy and serious. It could be nice for the kids too."

"You want to get married for the kids? You think they'll be bullied because their mother doesn't have a husband?"

"Sean, you're twisting my words."

"I'm just trying to make sense of how this has happened."

"Nothing has happened. I asked you a simple question."

"It's not a simple question, Lauren. You expect an answer right away?"

Some hope flickered. "No, not right away. I don't want to rush you."

"And how do you think we're supposed to get on with our regular lives with this thing hanging between us? How are we supposed to sit around the dinner table with our children? Look each other in the eye with this looming over our heads? And, more important, what happens if I say no?"

She hadn't considered any of this before, and now she wished she could take it back. Those dresses she'd tried on didn't seem worth it anymore.

"Nothing happens. It was only a passing thought."

He leaned toward her but didn't take her hand. It was almost as though he wanted to get a whiff of her. Like he could smell an unfamiliar odor coming from her. "I know you, Lauren. This isn't just a passing thought in your mind. You said it yourself, you've been thinking about it."

"But our life together means a lot more than signing a piece of paper. As you put it."

He almost seemed angry. His eyes bulged and he held the wineglass too tightly. He was usually so particular about holding it by the stem. Tonight he was holding it by the bowl, like he was about to slurp it down the way Harry ate soup.

"I don't know what to think of you anymore, Lauren."

He sounded disappointed in her. It wasn't like she'd done it on purpose. She didn't have any control over it; she'd simply spoken her mind. "You're right, we should talk about this later. Once we've both had some time to think."

"There is nothing to think about. I won't marry you. I can't marry you."

If she hadn't already been sitting down, she would have crashed to the floor. It would have been kinder if he had asked for more time and then let the idea die a natural death.

"Lauren, I haven't been faithful to you, and I can't marry you knowing this. I will most likely be seeing other people through the course of our marriage. I don't want to make false promises, which will be expected of me, to say in front of our children. If we get married, it would be a lie. That is not the life either of us wants to live, is it? I'm trying to do the honorable thing here."

She sat very still. She hoped that if she didn't move, it would all pass by her. Like a hurricane magically leaving her unscathed.

"Lauren, did you hear what I said? I'm cheating on you—isn't that the word they use to describe it? *Now.* I'm cheating on you now. I've cheated on you in the past, and I will probably do it again in the future."

"Who is it? Who are you sleeping with?"

She looked into his eyes, and she knew.

Sean left the room, and Lauren followed him to the kitchen. She watched him pour the wine down the sink.

"It's her, isn't it?"

"I'm not telling you this so you can go on another one of your witch hunts."

"Why won't you even look at me?"

He whipped around to face her, leaning against the sink, gripping the edge of the counter. "I'm looking at you now, Lauren. I'm looking straight in your eyes. I have nothing to hide. I want you to know everything."

"Except you won't admit it's her."

"I won't tell you who it is because of the way you've acted historically. I can't risk it."

"What are you so afraid of, Sean?"

"That you'll do something you'll later regret."

"How stupid do you think I am? Your sudden obsession with her. Coming to her defense. Admonishing me for some harmless things I've said. Did she go running to you all teary-eyed? Did you kiss it better?"

If she heard herself speak, Lauren would have laughed. Her words came out in stifled whispers. Like someone was trying to force her to eat her words by covering her mouth. She struggled against the force of those imaginary hands.

"We are discussing *our* relationship, Lauren. That is what we need to talk about, not someone else."

"But this changes everything."

"This changes nothing. You've always known . . . what I believe in. Who I am. You knew it when we first got together. There have been other women."

"But you stopped when Freya was born. I know you did."

"Yes, because I had my hands full. I couldn't focus on anything other than this tiny living thing I'd helped create. Then the dust settled, and I got used to having kids around. Lauren, I would never take it personally if there were other men in your life."

She searched her memory for signs and clues. She thought she knew him, that she would have noticed if he was being unfaithful.

Sean drew away from the sink to crack open one of the windows. The kitchen got suddenly cooler. "Look, I'm telling you this because I want you to remember what we are. Who we are. I can't marry you, because it wouldn't be right."

"And what you're doing is . . ."

"Is natural. Legally shackling yourself to another human being for the rest of your life is not. It's forced upon us, monogamy is. It goes against every law of nature."

She tugged at her cardigan, tightening it around herself. Sean came toward her. She flinched before he even touched her.

"Please, love, will you put this thought out of your mind? This whole marriage thing? I didn't mean to upset you. If you really think about it, you'll agree with what I'm saying. Give it some time, and you'll understand. I know you will. Just because we have children now, that doesn't change who we are as people, does it?"

"Don't talk about the children."

"I don't want our kids growing up thinking they smothered us."

"I have never stopped loving you."

Sean smiled at her, placing tentative hands on her shoulders. "Nor have I. Those are two separate things. How I feel about you has nothing to do with who I'm fucking."

"You're fucking *her*, Sean. I know you are. Why won't you just admit it? You've admitted everything else."

"I can't tell you who it is, Lauren."

"I have a fucking right to know!" She raised her voice for a fraction of a moment, and it was enough to wake Willow.

They heard her cry out, and Lauren covered her face with her hands.

"I'll go to her. You take a minute," Sean said. He was already making for the door to go to Willow's room.

"She doesn't want you. She wants me."

He stopped in his tracks. "Take a minute, Lauren."

He went into their daughter's room. She heard him whispering, then singing, then the floorboards creaking under his feet. He was pacing around with Willow in his arms. Lauren heard her whimpering, groggy and unhappy that it wasn't her mother holding her.

Chapter 22

September 15

IT WAS A MILD AUTUMN AFTERNOON, AND MISHTI WAS at the playground with the group, the only one swathed in layers of clothing. When she first came to Ireland, she hadn't pictured coming to know other women she could have lunch with, chat with outside the preschool at pickup, meet for playdates or at the playground. These women had welcomed her with their arms open, but Mishti had to wonder how much of that friendliness was to do with being chosen first by their shepherd.

Ciara stood in the middle of the group today, her arm elbow-deep in a bag of skin-care products she was distributing. A Danish brand had sent Ciara heaps of products to try out and review. Mishti guessed she got paid to do the reviews, because Ciara never discussed the terms and conditions.

"I wouldn't have known to use SPF daily if it wasn't for your tutorials," one of the women said. Ciara nodded sagely as she handed out sample-sized tubes. "It's only been a few months, but I can already see the difference."

"Not all of us are as lucky as Mishti, with her flawless skin," someone else remarked. They glanced at her almost sympathetically, even though this was meant as a compliment. She wanted to leave. She knew the others had been talking about her. They had all seen Ciara's photograph from the night before last. Mishti knew what they were thinking.

"Come on, it's our turn to watch the kids." Ciara appeared by her side. She linked an arm with Mishti's and gently tugged her in the direction of the children. "Don't worry, I've saved some real treats for you."

Mishti wanted to dig in her heels and refuse to be led away. She had never felt this enraged by Ciara before. She was acting like nothing had happened.

Ciara pulled her to the shrieking group of children before she could find the words to protest.

"We haven't had a chance to talk since dinner the other night," Ciara said. "I just thought it would do us good to clear the air. People around here can be so judgmental and small-minded."

Mishti's worst fears were being confirmed—everyone saw that post. If Ciara thought she needed to address the photograph, someone must have said something.

"I'm sure you know what I'm talking about. That photo I posted to my Instagram? The one of Parth and myself from that night."

"What have people been saying?"

"Nothing to me directly. No, they wouldn't dare. There have been hints. And then Lauren made that comment on the photo. I don't even know what she was trying to imply."

Mishti hadn't seen the comment. She couldn't make herself look through all the praises she knew people had showered on Ciara.

"I don't know what Lauren said, but it doesn't matter," she said.

"It does matter to me." When Ciara reached for her hand, Mishti drew it away. It surprised them both. Neither of them thought Mishti capable of rejecting Ciara's friendship. "It matters to me what you think and how you feel about me as a friend. Our girls are growing up together, Mishti. Maybe you don't realize this, but you've been a good friend to me. I would hate for that to change." Even though Ciara's words were meant to be kind, they carried an edge of threat.

"Do you think it's changing?"

"It shouldn't because of one stupid photo. It was stupid. I never should have posted it. I'd been drinking, obviously, and I thought it was funny and that we'd all have a laugh."

"Why would it be funny?"

Ciara let out a short sigh, as though she was frustrated by having to explain a simple concept to a child. "So you *do* mind. You *are* offended. You should have said something, instead of giving me the silent treatment all day yesterday and today. We could have talked about it."

"I haven't done anything on purpose."

"I know. I'm the one apologizing here, Mishti; you shouldn't have to. You're right, I should have come to you sooner. I thought the photo was funny. We looked funny, and I wasn't thinking straight when I posted it. I mean, I should have sent it to just you. Instead, I posted it online, like an idiot. I am an idiot." Ciara glanced at her feet dejectedly, like a child expecting to be given a warm hug and told she shouldn't be so hard on herself.

"Anyway, the point is, I didn't mean anything by it. These women have twisted it around. I don't even know what they're saying behind our backs, but I wanted to talk to you, so if you end up hearing any of this chatter, you'll know where I'm coming from . . ."

For the first time, Ciara's voice sounded more like babbling to Mishti's ears. She nearly burst out laughing. And Ciara was still talking.

". . . Just one photograph, taken in a moment of lighthearted fun. It isn't indicative of anything. You know that, don't you? You were there the entire time. It's not like we took a secret selfie without your knowledge. Why would I have posted it if there was anything to hide?"

Mishti couldn't recall the picture being taken.

The first time Mishti saw the picture was the next morning. The phone had fallen from her hand while she was scrolling through Instagram. Parth was sitting across from her at the dining table, munching on buttered toast and flipping through some notes. As she'd stared at the photograph, she hadn't recognized the man in it.

He didn't look anything like her husband. His smile was effusive, his arm slung around Ciara, so natural.

Parth had admonished her. "Be careful with that phone, Mishti. I'm not buying you a new one if it breaks because of your carelessness."

"Yes, I knew you were taking pictures that night," Mishti told Ciara.

"Exactly. That's what I want everyone to know. That's why I posted it without thinking much of it. I thought you'd find it funny too. Didn't we look silly with our big moony eyes?" Ciara chuckled, then paused to see if Mishti would join her.

"No, it didn't make me laugh. I didn't think it was funny. It looked like the two of you had been kissing."

Ciara's face fell. She looked up at the children but didn't seem to register their presence. "Mishti, I'm not having an affair with your husband."

"All right."

"I'm serious, listen to me. I'm not sleeping with Parth, if that's what you're thinking. I'm sleeping with someone else."

At first, Mishti thought this was one of Ciara's twisted jokes. The kind she made when she wanted to be cruel and hear herself laugh.

She heard Sean's name next, but she expected Ciara to break into a cackle.

One of the kids ran straight into Ciara's legs immediately after she'd said Sean's name. She had to detangle herself with some effort. There was discomfort on her face, in the way her mouth twisted impatiently. When the kids were gone again, Ciara sighed, peeling displaced hair off her forehead. "It's true."

"You're sleeping with Sean O'Grady? Lauren's husband?"

"He's not her husband. They're not married. Anyway, that's not the point. Yes, I've been sleeping with him for a few months."

Ciara looked around to make sure none of the other mothers were lingering near them. Two children started running around them in circles. It didn't matter what they overheard—nobody would take them seriously—so Ciara continued speaking. "I can see you're in shock. I don't blame you. If someone told me this about myself, I'd be in shock too."

"Why, Ciara?"

"I haven't been doing it out of vengeance against Lauren. As hard as it might be to believe."

"Why, then?"

"Because I was attracted to him. Gerry and I have been . . . I don't know how to describe it. Things have been off between us."

"So you start sleeping with someone else?"

"Yes." Ciara shrugged.

Mishti looked for Maya in the crowd of children. She found her daughter sitting on one of the swings. Bella was pushing her, and they were laughing together. "I don't understand," she murmured.

"What do you want me to say?"

"That you're making this up."

"I'm not, Mishti. Are you upset because I didn't tell you sooner? Because you can't be upset for Gerry's sake."

"I'm not upset. Why would I be?"

"You're acting like I've offended you. I'm telling you now so you believe it's not your husband I'm sleeping with. I want to be able to tell you this. I hope our friendship allows this. Whatever you suspect is going on between Parth and me is just your imagination."

"I wasn't thinking that."

Ciara arched her brows. "Yes, you were. You are just like the rest of them, Mishti. You saw that photograph of us and assumed the worst."

"I did not. Not because of the photograph."

"Why, then? We've been friends for so long. Don't you think you can trust me enough that I wouldn't do that to you?"

"But you'll sleep with Lauren's husband. Her not-husband. Because she's not your friend?"

They glanced at each other, but it was too difficult to hold the gaze. They went back to staring at the children.

"I didn't set out to hurt Lauren. I'm not trying to hurt anyone. Lauren's feelings are Sean's responsibility."

"And what about Gerry's feelings?"

"Since when do you care about Gerry? In all these years we've known each other, the two of you have barely ever spoken."

"No, we're not friends, but I want to know what you think of his feelings."

"I *have* given it some thought. What kind of a person do you think I am? I don't purposely want to hurt him."

"But you're being unfaithful to him."

"Do you think less of me now, because I told you?" Ciara asked.

"I don't think anything."

Mishti wished she could walk away. It wasn't that she'd considered Ciara incapable of cheating. She just didn't expect it to be with one of them, one of their husbands. She'd hoped Ciara would go looking someplace else, and Mishti wished she'd known about it sooner.

"I'm going to end it with him. I don't think he wants it to end, and that is a problem."

"Yeah, you've had your fun."

"Mishti, you're supposed to be my friend. You're the only person who knows, and I'm telling you because I hoped you would understand."

"Why would I understand?"

"Because you're not happy with Parth."

"Ciara, please."

"No, you need to be honest with yourself. I'm not letting you off the hook. You're not happy with him. He's the boss of you and flirts with me. Haven't you thought about what he's like with his students? Those pretty young girls who idolize him? He's a handsome man. Smart and successful."

"Stop."

"But he doesn't see you."

"Why are you doing this? I'm not the one cheating on my husband."

"But wouldn't you like to? Wouldn't you like to be seen by a man?

You can't keep this up all your life, Mishti, your mask of righteousness. Someday it will consume you. I didn't want it consuming me."

One of the children playing near them turned his head to look at them. They fell silent for a moment.

"I wanted to tell you because I thought you would . . ."

"Cheer you on?"

"Well, I suppose I didn't know what I expected from you. It wasn't this."

"I'm going to take Maya home."

"Don't be ridiculous. I'll leave."

"This is your party."

"This is not a party."

"It is always your party."

Mishti headed in Maya's direction, to the swings. She could feel Ciara's eyes on her as she pulled Maya off without a word and rushed her out to the footpath.

Walking home, Mishti tried to focus on the ground, one foot in front of the other. She just had to get them home. Her head was spinning with so many thoughts. Thoughts that Ciara had planted in her head. If she were to be unfaithful to Parth, who would she choose, and how? She hadn't spoken to Neel in years, and he was happily married back in India. Besides him, there was nobody else.

MAYA RAN UP to her room when they reached home. She used to follow her mother around, trying to participate in the household chores, but she was more independent now, and preferred playing by herself. Mishti was left alone again.

There were a few dishes to wash, so she did those, but the house had been recently cleaned, and there wasn't much else for her to do. Only a few days ago, she would have called over to Ciara's house if she was feeling this way. Maya would have been delighted too.

Today, Mishti looked all over the house for her earphones and finally found them in a box in her bedside table. She plugged them in her ears and searched for a Dylan playlist on her phone. On the floor of her bedroom, she sat down cross-legged, resting her wrists on her folded knees, with her fingers in the gyan mudra. She hadn't practiced these asanas in several years, not since Maya's birth. All she had to do was let herself relax, put a lid on that simmering pot, coach her brain into shutting off. The way she'd been taught by her grandmother. Today, however, she just couldn't seem to catch her breath.

Chapter 23

September 15

BACK IN COLLEGE, CIARA HAD BEEN SO UPSET WITH Eoin Brophy's inattentiveness toward her that at one point she wanted to drop out. She couldn't bear the thought of walking into class, having him ignore her again. This sexy, worldly-wise professor certainly noticed the other girls who threw themselves at him, but for some reason he didn't want Ciara, and she found that unacceptable.

Her friend Teresa gained his favor, which was particularly bad luck, because she was the only one who knew about Ciara's crush. Once, Ciara spotted Eoin Brophy and Teresa sharing lunch on the green. She saw the way he reached for one of Teresa's sandwiches, without feeling the need to ask her permission first. Teresa pretended not to see Ciara walk by; neither did she try to recover their friendship when it suddenly turned cold. Teresa chose Eoin Brophy over Ciara. A mister before a sister.

For days, Ciara found herself following in her mother's footsteps, remaining locked in her room, skipping all her classes, sleeping all day. She considered never returning to the college, leaving Cork City for good and finding work elsewhere. Dublin or London maybe. Berlin sounded nice. When it finally struck her what she was doing, after having categorically promised herself she would never turn into her mother, she picked herself up off the bed and took a hot shower.

Ciara returned to college because she wasn't going to let him win, even though he seemingly wasn't aware of being in the game at all. She began sitting in the front row at all his classes, smiling sweetly at him if he turned his gaze to her. She worked hard on all the essays he requested and never spoke to Teresa again.

On graduation day, he finally acknowledged her.

"Congratulations, Ciara." He was walking past her, while she stood in a group with some friends. They were just done taking a group photograph in their robes and hats.

"Thank you."

"What are your plans? For the future, I mean. What's next?" He had his arms folded over his scuffed leather jacket. He smelled of coffee and cigarettes and something eggy. Maybe mayonnaise. He had shoulder-length hair. It may have been a rich chestnut once but was now more of a boggy brown.

"I've been offered a position at Horizon."

"That's excellent, Ciara. Just excellent."

"Yes, I'm excited."

"You should come back here sometime, drop in whenever you like. I enjoy hearing from past pupils."

"Yes, maybe I will."

It seemed as though he had more to say, but he looked over her shoulder and saw her friends. They were waiting to take another photograph.

"Here, I'll take it. You go join them; nobody has to be out of the frame," he offered.

Ciara still had this photograph somewhere, the one Eoin Brophy had taken. They were smiling at the camera, hopeful for the future, with their arms draped around one another. She didn't have those friends anymore.

After Eion Brophy had handed the camera back and started walking away, Ciara caught up with him. "By the way, Teresa told me everything."

His eyes grew wide with confusion and then fear, then panic. She tilted her head to the side, watching his face change, like she was admiring a watercolor she'd toiled over.

"I don't . . ."

"Please, don't make a fool of yourself. You could lose your job over this."

That was enough to shut him up. She could see his tightened knuckles through the worn leather of the jacket pockets.

"Teresa is a lovely young lady," he managed to say.

"Yes, she is. I've always cared about her."

"I didn't mean to hurt her, if that is how she feels, if she thinks I've wronged her."

It gave Ciara joy that her gamble was paying off. "Don't worry, I don't think you've wronged her, and I've decided not to tell anyone. I know what it feels like to want someone and have no control over your feelings."

He obviously regretted talking to her, when he could have so easily avoided all this. "Is there something I can do for you, Ciara?"

"No, nothing. I'm on your side."

His neck was red and marked with burst boils, like a teenager's would be. It was something she hadn't noticed before.

"It was a mistake. It has never happened with anyone else. I would never . . . so I had to stop it. For her sake. I told her she's going to thank me one day, for ending it when I did. Right now she hates me, but she'll understand eventually. She's a bright girl."

Ciara smiled at him. "I'll talk to her, knock some sense into her."

"Thank you, Ciara."

They parted ways with a nod. He even looked back at her as he walked away. She knew he was breathing a sigh of relief, thanking the gods he didn't believe in for sparing him this time. The next time he was going to have to be more careful.

Except there wasn't going to be a next time. She had wanted to lull

Eoin Brophy into a false sense of security, for only a few hours. He was going to sleep peacefully that night, and the next morning he'd be dragged into a meeting with the dean. All his colleagues at the English department were going to receive a carefully worded letter overnight, outlining the story Ciara imagined had played out with Teresa. It was what she hoped had happened between them. What she thought Teresa deserved to have happen to her. Ciara signed the letter proudly; she didn't care for anonymity.

IT UPSET HER that all these years later she was still thinking about her professor. Especially now that she had unwittingly endangered her friendship with Mishti. Ciara didn't know how long it would take for the dust to settle, for Mishti to be ready to talk. They'd never fallen out before. It wasn't that she was afraid of Mishti telling on her; she didn't regret her confession. Now that she'd said it out loud and someone knew, it seemed even more ridiculous. She couldn't recognize the person she was, the person who thought Sean was a good idea.

The idea had first taken root when Bella was born, the idea that she needed a distraction. The sleep deprivation, the inexplicable crying at all hours, the mysterious rashes, pureeing and freezing vegetables, boiling and sanitizing bottles, making the house decent for Rita before she came to clean. And then there was remembering to hydrate, forgetting to shower, the strict diets she put herself on, no privacy in the bathroom, no privacy anywhere. Her body didn't belong to her anymore. She'd resented Bella's grotesque neediness. The carrying, patting, wiping, burping, cradle cap, pooping in the bathtub. Ciara didn't want to feel the same way toward Finn when he was born. She wanted to do things differently this time around.

She couldn't remember what life was like before the children, what she did when she didn't have a baby in her arms. She'd grown accustomed to drinking cold cups of tea. Feeling unattractive and sexless. Until she decided it was time to start caring for herself.

She used to watch Sean out in the garden, sitting with his feet propped up on a lawn chair, book in hand. She hadn't thought of Eoin Brophy in years, but she was reminded of him then. One afternoon Sean caught her looking, and she didn't look away. Even when he put his book down and walked up to the hedge, she remained standing at her kitchen window, staring at him. He wanted to say something, but she wouldn't make it that easy for him, so she didn't go out and meet him. She was going to make him wait. She was giving him an opportunity to change his mind.

A few days later, they saw each other at the shop in the village. Sean had the two older kids with him, a basket in hand, filled with multipacks of toilet paper. Ciara had Finn, sleeping in the buggy. They were at opposite ends of the dairy aisle and stared each other down again.

His first words to her were "I've been thinking about you." They still had a few feet between them, and he practically shouted.

"You've crossed my mind, off and on," she shouted back. Anybody could have heard them.

It started that easily. Living innocently as neighbors, rarely even so much as waving across their gardens. Their affair began like it was brimming under the surface the whole time. Plans were made quickly; not much else was discussed. They both knew what they wanted, and she had liked that. Ciara had recently purchased the cottage, and she made the call to Liz about watching Finn.

It was supposed to be a bit of fun. Something to do while the fog in her mind cleared. This way she was going to have something to distract her from the state of things. All those comments and adoration on her socials only fulfilled her so much. She needed physical appreciation, and Sean gave her exactly that.

Self-care. That was what her brand was all about.

If Mishti had asked for details, Ciara would have admitted she enjoyed herself for a while. For the first few months, they only ever met at the cottage, and they did very little talking. She had no plans of getting to know Sean.

"Your skin is flawless," he had said to her one afternoon. It was the first substantial thing he'd said, weeks into their liaisons.

They were lying on the lumpy cottage bed, naked. He was smoking a spliff beside her. She'd tried some of his weed before but didn't like how it slowed her down and did nothing more. She preferred her pills—they knocked her out right cold.

"I look after my skin." She eyed the ash he dropped on the floor.

"I'll clean it up, as soon as I can find a dustpan," he said.

"Don't bother."

"I've seen your videos," he said. "On Instagram. They're incredible, really. You're a natural in front of the camera."

"Thank you." She slid out of bed, but he grabbed her hip with one arm and pulled her back.

"And this waist. This itty-bitty waist. Your body is . . ." He kissed her shoulders, and she laughed.

"I work hard at it."

He forced her around and kissed her mouth, his tongue lapping greedily at hers, but she was bored. "How many women have you been with?" she asked, nudging him away.

Sean laughed, bringing the joint to his lips again. "Not as many as you think."

"How do you know what I think?"

"Okay. Well, I had a reputation."

"When you were young?"

"Jesus, Ciara. Yeah, in my youth."

He settled back on the pillows, which were as rough and thin as cardboard. He looked annoyed for a moment, then took another hit and smiled. He was thinking about all the women scorned. "Okay, I'll admit there were a few."

"And what about Lauren?"

"What about her?"

"What number was she?"

"I thought we don't discuss our partners."

"Did we say that?" She was enjoying watching him get all riled up.

He scratched the side of his face. "There have been others since I met Lauren. She knows about them. What about you?"

She shrugged and got off the bed, and this time he didn't try to hold her back.

"You're not going to give me an answer? How many men have you slept with, Ciara?"

She put on her shoes first. Navy loafers. Then the lace lingerie she'd bought especially for the occasion. She wasn't going to touch her secret wardrobe for this. Sean had his jaws clenched tightly as he watched her. "How many men since Gerry?"

She picked up the wrap dress from the floor and arranged it perfectly around her body.

"It's just been you, Sean."

He sat up in bed, dropping the spliff to the floor, where she could still smell its mulchy scent as it burned.

"Fuck! Are you serious?" He ran a hand through his hair. His smile made her want to eat her words. She regretted admitting it. She hadn't planned on making him feel special.

He came to her, hooking a finger under her chin and guiding her face toward his. She let him undo the dress, take off her lingerie all over again.

"I've wanted to fuck you from the moment I saw you," he groaned between smothering her with his mouth.

The first time she saw him, she thought he was entirely insignificant.

Chapter 24

September 15

LAUREN WAS SIX WHEN SHE ATTENDED HER FIRST AND last birthday party. She wasn't invited to another one again. It was as though the village had collectively decided that they'd done their good deed for the decade by inviting her to the O'Briens'. Her parents either didn't notice or weren't curious why she didn't have any friends or why she spent so much time crocheting with her gran. When they did see her, on Sunday evenings usually, her mother lectured her on keeping the house clean for her gran so she wouldn't mind having her stay. Her father and Evan spent that time arguing loudly and slamming doors.

Lauren was fifteen when her classmates started having sex. Molly O'Brien was the first one, or at least the first one Lauren came to know about. The only reason she found out about it was that she'd seen the other girls making kissing faces at Molly when she went off with Johnny Fitzpatrick.

She saw them walking into the woods together one evening soon after this, and it almost felt like an invitation. They were going down the path that was overgrown, the one nobody took with their children or dogs. Lauren had been lingering in the woods alone when she saw them, then followed them at a distance.

For several minutes, she listened to Molly's giggles from behind a tree. She heard the sounds of Johnny fumbling with his belt buckle and the rustle of clothes and shoes on crumbly leaves. When Molly's voice turned to a whisper, Lauren stepped out from behind the tree. She didn't want to look at them; that wasn't what she was here for. She leaped for the bundle of clothes and ran. Johnny shouted and Molly screeched, but Lauren was already flying. One of his socks fell out of her hand, and Molly's satiny padded bra wrapped around her forearm as she ran out of the woods. She wasn't laughing; this wasn't funny to her. It was war.

There were some whispers in school the next day. She'd wanted to stay home but didn't want to worry her gran.

"You crazy bitch!" Molly confronted her at lunchtime. Her posse stood behind her but kept their distance, letting her take care of it herself. Molly's sister, Daisy, looked like she was ready to rip Lauren's hair off her skull. "You think I'm going to let you get away with what you did?"

Lauren flipped her off, the way she'd seen her brother do to their father. Molly came at her, and at first Lauren held her arms up in defense. The moment Molly put her hands on her shoulders, she knew what to do. She grabbed Molly by her ponytail and swung her around to the ground, where she fell on her face. Daisy and the others came shrieking to Molly's rescue, too concerned for her welfare to worry about where Lauren had run off to.

So Lauren knew what it meant to grow up without friends, and the time had come to admit that she might be leading her children down that same path.

SHE STAYED UP at night thinking these thoughts, how she wanted a different life for her children. She stood over the sink, moving a crochet hook blindly across a hat for Freya that was nearly complete. Then one moment she was standing in her kitchen, listening to Sean snoring in their bedroom in the silence of a house with sleeping children. The next moment she was standing in Ciara's garden with no shoes on. Blades of dew-wet grass were stuck between her toes, and Lauren turned to look back at her own house. She could barely see anything but its silhouette in the dark; there were no lights on. She couldn't recall sneaking out of the house, but she had to have done it.

She looked up at Ciara's home, and it seemed that she'd walked a few paces forward without her own knowledge. The wall was right up against her nose now. She gasped and stepped back. A light came on and she nearly cried out—there was a dim glow from somewhere in the house, coming in through the open door of the dark sun-room. She wasn't standing by the wall anymore. She was right at the glass doors of the sunroom, where she could look in. Her eyes adjusted quickly to the things there. The reading chair. The storage compartments for the toys. A Waterford crystal vase on the ledge, arranged with English lavender from the garden.

Ciara's silhouette suddenly appeared at the door. Lauren froze on the other side of the glass, certain that she'd been seen. Then she saw the sway in Ciara's steps, the glass of wine being raised up to her featureless face. Ciara walked into the dark room, the long cord of her dressing gown trailing behind her. Lauren's breath fogged up the glass when she breathed again, just as Ciara threw herself into the big armchair. She wasn't turned to face Lauren, nor was she turned away from her. She was just looking straight ahead at the spot where the children probably played on the rug.

Lauren watched as Ciara took another sip of her wine, then hung her head over the back of the chair, stretching her graceful, pale neck.

Reaching out a cold hand, Lauren cupped her palm over the glass and left a damp fog there. She then pressed her middle finger in its center, leaving a perfect imprint on the glass. In a few moments, the fog would clear and take her mark away along with it. But Lauren would remember she'd been here.

Chapter 25

September 21

CIARA'S DOORBELL WAS RINGING, AND SHE WAS hoping it might be Mishti, come to make up. But when Ciara opened the door, she cursed for not having looked through the peephole first. She wouldn't have opened for Sean. Not in broad daylight, for anyone passing by to see.

"Ciara, we have some talking to do."

He stepped up to the threshold and she tried blocking him. Finn came up behind her, and she reached for her son. She felt the urge to cover his eyes, like she didn't want him to ever take a good look at Sean.

"Why are you here? I'll talk to you later."

"No, we need to talk now. This can't wait a week."

"What's happened?"

"Can I at least come inside?"

He caught her looking over his shoulder and down the street, checking to see if their neighbors were around.

"This would be much easier if you just let me come in."

As much as she wanted to push him out, she pulled him inside instead.

"Hi there, little buddy." Sean smiled at Finn lingering around his mother's legs.

"Do not speak to him."

He looked up at her sharply, offended by the tone of her voice. "You are overreacting, Ciara. This is fine. We are neighbors. Why can't we be friends too?"

"You would fool nobody with that spiel."

Sweeping Finn off the floor, she hurried to the kitchen to make sure Lauren wasn't in the garden. Once in there, she rolled down the blinds. Then she rushed to the sitting room to draw the curtains as well.

Sean remained in the foyer, looking around like he'd stepped into a museum. Photographs from Ciara and Gerry's wedding and portraits of the children covered the walls. They were carefully arranged to produce a meaningful narrative.

Ciara returned to Sean, holding Finn close to her. "You really shouldn't be here. Lauren could have seen you, anybody could have seen you walking up."

"Don't worry. I made sure the coast was clear." He spoke in a put-on spooky voice that would have made her laugh a few weeks ago.

She didn't appreciate how lightly he was taking this. "You don't care if anyone sees you?"

Sean shrugged. "Would it really be the worst thing?"

"Lauren finding out *would* be the worst thing. Do you even hear yourself?"

"Lauren knows," he said.

"No, she doesn't. How could she possibly know?"

"I told her."

"Sean, you didn't."

"I had to tell her; it was time. I couldn't keep lying to her. Maybe you can lie to Gerry, but my relationship with Lauren is different."

"And she let you just come over here for a chat?"

"She doesn't know I'm here."

"Why are you here, Sean? Have you come to end things now that she knows?"

"On the contrary, my darling. I'm looking at it as a new beginning."

She waited for the punch line—it sounded like a joke. Sean was smiling too, but she soon realized he was deadly serious. "Excuse me? What new beginning?"

He stepped toward her, and she swung away. She positioned Finn away from him too. "You need to stand back."

"Ciara, come fucking on, love."

"And you need to watch your language around my son."

"Okay, all right, I apologize. I'm sorry, Finn."

"Sean, I think you should go. You're going to upset him."

He held up his hands in surrender and took a few steps back. "He's fine. He doesn't seem upset."

"You're going to stand in my house and claim to know my son better than I do?"

"Ciara, please stop this. I'm trying to have a conversation with you about our future."

"What future? There is no future. You're leaving now."

She started for the door, but he didn't budge. Finn clutched the sleeve of her top.

"No, Ciara, I'm not going anywhere until we've talked this out."

"The only person you need to talk this out with is your girlfriend. What are you even doing here when you say she knows about us?"

"She knows about the affair. She doesn't know it's with you."

Ciara's arms sagged with relief. "Okay, if you haven't told her about me, then you need to keep it that way."

"I wanted to tell you my plan, before I told her."

"Sean, you cannot tell her! It will ruin everything. I'm not going to beg you, but think about what this could do to my children, to your children. Lauren is not going to take it well. She hates me."

"It's the only way forward for us, Ciara."

"There is no us. There never was. We had sex a few times." She lowered her voice, even though Finn was right there in her arms and could hear everything.

"It's been more than a few times, and Ciara, you know it's more than just sex. We have gotten to know each other in these past months."

Her back was pressed to the door. She clung to Finn as though he was the only one who could save her. "I have gotten to know my cleaning lady too. That doesn't mean I'm planning a life with her."

Sean smiled, even though she wasn't trying to be funny.

"Can you put Finn down, Ciara?"

"No. I am not putting him down."

"I want to kiss you."

"That is not going to happen."

With Sean watching her closely, Ciara put Finn down in the playpen. They stood apart in the kitchen.

"All we have to do, Ciara, is be honest with the people in our lives. Lauren, Gerry, the kids."

"Honest about what? That the sex was good while it lasted?"

"Yes, the sex was good. It *is* good."

"I have nothing to say to anyone."

"Lauren can't . . . she won't stand in my way if I decide to leave her. It doesn't mean I'll be leaving the children. It could be the same for you and Gerry."

"I told you before, Sean, I am not taking the kids away from him. They need their father."

"Do you love him?"

"You can't ask me that. There is no right answer. You, more than anyone else, should know how complicated the answer is. I know you have feelings for Lauren."

It seemed to work. Sean appeared perturbed. He rubbed a hand over his face and neck, leaning a little to the side. It was like an invisible force was pushing his body to bend.

"Okay, yes, it is complicated. My feelings for Lauren are all over the place, but I know how I feel about you."

All she felt for Sean now was embarrassment, and she wished he'd just stop.

"Once everyone finds out about us, we won't have to hide. You're worried about the children and Gerry because you think we'll have to run away, live in hiding. But we won't have to."

"I'm worried about how delusional you are."

She glanced at Finn, who surprisingly hadn't made a peep yet. He was enthralled by the drama unfolding before his eyes. She wondered if her words were being processed in some corner of his growing brain. Would they echo in his life repeatedly? As a grown man, would he wake in a cold sweat with these words ringing in his ears? *The sex was good. I know you have feelings for Lauren. Watch your language around my son.*

"You're saying I've imagined everything that's happened between us?" Sean sounded hurt, and it didn't suit him.

"You've imagined the feelings. Whatever it is you think was being said between the lines, I wasn't saying it. I wanted to have sex with someone other than my husband. You happened to be right there, literally in my line of vision."

She couldn't quite remember his exact complexion anymore; his face appeared ashen now. "You're not serious, Ciara. Do you know what you're saying to me?"

"Of course I do, and I hope you're hearing me. I don't know how else to make myself clear. This is the end."

"Fuck!" he shouted, then glared at Finn. "Fuck, I'm sorry. Damn it, Ciara! Put that kid somewhere else, will you?"

"This is his house. You're the one who needs to go somewhere else."

He looked about the room, panic-stricken, like he was searching for something to hold in his hands. For a moment, Ciara worried he was going to do more. "Gerry might come home any minute," she said. It was the best she could come up with.

Sean looked at her again, dazed. "What?"

"I said, Gerry will be home soon. You need to go."

"Maybe I'll stay right here in that case. We can get him up to speed."

"You need to go home and have a good long think about what you're saying. Do you want to lose your children? It will happen. You keep this up, and Lauren is going to take those children away from you."

"She won't do that. She understands."

"She understands why you need to sleep with *me,* of all people? I don't think so, Sean."

Finally, Finn cried out. She rushed to him. "Look, you've got to go. We'll talk later."

"You're saying this is over?"

"Yes, that is what I'm saying, Sean. This is over. I never intended to carry on with you for this long. Things are getting out of hand."

"You mean I'm falling in love with you, and you want me gone?" He sounded like a child who was sad about a holiday coming to an end.

"What you feel for me is not love. Listen to yourself, Sean. You have Lauren. You have Freya, Harry, and Willow." She hoped that saying his children's names would pull him out of it.

"My kids are—"

The doorbell rang before he could finish the sentence.

"Fuck!" They cursed together.

Ciara knew it wasn't Gerry. He had no reason to ring the bell.

"Go in there. Just go. Shut the door and don't make an f-ing sound." With Finn in her arms, she shoved Sean roughly in the direction of the utility room with the washing machine. He didn't protest as she slammed the door on him.

Then she took a deep breath and smoothed the top of her hair.

Ciara racked her brain for her latest online orders, hoping this was just a package being delivered.

When she opened the door and saw Lauren, she nearly slammed it shut again.

"Can I come in?" Lauren sounded determined.

She listened for any sounds coming from the kitchen but heard none. Sean had to have been more uneasy about this than she was, and it put a smile on her face. She decided he needed to hear whatever Lauren had to say.

"Fine, come in. I was about to put the kettle on," she said, pulling the door wide open.

Chapter 26

September 21

CIARA STEPPED ASIDE TO LET LAUREN INTO THE foyer. Finn was perched on her hip, and she held him to her tightly—excessively so, thought Lauren, like he might fly away if she let go.

In all the years they'd been neighbors, Lauren had never been inside the Dunphy house, always hovering outside, peeping in when it was dark. It was spectacularly clean and pristine, just as she'd observed it to be. She was reminded of a model home for display purposes only, rather than a living, breathing home that housed two children under the age of five.

Ciara was leading her to the kitchen. "I suppose I'll make some tea."

"Well, okay."

Lauren untied Willow from her back, and Ciara put Finn down. The children gravitated to each other, taking tiny unsteady steps, staring in silence, like caged animals being introduced to others of their species for the first time.

"This is going to be the only time in their lives when it's perfectly acceptable to stand and stare at someone," Ciara said.

"It's sweet."

"Yeah, I suppose it is. In a few years' time, the world will have beaten that innocent curiosity out of them."

"Isn't it sad?"

"Extremely. The worst part is, they don't even realize how good life is for them right now."

Lauren caught herself smiling, but Ciara's back was turned to her.

"I suppose I'm a bit confused, Lauren. What are you doing here?"

Ciara handed her a mug of tea. It was made using a tea bag that had barely been left to brew. When Lauren tasted it, she was reminded of the Earl Grey incense diffuser she'd once bought for the bathroom. It was a scent that didn't belong there, leaving her with a strange taste in her mouth every time she went in for a shit.

"You can't be that confused by it, Ciara. We've been locking horns for a while."

"Exactly; this is nothing new. You haven't knocked on my door before, no matter what's been said between us. So why now?"

They both knew the answer to that, no matter how innocently Ciara asked it.

"I'm tired of battling it out with you," Lauren replied. She wasn't going to play the trope of the lunatic woman accusing her of sleeping with her man. Wouldn't Ciara have just loved that.

Ciara licked her lip after sipping the tea. "Are we in battle, Lauren?"

"Are we not? It seems like you've gathered the troops."

"I have done nothing of the sort. It's not my fault that I have more friends than you do." It sounded childish, but Ciara made a fair point.

"It's not about how many friends you have." Lauren could feel a pinching sensation behind her eyelids, making it difficult to keep them open. Whatever happened today, she couldn't let Sean find out about this. She needed to remain focused. She needed to remember what was being said, the things she would have to do.

"Well, there is some strength in numbers. Maybe the reason why you feel you're being attacked is because you're alone."

"I'm not alone. I have my family."

Ciara smiled at her indulgently. "Of course, Sean and the kids."

"Yes, them. I put my family first, before everyone and everything else. Maybe that's not how you feel about yours."

Ciara's stare turned dull, as though she found this whole conversation tedious. "Well, I don't want to be rude, but you are in my home. If you've come here to insult me, then I suggest you leave."

"It seems to me that you have no respect for me, or really for anyone who doesn't happen to worship you."

"Believe me, Lauren, I can handle criticism. I have dealt with criticism all my life. It hasn't been a bed of roses for me. Well, maybe it has, if you consider the thorns."

"And that gives you the right to treat people however you want?"

"When have I ever mistreated you?"

Lauren knew there were thousands of instances, but her mind was hollow now.

Ciara nodded. "You can't come up with one, because they don't exist."

"You've made it impossible for me to have friends in the neighborhood."

"What other people think of you and your family is not on me. You've known these people a lot longer than I have. I'm not preaching to a congregation every week. When we all get together, we rarely ever talk about you and your family. There are far more interesting things to discuss. I wish, for your sake, that you would stop making it all about yourself."

"I wish you wouldn't bring my family into this."

"That is not what I'm doing."

"Just don't mention them, especially the kids." It was an invitation extended to Ciara to say something about how Sean was the one who was hurting the kids. She hoped to push Ciara to the brink where she'd have no choice but to admit she was responsible for Sean's disloyalty.

Ciara stood leaning on the kitchen counter, with the edge digging into her hip. She didn't seem to notice. The mug of tea shook in her hand, threatening to spill. Lauren focused on that, instead of on Ciara's darkened and narrowed eyes.

"We're not talking about the children, yours or mine," Ciara said. "But speaking about kids *in general,* the advice you spout on the group chat is absolutely ridiculous. Giving advice based on some bogus studies. None of it has any scientific research to back it up."

"Nothing I have said could be deemed as dangerous advice."

Ciara rolled her eyes. "Not yet. Keep this up and, someday soon, one of these mammies is going to come at you with a pitchfork. I'm sorry to break it to you, but breast milk isn't a magic potion, and almond milk isn't an appropriate substitute for real protein. And many children are allergic to it—you could do some serious damage. What's next, telling people to cure their children with amber bracelets and positive vibes?"

Lauren considered how easy it would be to pick Willow up and walk out right then. However, this was probably going to be her only chance to get a confession out of Ciara. She had a feeling she would never be welcome in this house again.

"How very hypocritical of you. Do you even know what's in all those beauty vitamins you push on Instagram? Just because someone has the money to pay for a cool marketing campaign doesn't mean what they're selling is backed by science either," Lauren replied.

"I thought you came here today to apologize."

"No, I did not. I wanted us to talk, and that is what we're doing."

"This isn't going anywhere, Lauren. It's a waste of time. We used to at least be civilized with each other, but it looks like we've crossed that line."

Lauren searched Ciara's face for any signs of Sean. As though he may have left some traces of himself on her. "So, how are things with Mishti?" she tried.

"That is none of your business."

"Has she decided to look the other way?"

"I'm not having this."

"It's very obvious to me, and frankly everyone, that you like to play temptress with the men in this village."

"I can't believe this. Get the fuck out, Lauren!"

She watched Ciara's shoulders heave with fury, and it brought her some satisfaction. Then Ciara tipped her head backward, just to lift her chin up farther. She'd thought of something.

"It's quite funny that you bring this up, when the father of your children has never been faithful to you. You're the one who has chosen to look the other way."

"How would you know that?"

"Come on, Lauren, he has a reputation."

The two women fell into silence, spent.

"So how did you picture this conversation going?" Ciara began. "Us talking it out? Did you think we'd decide this was all a misunderstanding and we can be friends after all?"

"I expected some hospitality."

"I offered you tea."

"Okay, the truth is, I came here because I wanted to see it for myself."

"See what?"

She was *this* close to telling Ciara she knew. It was on the tip of her tongue. She knew Sean was sleeping with her and that the bitch was going to pay the price for ruining everything. "The inside of your house," she said instead. "I've heard such great things about it."

Ciara stared at her, her eyes like little raisins. She had her mouth puckered up, as though she were collecting spittle.

"You're joking," Ciara finally said. She might as well have spat the words out.

"No, I'm not. You've never invited me into your home before. I thought I'd take this opportunity to have a peek inside."

"You need help, Lauren."

Laughter rose in Lauren's throat. She had to cover her mouth with the back of her hand to stop from exploding. Ciara's face grew redder. She took a step away from Lauren.

"If there is anything substantial you want to say to me, Lauren, this is your chance. I doubt we'll be speaking to each other after this. You are such a weirdo—they all warned me."

Lauren waited while Willow toddled back to her.

"Thank you, Ciara. I look forward to never having to speak to you again."

Ciara didn't see her to the door, and Lauren stood in the foyer for a few moments strapping Willow to her back, taking her time. The gilded mirror was opposite her against the wall, and Lauren watched herself. There were dark circles under her eyes; her back was curved, not strong and straight like Ciara's. Now that she was sure it was her, she could see what Sean saw in Ciara.

After all these years, she finally understood what Sean meant when he said he would never choose another woman over her.

He would choose someone else in spite of her.

Chapter 27

September 21

MISHTI HAD BEEN AVOIDING CIARA IN THE DAYS since they spoke at the playground. It had been nearly a week. In the mornings, she'd drop Maya off at preschool and then swiftly collect her a few hours later, avoiding the usual pickup chit-chat with the other mothers.

Ciara hadn't reached out to her either. Not even a text. She'd been posting fervently on Instagram, however. There were several photos of Ciara posing with the other mothers, which Mishti felt were secretly aimed at her—arms draped around one another in a half hug, holding their coffee cups up in a mock toast. Mishti did feel envious, even though she could smell Ciara's passive-aggressive bullshit from a mile away. Still, it hurt.

However, today was her day to give Bella a lift home from preschool. She hadn't discussed with Ciara any change in their plans. Bella didn't deserve to be left stranded because Mishti had fallen out with her mother—temporarily fallen out, she hoped, because she did still hope to resolve it, to be proven wrong about everything she now thought of Ciara.

The girls were in their booster seats in the back of Mishti's car, singing silly songs and then dissolving into giggles. If she didn't make amends with Ciara, Mishti worried, Maya would lose her best friend.

Just as Mishti pulled up to the Dunphy house, Lauren stepped out of the front door, smiling to herself.

"Oh my God," Mishti groaned under her breath as she killed the engine. This couldn't be good.

Lauren stopped in her tracks, and Mishti had no choice but to get out of the car.

"Hi there," Lauren said.

"Hi," said Mishti. "I was giving Bella a lift. We take turns." Mishti winced at her own defensive tone.

"That's a nice arrangement."

"I'm not doing her a favor or anything."

"That's good, because she doesn't deserve any favors from you."

Mishti glanced at the front door, wishing she had the courage to ask Lauren what she was doing here.

"Has she apologized to you yet?" Lauren asked.

"Why would she apologize to me?"

"Because she insulted and embarrassed you by posting that photograph."

"It was just a joke. We laughed it off."

"You mean Ciara and Parth laughed it off?"

"I've got to take the girls in."

"Yes, you do that. And when you speak to Ciara, make sure you ask her what she was doing in the house that night while you and I were talking in the garden." Lauren stepped closer to her, with bloodshot eyes and a tight smile. Willow peeked innocently over her mother's shoulder. "Don't stand there and take it, Mishti. Don't let her do this to you."

Mishti wished she had the guts to tell her what she knew about Sean, but Lauren had already spun on her heels and was heading down the driveway, throwing a hand up in a wave.

"Think about it, Mishti. That's all I'm saying," Lauren said over her shoulder. Willow threw her a sweet smile, and they continued on their way.

Something like bile was rising in Mishti's throat, and she thought she was going to be sick. Then she heard the front door open. Ciara stuck her head out.

"Mishti? Oh, thank God, get in here! Bring the girls in. Hurry!"

Mishti quickly went to the car and herded the girls out, untangling them from backpacks and seatbelts. Once free, the girls sprang out of the car like wild antelope and made for the house. Maya followed Bella in, and both girls disappeared up the stairs. Mishti took one step inside, and Ciara slammed the door behind her like a trap. Mishti was startled, but it was nothing compared to how she felt when she saw Sean emerge from the kitchen.

Her first instinct was to back away, then she called for Maya. They had to leave. Now.

"Let Maya be. They're upstairs, they'll be fine," Ciara said.

Mishti couldn't take her eyes off Sean. He was standing at the other end of the foyer, unsure of what to do with his hands.

"Hello, Mishti." He spoke gravely.

"Hello."

"Did you see Lauren? She was just here," Ciara said.

"Yes, I met her before she left. What . . . why was she here?"

Ciara sighed, then raked her fingers through her shiny, silky hair. It messed up her ponytail. "You wouldn't believe it if I told you." Ciara turned to Sean accusingly. She crossed her arms over her chest, like he owed them an explanation. "Apparently, she wanted a tour of the house."

"That is obviously not the real reason; it's not like she's insane," Sean said.

"Exactly. So, why was she here, Sean?"

"I don't know, maybe she suspects something."

"You said she doesn't know."

Sean glanced at Mishti, and she looked away, embarrassed. "I'm going to leave," she murmured.

"No, you don't have to go. Sean was just leaving," Ciara said.

"I wasn't. We still have things we need to iron out."

"I've done enough ironing for one day, Sean. You and your family have overtaken my house. I need you gone."

Mishti inched toward the stairs.

"Where are you going? I said, leave the girls alone!" Ciara hissed.

They all heard Finn's voice coming from the kitchen. Ciara had presumably left him in his playpen, and now he wanted out.

"I'm going to check on him. Mishti, don't you dare go anywhere! Sean, get out." Ciara strode away, leaving the pair of them alone together. Mishti couldn't remember ever speaking to Sean or even looking at him closely.

He waited until Ciara was gone. "She listens to you."

"No, she doesn't."

"But she wants you here and wants me gone. That must mean something."

Mishti wondered if he wanted her to comfort him for being rejected by Ciara, his other woman. "You should go. This is her home. This is what she wants."

"And you should tell her this is not over. Not this way. I want a fuckin' explanation for why she's putting me through this. She doesn't even know what I'm risking here. What I'm putting on the line for her."

"Then why are you doing it? Why are you risking your family?"

"Because I fuckin' love her, don't I?"

He waited for her to respond. When she didn't, he loped to the door, as though he'd been trying to get away all along.

The front door shut just as Ciara stepped back into the foyer. She'd timed it perfectly.

"He was hiding in the utility room the whole time," Ciara said, laughing.

THEY WERE IN the kitchen again, and Ciara had forced a cup of tea on Mishti. She couldn't bring herself to drink it.

"And she stood here, where you're standing now. She didn't have a clue her boyfriend was in there, only a few feet away."

Mishti was disgusted and kept her face downturned to the cup in her hand. Ciara finally gave up, sighed, and put hers down on the table.

"I didn't know what else to do. He barged into the house, and I couldn't get him to leave. Then *she* showed up. It wouldn't have been pretty if she came in here and saw him."

"Why was she here?"

"I don't know. She threw some accusations at me, pretended to be concerned about *your* welfare and our friendship." Ciara waved it off. "I think she was after something more. I think she's maybe onto us."

"Why? What did she say?"

"She basically called me the village whore. Can you believe it?"

"So it wasn't about Sean?"

Mishti had seen something in Lauren's eyes today. It was a ruthlessness without fear of consequence. She didn't know whether to be afraid of her or afraid for Ciara.

"Maybe it was, I don't know. Maybe she knows. Sean told her he's having an affair." Ciara shook her head, like she found him despicable. "But he didn't tell her it's with me."

"She's figured it out," Mishti said.

They stared at each other. Ciara covered her face with her hands briefly. "Yes, maybe she has. Maybe she saw Sean coming here and followed him. Maybe she just wanted to talk to me and see if I'd confess. Of course, I wouldn't. Why would I do such a thing?"

"What will you do now?"

"Nothing. I don't know. Yes, nothing. What can I do? Other than make sure Sean gets it in his head that it's over between us. He still wants to talk about it. He won't take no for an answer."

Mishti stopped herself from repeating what Sean had said. Perhaps he did love her.

It couldn't be. It was lust or something else, but not love. Not everybody fell in love. It wasn't essential for survival, like breathing, or learning to walk, or digestion. Not every human was destined to experience this thing that nobody could even put into words. Neel and Parth had both offered Mishti a means for escape, and neither had delivered. Even when she was with Neel, she knew it couldn't be just love, plain and simple. What she felt for Maya was the only real love she'd experienced, and she was almost certain it wasn't what Sean felt for Ciara.

"He will have to come to terms with it. Maybe if I give it a few days. A few weeks, maybe. He'll see how foolishly he's been acting. His place is with his family. Just like mine is here—"

"I am sorry, but I have to go," Mishti said, interrupting her.

Ciara's mouth was open, mid-sentence; her fingers were splayed in the air, in the middle of gesticulating vigorously against Sean. When Mishti went to leave, Ciara stopped her.

Ciara's hand on Mishti's shoulder felt alien. Detached from her body. "Why are you leaving, Mishti? I need you. I've been there for you when you've needed me in the past."

"I don't want to be a part of this."

"A part of what? You think I'm asking you to participate in my depravities?"

"Ciara . . ."

"What is it, then, Mishti? Tell me why you won't get off your fucking moral high horse and just hold my hand for a minute."

"How can I help you? What am I supposed to do? Should I tell you everything will be okay? Will it? You're cheating on your husband. How many times have you been unfaithful to him? With how many men?"

"There is nothing going on between Parth and me. That's what you want to know, isn't it? That's what this is all about. You've seen the way he looks at me. You've noticed how we talk to each other. You're jealous."

"I'm not jealous of you, Ciara."

"Then what is it?"

Mishti couldn't believe it. She was seeing tears in Ciara's bright-blue eyes. They were wiped away quickly, but the tip of her nose was undoubtedly red. Even her lower lip trembled for a moment. Mishti blinked, and then all traces were gone from Ciara's face.

"I wasn't trying to hurt anyone. Least of all you," Ciara said.

"I'm not hurt."

"And yet you're done with me." Ciara plonked herself down on one of the barstools, spinning slowly. "I need you right now, Mishti. For fuck's sake. I'm a mess."

Mishti took a few moments. She was so close to getting away. "I'm sorry, Ciara. I can't stay."

Chapter 28

September 22

CIARA WAS MAD AT EVERYONE, INCLUDING HERSELF. She'd let it all get terribly out of hand. Now she wasn't sure if she could get rid of Sean as smoothly as she'd initially planned. She wasn't even sure if she had Mishti anymore.

She'd spent the previous night, after Lauren, Sean, and Mishti had all left her house, arranging and rearranging outfits in her wardrobe, matching shoes to a knitted body-con dress she didn't have the figure for anymore. She'd draped a fuchsia silk scarf around the neck of a black button linen dress. Tucked in a plain white tank top under a pinstripe pinafore. Then she stood back and stared at her wardrobe, imagining living a life where she could wear these clothes every day again, all the time. What was stopping her? She had nowhere to go.

In the morning, she picked out an outfit from her collection she'd never worn before. A white peasant dress, ruched around the waist, with great showy batwing sleeves. She wore it with a pair of sandals that hadn't been broken in. The pink lipstick had looked punchy under the lights of the Debenhams counter a few months ago. It looked a tad flamboyant in her bathroom, but she put it on anyway.

She was going to drop Finn off at Liz's place.

Like a dog being taken to the vet, her son knew where they were headed as soon as she buckled him in his seat. He fussed and cried the whole way, making Bella complain on her way to preschool.

Outside Liz's house, Ciara kissed Finn's forehead. She wiped the lipstick residue off his skin with some spittle. "You'll have a grand ol' time with Gran, won't you?" she cooed.

Liz came to the door in her dressing gown. There were biscuit crumbs around her mouth and a jam stain on the lapel. "Oh, it's you! And there's my sweet boy." She reached for Finn, who clung to his mother. Ciara felt rather like a sinking ship as she peeled him off.

"I wasn't expecting you today. You never rang."

"Yes, it's a last-minute thing. My hairdresser rang about a canceled appointment, and I thought, why not!"

Liz examined her closely, while patting her grandson's bottom. He wasn't a child who liked having his bottom patted, but Ciara said nothing. If Liz hadn't figured it out by now, then it was too late to change the habit.

Ciara's lipstick, the clothes, her hair left loose, had all caught Liz's attention. "You're going to the hairdresser's?" She omitted *in that.*

"Yes, and then I'm meeting some friends for brunch. I won't be long, I promise. It won't be for the whole day."

"I just wish you'd given me some notice."

"I thought you'd be happy to spend some time with your grandson."

"Of course I am. It's not that."

"Don't worry, you'll have some time off from watching the kids when we buy you those tickets to Lanzarote in the summer."

Ciara brushed Finn's hair quickly before walking to the car. She knew Liz had nothing more to say. She blasted the music as she drove off, keeping an eye on her rearview mirror. Liz waved, in an attempt to get Finn to wave too. He just stared at the car, like he knew his mother was watching.

On the way to the city, Ciara stopped at one of the viewpoints that dotted the West Cork coastal drive. She propped her camera on the dashboard and touched up her lipstick first. Then she started recording a live video on Instagram. She'd been planning the speech all morning, saying the words out loud in the shower and as she'd gotten the kids ready, imagining Mishti listening, really paying attention this time.

"Hi, guys. I just wanted to quickly come on here with an update. First of all, I want to apologize for not posting as regularly lately. I know a lot of you have been wondering what's been keeping me away. I want to reassure you that I'm doing okay, hanging in there." She smiled weakly, then panned the camera out of the window so her viewers could take in the breathtaking scene. Green cliffs and crystal waters underneath.

The wind whistled in the background, and it added to the drama. She brought the screen back to her, glancing quickly at the rising count of viewers. "I don't want to get into the particulars, not yet anyway, but I'm here to remind anyone who needs to hear this." She looked directly at the camera, making eye contact with these women who believed they could see her soul. "Don't let bullies beat you down. I'm only speaking out because I know it will help you guys to know that Instagram isn't reality, and despite what my pictures look like, I've really been struggling. There are some toxic people . . . who can't stand seeing someone else succeed. The worst is when women bring other women down. The people closest to me know what I'm talking about, and I'm lucky to say I have an amazing support system. Just the very best of friends." She shut her eyes for a moment, focusing on the image of Lauren in her own kitchen, then she smiled again. Sean was right: She was a natural in front of the camera.

"Now, don't you guys worry about me. I'm just taking a few days off to take care of my mental health." She took in a deep breath. "I'll be back soon, and I'll have an exciting announcement. I've been working behind the scenes with a brand that you will all love. A brand that pays attention to what women want and need."

She'd spent the last few weeks working on a new deal, and this video was going to generate a lot of interest in it. She was building up anticipation. Her followers would be searching for clues to her personal drama in anything she posted now, thereby pulling traffic to the brand she was being paid a lot of money to start promoting.

"One of these days, I'll be ready to talk about what I'm going through. Until then, you stay strong, protect your energies, and continue to lift one another up in this little community we've built. Most important, remember to wear your SPF today." She blew a kiss at the camera with a wave, then ended the video.

She felt a lot better already.

Chapter 29

September 25–26

WHEN SHE THOUGHT ABOUT IT NOW, LAUREN knew she should have ended it with Sean when Freya was born. It was her last chance to be rid of him. The gnawing desperation she'd lived with, ever since the first time he kissed her, had evaporated when she set eyes on her baby. All it took was being handed one purple bundle of human flesh.

Before giving birth, Lauren had felt detached from her own self for several years. It was the effect he had on her. She couldn't think straight. She had become forgetful, willing to forgive, willing to mold and shape herself to his needs, as long as he allowed her to orbit his sun.

Then she looked at Freya, while her breasts dampened her caftan. She was prepared to relinquish her soul and body to this child. Different bits of her were floating around, suspended in air. She had been successfully untethered from Sean. For the first time since she had met him, she didn't care if he stayed or left.

After he left without a word, she was surprised to see him turn up at the hospital, smelling of revelry. If he hadn't shown up, she would have shrugged and moved on. By giving her this child, he had released her.

Now, two births later, Lauren wished he hadn't returned to the hospital that day. She could have raised Freya alone. In fact, it would have been easier that way.

It wasn't until Harry was at least one that she wanted Sean in the same way again. It returned to her in a rush. She couldn't explain it. Her desire for him was like meeting an old friend, familiar but awkward. So much had changed since the last time she had wanted him like that. He was older and arguably less attractive. She was older too, with a squishy belly, thinning hair, and stretch marks crawling up her torso and arms.

She was waking him up every night with her hand on his cock, stroking him until he groaned and gasped and pulled her on top of him. He'd be cooking a meal for the kids, and she'd wrap her arms around him. Pressing herself into his back, sliding her hand down his jeans. He'd eventually turn off the hob. He'd laugh or curse at her. Usually he did both.

Even if he wanted to leave, she wouldn't have let him go anymore.

They had only exchanged a few words since their big talk eleven nights ago. Whenever they did speak, it was in relation to the children, usually in front of them too. Mostly for their benefit.

Lauren had barely left the house since their fight, and neither had Sean, as though they were both guarding their territory. Except he seemed to have forgotten that he had no legal right over this physical space. Her gran's house belonged solely to her.

They went to sleep beside each other, although she only came to the room after she was sure he was asleep. She barely slept anymore; instead, she replayed all her recent encounters. She waited with her eyes open in the dark for Willow to cry out, for one of her children to need her. It gave her a reason to leave their bed, to get away from her thoughts. He, on the other hand, was sleeping just fine.

When the older children were at school, they silently battled each other for Willow's attention at home. Sean brought out the big guns—the chunky crayons they rarely allowed her to play with. The first thing Willow did was start scribbling on the walls. Lauren positioned herself strategically on the corner of the sofa Willow was most attached to. Willow would inevitably and quickly find her way there, snuggling into Lauren's lap, looking for the comfort of her breasts. For every sticker book and jar of kinetic sand Sean presented, Lauren trumped him with cuddles, songs, and her boobs. Willow was too young to be bought by material things. Lauren reckoned she had a few years until her youngest gravitated toward her father too, like the older ones had.

In the evenings they sat around the kitchen table, passing bowls of food between them. They asked Freya and Harry to describe their days at school, each more eager than the other to come up with the right questions. So far, the children seemed to be buying it, but they couldn't carry on like this forever.

They bumped into each other in the bathroom one night, having carefully avoided sharing space alone for many days.

"Shit. Sorry," Sean mumbled. He'd walked in and found her on the toilet. It was the first non-child-related thing he'd said to her all week. Lauren quickly wiped and stood up. He'd stopped at the bathroom door, keeping his back to her. He may have regretted apologizing.

"It's fine. Whatever." She washed her hands and began brushing her teeth. He took a moment to hang his head, then slowly turned to her. The mirror above the basin was covered in flecks of dried toothpaste. She began digging them off with her nails.

"I knew this was going to happen when you brought up the wedding," he said.

She spat out the froth and washed her mouth. "Of course you did, because you knew you were cheating on me. I wasn't aware of that minor detail."

He was right: His rejection hung over them like he predicted it would. Something else hung over them too. It was the stench of deception. Ciara's invisible perfume.

"What do you want me to do about it, Lauren? I've tried to be as honest with you as I can. You're not thinking about the kids."

"And what exactly would you have us do for the sake of the kids?"

He brushed his hair and shut his eyes. "I just want you to be reasonable."

She'd been fantasizing about a wedding; wildflower arrangements, a lavender lace dress, scrolling through Instagram accounts for the perfect set of wedding rings. Silver, not gold. Sean would never go for yellow metal.

She felt foolish now.

"So this is my fault?" she asked.

"I'm not blaming you for what I did. I'm taking full responsibility for that. However, we need to move past it."

"And what if I don't want to move past it?"

"What are you saying, Lauren?"

"I'm saying, I don't know if I want you living here anymore. You're doing nothing for me."

"Are you fuckin' serious? You're going to kick me out?"

"Am I being unreasonable?" She dried her hands on the towel she'd used in the shower earlier, then walked past him. He followed her into the bedroom.

"Yes. You're being fuckin' unreasonable. You want to end our relationship? Ten years. Three kids. Our life together? You want to end all that because I slept with someone? There have been others in the past and you didn't care. What has gotten into you, Lauren?"

"I don't know, Sean. I guess I've just had enough."

ON SUNDAY MORNING, the kids woke up demanding to go to the city.

Freya claimed there was a fair with special rides. All her friends from school were going to be there. It hadn't taken Freya much to convince Harry this was going to be a once-in-a-lifetime opportunity. They'd even managed to teach the word *fair* to Willow. She was now repeating it incessantly as she raced around the house.

"Sure, we can take the bus into the city today, can't we?" Sean was saying when Lauren walked into the kitchen. He had Willow up on his shoulders and was scrambling some eggs in a pan.

Freya and Harry clapped their hands. She imagined them applauding as their father drilled the final nail in her coffin. It was the first time she experienced a genuine distaste for her children.

"We are not going to the city today," she said, slamming a stale mug of coffee on the table. She'd found it wedged underneath Sean's side of the bed. She'd considered throwing it at his face. None of them understood; they couldn't go out, they couldn't show their faces in public. Not after the video Ciara had posted.

"Mammy! Why?" Freya whined. Harry lunged out of his chair and began bouncing—it was his version of stomping his feet. Willow couldn't have understood, but she slammed her hands on Sean's head in protest, in an attempt to be a part of the mob.

Sean caught Lauren's eye. He was smirking like a rebel.

"Why can't we go? Everyone is going. Everyone!"

"Yes, Mammy. There will be bouncy castles and lots of rides."

"And Eilish told me she ate kangaroos on sticks there."

"Kangaroos on sticks? I can't remember the last time I saw a kangaroo in Ireland," Sean cut in, and the kids pouted harder.

"But Eilish said they were delicious."

"We're not going out," Lauren said.

"Why not?" It was Sean. It looked like he was enjoying this.

"Because I've already planned a picnic for us."

"A picnic? Where?" At least Harry sounded excited. Sean looked suspiciously at her, waiting for an explanation. He knew she was pulling it out of her arse.

"In the garden. I'm baking a strawberry tart, and there will be ice cream. Lots of sandwiches and sweeties. It'll be fun." She knew she wasn't doing a great job of selling it. She could barely get her voice to rise higher than a murmur.

Freya and Sean exchanged looks, like they were in on it together.

"What kind of sweeties?" Harry was sucked in.

"Check the press. I've been collecting them for weeks."

Harry ran over to look where he knew the treats were stored. He pulled out a bag containing a handful of fizzy cola bottles and Love Hearts. He was disappointed. This wouldn't compare to a fair in the city.

"I'll go get more. Why don't you make a list?" Lauren suggested. The children had never been given this much power before. She could see their little minds whirring.

As they joined heads to draw up a list of all the sweets and snacks they wanted from the shop, she fixed her eyes on Sean. He was starting to look uncomfortable with Willow still perched on his shoulders, but he wasn't going to put her down, because he didn't want to let her go.

"Fuck you," she mouthed to him.

LAUREN WAS NERVOUS about leaving the house, but now she had no choice and hurried to the shop. Just like everyone else, Lauren had watched Ciara's video. Just like everyone else, she knew who Ciara was talking about.

Ciara's call to arms had been answered. The previous evening, when Lauren was walking with the children, Molly O'Brien and Erica Dunne were jogging behind them. Every time Lauren looked over her shoulder, their eyes bored into her, and they spoke to each other in hushed tones through their pinched little mouths.

She'd been at the receiving end of enough of their sneers growing up to make an informed estimate of what they were saying. They'd start off by commenting on what Lauren was wearing, ridiculing her choice of clashing colors, the state of her hair; then they'd move on to the root of the discussion—how Lauren had insulted Ciara, how senseless she was in her attack. They wouldn't shy away from using words like *attack* and *abuse*. Lauren had heard it all before.

She'd nearly skidded in an attempt to hurry the kids along last evening.

She returned home today with bags of sweets, pretzels, black-currant cordial, and popcorn from the shop. The strawberry tart she'd promised was replaced by a store-bought pound cake. She'd been so worried about being accosted at the shop by the other women that she grabbed whatever she could find easily and ran out of there. She was going to ice the cake and cover it in sprinkles. It would have to do.

When the children saw her unpacking the shopping on the kitchen table, they sighed and whined. It was like the life force was being sucked out of them, and for a moment Lauren wished she could be in Sean's place. The fun parent.

Sean sat by the kitchen window, leaning back in a chair. His feet were up on the edge of the dining table. He had a book in one hand and a coffee mug in the other. He watched with amusement as she attempted to placate the children with more promises.

"I could take them to the fair myself if you don't want to go," he finally said, dog-earing a page.

"I've already planned the picnic, and I want us all to stay home. Is it so hard to get on my side for once?" It was one of the rare occasions she'd snapped at him in front of the children. Freya and Harry stared at her in surprise.

"I *am* on your side, Lauren, and I understand if you just want a break from the chaos. Which is why I'm suggesting you don't come with us."

"And let you take the children all by yourself? To a crowded city center?"

"What are you suggesting?" His voice was calmer than hers. She hated him even more for it.

"It's not a suggestion. I believe I'm making myself very clear. I have no faith in you. You'll lose one or all of them as soon as you get there." The longer she stared at him now, the more convinced she was that she'd been deceiving herself all these years. Sean was only a good father when he wanted to be. He rarely ever took the children out by himself, and if she left them alone with him in the house, she always had a nagging feeling that he would have bad news upon her return.

Sean laughed, loudly and bitterly. "You're being dramatic, Lauren. But go on, let's have your little picnic."

He slid his book across the table and stood up, heading straight for the garden. The children followed him outside like he was the Pied Piper of fucking Hamelin.

Chapter 30

September 26

CIARA WAS IN THE CITY ON SUNDAY AGAIN, AFTER Gerry left for the office. If he really had gone to work on a Sunday, she hoped that he at least got to fuck his assistant. She dropped Finn and Bella off at Liz's place first. Ciara decided she was going to bring up what Liz owed them in clear terms the next time she fussed about having to watch the kids. Not just her summer getaways, which they funded, but also the check for brand-new tires that Ciara had noticed in Gerry's office a few weeks ago. Her mortgage, which Gerry had paid off years before.

Ciara's usual table at the café was unoccupied. She slid into a chair, bringing her tailored coffee with her. She hadn't planned to meet Parth here today but hoped he would turn up anyway. She'd seen him drive off in the morning, and if he wanted some quiet time away from the family on the weekend, this would be the natural choice.

Ciara kept her head down, but her eyes darted to the door every time someone came in. It reminded her of how she'd once boasted to a friend in college that she never waited for men. That she always made them wait. It used to work when she was younger, when the scales were tipped on her side. Now the years were passing her by, and the scales were falling the other way. Someday soon she was going to be too old, even for a man like Sean. One more decade and she'd be competing with girls who wore her favorite jeans ironically. No matter how hard she tried to keep up and fill her closets, she was going to eventually lose the race. She saw it happen to her mother. It had never happened to any man she knew.

Lost in thought, she didn't see him walk up to the café doors. She only noticed him when he was already in the queue, waiting to place an order.

Parth looked clean. Unlike Sean, he didn't look rumpled or tired. He was solid, confident in his gestures, even when he wasn't aware of being watched. The woman in front of him took a few absent-minded steps backward. She nearly knocked into him, but he only smiled at her. He made an obvious effort to be polite when he placed his order. He glanced at his phone only once while he waited for his coffee. Nearly everyone else in the queue was glued to their screen.

After the barista handed him his coffee, he turned and saw Ciara in the corner. He stopped in his tracks. She waved him over. It wasn't like he was going anywhere else.

"Surprise!"

He didn't seem to share her enthusiasm, but he sat down beside her, nodding lightly.

"You didn't expect to see me here, did you? I had some shopping to do, and I always come here when I want a coffee."

"No, I didn't expect to see you."

"Not working on a Sunday, I hope?"

"Yes. I have an appointment with a client in twenty minutes." That was how much time he was willing to give her today. It was more than enough for what she needed from him.

"You can relax, Parth. I'm not here to talk about what happened that night. We both had a little bit to drink. We were being silly."

"I know you're good friends with my wife. I wouldn't want things to get awkward between us all."

"It won't. I'm not going to tell Mishti. I don't intend on telling anyone."

He visibly relaxed after that, sitting back in his chair more comfortably. He obviously hadn't seen the photograph of them she'd posted.

"Okay, I confess I was hoping to bump into you today," she said. "I don't know who else to go to with this."

"With what? Is there a problem?" The way he looked at her reminded Ciara of Eoin Brophy, when his eyes would fall on her in class. As though he wished she wasn't in the same room as him, distracting him.

"Yes, it has turned into a problem of late. I can't sleep," she continued.

Parth understood almost immediately. She watched his face as it all clicked in place. He looked away, shaking his head again. He was most likely disappointed in himself. He should have seen it coming, as a trained professional.

"I know what you're going to say, and I have considered going to my GP. It's easier this way," she added quickly.

"If you're asking what I think you're asking, Ciara, then I'm going to save you your breath. I'm going to tell you that I can't help you. It goes against everything I stand by."

"It doesn't seem to me that you stand steadfastly by much. Where does cheating on your wife place on your moral compass?"

"I thought we weren't going to discuss that. What happened that night was a drunken mistake, and like you said, it won't happen again. Nothing really happened anyway."

"That is not what I said. I haven't decided if it will or won't happen again." His eyes brightened; she'd caught his interest once more. It didn't take much.

"I'm not sure if we should be meeting like this," he said.

"I'm sure we shouldn't, but isn't that half the fun?"

"I'm not exactly having fun right now."

She laughed at that, and finally he smiled too. "It's a little bit fun, watching you squirm in your seat. Honestly, you have nothing to worry about." She reached for his knee and patted it gently. He relaxed a little.

"Okay, okay." Now that he knew she hadn't come to threaten him with exposure, he was more open to listening. All men were the same.

"Honestly, I don't know what to do anymore," Ciara said, taking in a deep breath, making her lower lip quiver. "I feel like I'm losing my mind."

This time he rearranged his face to express concern. He leaned toward her. "Tell me what's bothering you."

"It's hard, trying to be a good mother, a good wife, to look after the house, and give Gerry the space and freedom he wants. It feels like I'm raising these children by myself."

"Mothers today put a lot of pressure on themselves."

"Mishti is very lucky to have you. To have someone who understands."

"I hate to think you're selling yourself short. You're a great mother. Doesn't everyone think so?"

"And it feels like too much to live up to. I'm competing with myself." She focused on his hands, admiring them once again. His nails were smooth and appeared manicured. She reached for him. Their fingers brushed, then they pulled away.

"Have you considered speaking to someone? A professional?"

"I'm speaking to one now, aren't I?"

"I would encourage you to take this seriously. Think of a long-term solution. I can make some recommendations."

"Can't we see each other more often? Maybe I can make an appointment with you?" Her GP prescribed sleeping pills, but they weren't enough anymore. Not for the mess she'd gotten herself into. She needed more, and fast. She didn't have the time to go through the procedure of being diagnosed for more pills, even if her GP did recommend her to a psychiatrist.

"That would be unprofessional, since we are personally acquainted. You need to be able to speak freely."

"Thank you, Parth, I really appreciate it. This is all such good advice."

He touched her knee briefly, then raked a hand through his hair. Like he was trying to transfer her touch to his body.

"I want to be able to help you, Ciara."

"Then help me now. You know you can. If I could just get something to help me sleep, it would make all the difference." This wasn't a lie.

"Ciara, I . . ."

She was noticing for the first time how long and thick his lashes were. He was an elegantly handsome man. If things were different, if there was no Mishti, she would have invited him to the cottage today.

"Please don't say no, Parth. I wouldn't be here, baring my soul, if I didn't think you were the only one who could help me."

"You need the right kind of help. I can connect you with—"

She shook her head, feeling the pangs of rejection she rarely ever experienced. They nearly brought her to real tears. She just had to lean into that sensation a little longer, and the tears would come. That would do the job.

Parth stopped speaking. He'd seen her wet lashes.

"I don't know how much longer I can wait." She spoke in a shaky voice. "I don't know if I can be the mother my children need when I'm feeling this way. Like a failure."

He hadn't looked at his watch at all. He'd forgotten about the client he needed to see in twenty minutes. "I want you to promise me that you will get the help I want you to get. All you have to do is make one phone call and set up an appointment."

She nodded. She was like a small child with an open palm, waiting for him to place a sweet on it.

"In the meantime, I can give you something to tide you over," he said.

Chapter 31

September 26

IN THE GARDEN, LAUREN LAID OUT THE FOOD ON ONE of her gran's old tablecloths. Harry knocked over one of the jugs of black-currant cordial. Freya barely had a bite to eat. Sean had his book stuffed in the back pocket of his jeans.

It was a bright day. It would have been perfect for walking around the city. She was beginning to feel guilty for forcing them to stay home. Especially since Freya and Harry were more enthusiastic about Sean's cartwheels than about spending any time with her. He wasn't even good at it. He barely managed to get his legs up in the air before he came crashing down. The children laughed and applauded him for his effort. Lauren had to look away. She wondered if she'd only been imagining it, the other women gossiping about her. Could it be that none of them had a clue who Ciara was talking about in the video?

Willow pointed at her father while her siblings laughed. Lauren stroked her daughter's wispy hair and kissed the tops of her ears. "Daddy's just making a fool of himself."

Freya found a Hula-Hoop half buried in the patch of chrysanthemums. She was showing off to Harry, and very soon it turned into an argument. Sean was eventually out of breath, and he ignored the quarreling children and walked toward her and Willow.

"You want to go play with your brother and sister, Willow?" he asked, sinking down beside them.

"She's fine over here." Lauren was embarrassed by her streak of possessiveness, feeling more and more like she couldn't recognize the person she'd transformed into.

"We have to stop, for the sake of the kids," he said, loosely eyeing Willow.

"Stop what? Are you going to stop sleeping with her?"

Sean smiled at Willow. He was picking crushed daisies off his jeans. "You have to stop talking like this, Lauren."

"Isn't it the truth? I mean, you told me yourself."

"Okay, if it makes any difference to you, yeah. I'm not sleeping with her anymore."

Surprisingly, it made her laugh. It wasn't the reaction she expected she'd have. He was so close to saying her name. She'd laughed loud enough to catch Freya and Harry's attention. They stopped hula-hooping for a moment. They would find out eventually, anyway, she thought. She was already losing her will to keep up the show. "What happened? Did she tell you I went to see her?"

Sean turned his face up to the sun and pressed his eyes closed.

"If you went to see Ciara Dunphy, and you did something or said something stupid, then you've only made a fool of yourself."

"Just say it, Sean. Say the words. She practically did."

Sean met her eyes; his face was stone. He looked like a beast crushing its prey with its bare teeth. "No, she did not *practically* say anything of the sort."

It was all she needed to hear, she was sure he'd talked to Ciara. How else could he be so certain?

"Because why would she? It would be a lie if she even implied anything." He was backtracking. Panicking. He threw another glance in Willow's direction. She was swinging her gaze from one parent to the other, like an observer at a tennis match.

"I can't believe you picked her, Sean. Fucking Ciara Dunphy. Of all the women you could have banged. And let me guess, she's chewed you up and spat you out. She doesn't want to have anything to do with you now, does she? Because who really wants to be with a man like you? A no-talent washed-up bookseller. Other than stupid ol' me. All these years I've wasted on you."

"And what about me? I overlooked the crazy and settled down with you anyway. In this house, this back end of nowhere. With a brood of children running around."

"You knocked me up, Sean. That's what happened. You think we would still be together if we didn't have the kids?"

"You're being ridiculous, Lauren. We have a life together. I wouldn't be here if I didn't want to be."

"Maybe you did, at some point. Now you want Ciara. Does her husband know? Has Gerry put an end to it? Now you have no choice but to get stuck with us again."

"Does it look like I'm stuck in this life?"

"No, because you couldn't possibly have it this good anywhere else. You have a good life, Sean, and it's all because of me."

He stood up again. He looked at Willow but didn't smile at her this time. "Why don't you keep sitting here and think of all the nasty things you'll say to me the next time I want to resolve this."

"The next time we talk, we'll be discussing your living arrangements. You're not going to live here anymore. You're gone. I'm glad we never got married. It'll make things a whole lot easier."

He stood there, at a loss for words. His expression alone felt like a victory to her.

Then he turned and moved out of her vision, quickly heading toward the other children, clapping at Freya's hula-hooping attempts. He was going to pretend this conversation didn't happen; there was no way he was going to simply accept her decision to kick him out. She only hoped she had the strength to stick by it.

Lauren pulled Willow into her arms, draping her over her shoulder. She needed a hug.

"Man," Willow said. Her voice was muffled but clear enough.

Lauren craned her neck to see what her daughter was pointing at. Willow didn't always get her words right.

This time, she did.

Gerry was standing at the door of his shed, in the corner of his garden. A string of fairy lights hung off the low-lying branches of the tree above him. They encircled his head like a miserable crown. He was staring at them. Even as Willow continued to point at him, he didn't move or look away.

He'd heard everything.

Chapter 32

September 26

AT HOME THAT NIGHT, MISHTI WAITED UNTIL PARTH and Maya were asleep. Then she checked the Facebook app on her phone. She'd considered going through Parth's liquor cabinet; everyone spoke so favorably of liquid courage. She decided against it, though. Alcohol only made her feel stupid, never brave.

She was sitting in the kitchen, fidgeting with her hair and clothes. She couldn't remember how many years it had been since she last spoke to Neel. It was likely he wouldn't take the call.

She battled with it until the last moment. She thought of Neel often, stalked him online, but it had never come this far.

There was something pitiful in the way Sean had spoken about loving Ciara. Neel had the same look in his eyes on their last day together. Was she the same as Ciara?

She tapped on the little bubble that had his face on it. She'd never called anyone through the Facebook app before, and the ringtone startled her. She nearly changed her mind about the whole thing. She was about to hang up, but then he answered.

"Mishti?"

It took a few moments for his pixelated face to appear on her screen. His mouth didn't move at first. He was frozen. Then, all of a sudden, everything cleared up.

"Mishti? Are you there?"

"Yes, it's me. I'm sorry. This mustn't be a good time."

"It's fine. I'm on my way to work." He meant his wife wasn't around.

When he was moving on the screen again, she saw white earphone cables strung over his shoulders. His background was busy. Familiar, but distant to her. The sound of a bus blaring its horn filled her quiet kitchen.

"Where are you?" he asked. His eyes narrowed as he tried to decipher her scene. The lights were all turned low in her kitchen. She didn't want him to see her in full brightness, in her unflattering fleece sweater, her torso misshapen by rolls, her face flushed with excitement.

"In my house. It's the middle of the night here."

She assumed he knew where she lived. He may not have, if he hadn't snooped around online like she did, but she had a feeling he'd looked too.

"How are you, Mishti? It's nice to hear from you after all these years."

"I'm fine."

He looked up and away from the screen, adjusting the bridge of his glasses. His cheeks had filled out; his lips were dark and crusty from all the cigarettes he undoubtedly still smoked; wisps of hair peeked from around his shirt collar. The sweetness was gone—there was a harshness about him. She saw him walking through a thick throng, pushing people off him with his elbows, the way he used to do for her.

"It's nice seeing you after all these years too." She spoke when it seemed like he had finished battling the crowd around him.

"When was the last time you were home? In Calcutta, I mean."

"A few years ago. Have you been back?"

"Same. I went over to help Ma make the move. She's living with us now."

"Congratulations, Neel. On everything."

"To you too. I've seen a picture of your daughter; you posted it awhile ago. She's beautiful."

"Thank you. Yes, she is."

"Does it suit you? Motherhood?"

"If you're asking if I'm any good at it, then I'm not sure, but I'm trying my best. Am I happy being a mother? Yes. She makes me very happy."

"That's all I wanted to hear, Mishti. I'm happy for you."

Neel stopped walking. He changed the angle of his phone, so she was able to see a little more of what was around him. She didn't recognize any of it, since she'd never been to Delhi. However, it looked more like home than Ireland did.

"I'm sorry. I don't know why I decided to call you tonight," she said. They were silent for some time, but it didn't make her uncomfortable. They'd spent enough time in silence together, with music in their ears, eating onion pakoras glazed with what may or may not have been tomato sauce. Neel had told her that a lot of places used pumpkins instead of tomatoes to make their ketchup. Pumpkins were cheaper.

"It doesn't matter, Mishti. I'm glad you called. I wasn't happy with the way we left things that day, you know? I shouldn't have walked away from you like that. I should have tried harder to convince you to come away with me."

"Then you wouldn't have your beautiful wife now." She was smiling at him. She also hoped he'd take this opportunity to tell her he hadn't forgotten her. That his wife would always be second best. Yeah, she was no better than Ciara.

"You're right. You have Maya, and I have Kiran. Everything happens for a reason. This is for the best."

Mishti wondered where Maya's soul would have gone if she'd had a child with Neel instead. He looked away from the screen again, and she knew what he was about to say.

"I wish you'd called at a different time. I need to get on the metro or I'll be late for work."

"Of course, go. I'm sorry for keeping you. I wasn't mindful of the time difference."

"Really, Mishti, I'm glad you called."

"Maybe I shouldn't have. This feels wrong. I think I've made a mistake."

"We can pretend it never happened."

"Can we?"

"I'm going to try, and so should you."

"It would be nice to take back the last few minutes. It felt right at the start, when you answered. Now it feels sad."

"You shouldn't feel sad, Mishti. This is what you wanted. You wanted to make your parents happy, and you have. Grandchild and all. This way, everyone gets what they wanted, except me."

"Neel, I'm sorry about that day, for not going with you to the train station."

"You're right, this doesn't feel good anymore. You shouldn't have called. Not after what you did to me."

"Neel, please."

"I hope your parents are happy with the son-in-law they chose for themselves."

He ended the call, and she lost her chance to say what she wanted to say.

She'd been wrong about everything.

Part Two

NOW

Chapter 33

September 29
9:06 P.M.

IT WAS HER OWN FAULT. MISHTI SHOULDN'T HAVE told her mother about her plan to run away with Neel. If she'd never known what it felt like to hold Maya in her arms or hear her voice, she wouldn't have known what she was missing. Now that she had Maya, she could never leave. Mishti wondered, though, if maybe she was at fault for the way her marriage to Parth had deteriorated over the years. Or, rather, the way it had never even begun.

She was in a marriage she had hoped against. She wasn't expecting to replicate what she had with Neel, her marriage to Parth was arranged by other people. However, she'd hoped for more than it turned out to be. It didn't look like the ones on TV, where the husband announced his arrival when he walked in after a day's work and gave the wife a peck on the cheek. They never cooked together, swirling wine in glasses, or had lighthearted food fights with pizza dough that turned into passionate lovemaking on the kitchen floor. He had never wanted her so much that he came into her shower and took her right up against the wet tiles.

She could picture Ciara and Gerry having sex in the shower, though. They probably did it all the time. All these women in the

village were probably having sex on their kitchen floors with their
husbands, or lovers, or both. And if there was no sex in the marriage, at least they had help with grocery shopping and taking the
children to the playground on the weekends, and had a drink together once the kids were asleep.

Her cousins in India had arranged marriages like her own. Mishti
wasn't naïve enough to think they were having rampant sex all over
the house while living in joint families with their in-laws. However,
their lives sounded full: loud, busy homes, with their husbands
rushing home from work to eat with the family, fathers going over
homework with the children, going on family holidays to Shimla
and Goa and Switzerland.

Her husband didn't fit in any of those pictures.

"WHY AREN'T YOU eating with me, Ma?" Maya asked. They were
sitting together at the kitchen table.

"I'm going to eat later, with Baba."

Maya screwed up her eyes in surprise. She scanned her mother's
face the way an adult would. In a lot of ways, Mishti saw wisdom in
her daughter far beyond her years.

"When will he be back?"

"In an hour or so, I would think."

"Will you read me a story in bed?"

"Of course. I'm still going to tuck you in, don't worry about it."

After Maya's dinner, Mishti helped her in the shower. They chatted about Maya's friends while she brushed her teeth and got dressed
for bed. Then Mishti read a story while Maya's hair dried. She was
turning the lights off in the room when Parth's car pulled in.

Mishti went downstairs to find him setting his laptop on the
kitchen table. His eyes were droopy and tired, and he didn't look up
when she came in.

"What's for dinner?" he asked. He'd seen the pots on the hob and
must have picked up on the familiar mix of spices wafting through
the house.

"It's a surprise. I'll be eating with you."

"Where's Maya?"

"She's in bed, asleep."

"So you didn't eat with her tonight?"

"No, I wanted to wait for you."

The rice was ready and left piping hot in the pressure cooker. She pulled the lid open and steam rose up, dampening her cheeks, making her smile.

Parth tapped the keyboard. He kept his eyes on the screen while she carried dishes to the table.

"Tell me what you think. Everything is hot now, so we should eat."

He finally dragged his eyes away from the screen and looked at the dishes.

"I know how much you like kosha mangsho. I'm not sure if I've got the right lamb cuts, but this is your mother's recipe. She taught me how to cook this a long time ago, when we were first married."

Parth stared at the heap of curry in the big porcelain bowl. The pieces of slow-cooked lamb were so soft they were melting in the gravy like butter. An identical bowl contained basmati rice, puffed up perfectly, fragrant and firm. A smaller wire basket was lined with some paper towels, with onion pakoras stacked high. Mishti had spent hours on the food. She wanted to sit with him and talk, like they sometimes did when they'd first moved into this house. Those were her only pleasant memories with him, when she still had hope.

The guilt of ringing Neel was nibbling away at her. All these years, she'd blamed Parth for not being Neel. This could be their chance to start over, and his mother always knew what he needed, so she'd followed her advice.

"Won't you sit down?" she urged him.

Parth remained standing, staring at the food awhile longer. "What's going on, Mishti?"

"What do you mean?"

"I mean, why are you doing this?"

"*Why?*"

"Yes, what do you want from me?" he asked. He stepped closer to the food, even brought his face down so he could give it a good big sniff. Then he stepped away and threw his arms out. "What has gotten into you lately? All these years, you never cooked anything like this, and now, all of a sudden, you want to go to India and you cook all this food."

"I just wanted to cook something special."

"Is that all, Mishti? Is that really all? You're not going to admit the truth? That this is an attempt at convincing me to go to India?"

"How can they be related?"

"You're trying to remind me of home. You've cooked one of Ma's recipes. One of my favorite dishes. How did you think it was going to make me feel?"

"Happy?"

"I am not going to give in to your tricks," he snarled.

"I am not trying to trick you. I just wanted us to share a nice Bengali meal together. We haven't done this in a long time."

"We haven't done this ever."

She could barely meet his eyes. All she saw in them was contempt.

"You could have cooked anything. What made you cook this particular recipe tonight? You're trying to torment me."

"I am not! Why are we fighting, Parth? I wanted you to enjoy this food. I wanted us to sit together and talk."

"Aha!" He snapped his fingers, the way Archimedes may have done in his bathtub. "You want to talk. I knew you did. What do you want to talk about? Let me guess. You want us spending thousands of euros on plane tickets to India."

"I don't want to go to India," she said. "I don't want you to buy tickets. We don't ever have to go back there. Not ever again."

Tears filled Mishti's eyes, choking her, and she dug her nails into her palms.

Parth shook his head, a gesture he had clearly perfected from his years in the teaching profession. She could picture him now, shaking his head at a young student who'd raised her hand and asked a silly question.

"I hate it there. I've always hated it. The noise, the pollution, the

heat, the small-minded gossips, the judgment. Someone's always listening. I feel claustrophobic in Calcutta. When I'm there, I want to
pull my hair out. To shout at Ma and Baba for the way they brag
about me." His voice shook, and that was a first.

She felt sorry for him. "You've never told me this, Parth. I didn't
know this is how you feel about Calcutta."

"It doesn't matter."

"You don't have to go back."

"You're not going there either. And you're sure as hell not taking
my daughter there." The moment had passed.

She opened her mouth to speak, but he interrupted her.

"Whatever you're trying to do here, Mishti, it's not going to work.
In fact, I don't think I'm hungry at all tonight. I'm going to take a
shower. You sit here and enjoy my mother's kosha mangsho in
peace."

She wanted to stop him, but there wasn't anything she could say.
She knew there was no chance he'd open up to her any further, not
when he was convinced he was being persecuted.

Mishti sat down at the table, waiting for his footsteps to fade as he
went upstairs. Then she went for his mobile almost immediately.
He'd left it next to the laptop. In his temper, he'd forgotten about it,
and now she shut the kitchen door.

The security code on his phone was the same as his debit-card
PIN, which she had access to, for household expenses. Mishti stood
with her back pressed to the door, scrolling quickly through his texts
first. There were conspicuously few of them in his inbox. He had to
have been purposely keeping his inbox empty. He didn't seem very
active on his socials. There were barely any messages in those in-
boxes either. The longer she spent looking through his messages,
the more frustrated she grew. She wanted to find something. Just
so she wouldn't feel as crazy as she did.

Then there were the emails. Her fingers shook as she tapped
the screen lightly. She was expecting to lock eyes with a name in the
inbox she didn't want to find and wanted to confirm at the same
time. In there too, everything appeared to be of a professional na-

ture. There was a chance that the subject lines had nothing to do with the content of the emails, but she didn't have time to check.

Finally, there were the pictures. She breathed in deeply, knowing this was where she was going to find what she was looking for. The answer to why she wasn't good enough for Parth and had never been. Strangely, like with a loose tooth, she was looking forward to the pain that was about to come when she yanked it out.

She didn't know what exactly it would be. Evidence of her husband's other life? All these years, the voice had been a faint buzzing at the back of her mind. Now it was bellowing right into both her ears. It sounded like Parth's laughter in the distance.

But all she found were photos of feet. A series of them. Only feet.

Pale white feet. Narrow and shapely, a woman's. In some of the photos, the nails were colored in deep scarlet or a sweet coral. In some, the nails were nude. They were always manicured and pristine. The photos were endless, or so they seemed to her. She scrolled through them slowly. With each flick of her forefinger on the screen, she grew more numb. It should have made her sick. Not only was her husband being unfaithful, but he had a kink she didn't understand. Her own toes curled in her woolly slippers.

It appeared to be the same pair of feet in every photograph. Parth's photo gallery contained no other images, not even of Maya, which was some relief. If photographs of their daughter interrupted the stream of feet, she was sure she would've broken the phone.

She couldn't tell if these were posed for, but they were certainly intimate. The owner of the feet angled them in a way that looked like she was modeling a pair of stilettos, arching them seductively. Sometimes they were laid flat on a carpeted floor, big toe crossed cutely over the long one.

She locked the screen with a jerk, then put the phone back beside the laptop. There was nothing else she needed to see.

Chapter 34

September 29
8:11 P.M.

CIARA HAD ACQUIRED THE PILLS FROM PARTH THREE days ago, but she hadn't had a chance to truly enjoy them yet. Finally, this afternoon, Gerry told her she was going to have the house to herself. He wanted to take the children to spend the night at his mother's place. Something about it being her birthday. Liz didn't want Ciara there, which he didn't say, but she guessed. The timing couldn't have been more perfect.

A night like this didn't come around too often.

"How are you going to get Finn to sleep?" It was the only question she asked Gerry. She was chewing her lip, trying to not laugh out loud. There was no way he and his mother were going to get Finn to go down easily, and she enjoyed the thought of that.

"Mam will manage. Same way she gets him to nap when you go to the city."

If she hadn't known any better, she would have taken offense at the hint of accusation in his voice. However, he was also simply stating a fact. She wasn't going to pick another fight with him, not when she had a night to herself to look forward to.

Ciara had the children ready when Gerry returned from work

that evening. Their bags were packed, and they were already changed for bed. As was slowly becoming the norm, Bella was delighted to see her father. She flung herself at him when he came through the front door. Finn, in the meantime, had sensed something was wrong. When Gerry peeled him off Ciara and took him to the car, he was screaming. She did not envy the drive Gerry would now have to endure.

There was a time when she would have even been jealous of him spending the night with the kids. Tonight was not that time.

"Bella!" She shouted her daughter's name just as she was about to jump into the back of the car. They'd been at loggerheads all day.

Bella turned to her, and there was something like scorn on her face. Like she couldn't get away fast enough. "We'll go get your ears pierced this weekend." She'd been begging for it all day, and it was the only thing Ciara could think of offering. Bella's face opened up and her eyes shone for a moment, and it reminded Ciara of the way she had looked as a baby. In the next moment, she shut herself off. Ciara could feel the rejection coming. "I don't want my ears pierced anymore."

Then they were gone. After she'd shut the door behind her, she wasn't so sure she wanted to be alone.

She kicked her runners off right there in the foyer. She didn't pick them up either. From the corner of her eye, she saw the way the sitting room was littered with toys. She walked past that door as well.

In the kitchen, there were dishes from their late lunch. The floor could have used some hoovering and a mop. All Ciara did was roll the blinds down over the windows. Then she picked out a bottle from the wine rack.

Her handbag was hanging off one of the chairs. In it were the sleeping pills she'd collected from the pharmacy.

When she held the bottle up against the light, she saw the tubular pills inside. It was a joyous sight. The idea of tranquility, of spinning out of control with her feet still stuck to the ground, of laughing out loud at a horror film she'd watched several times. A night of sweet release and clarity, and then things could return to normal.

She placed one pill on the tip of her tongue. Her taste buds puckered, protesting the bitterness. She washed it down with a large mouthful of wine. When Gerry returned the next day, she would propose the idea of going away on a holiday together. Maybe they could go to Greece with the children. She couldn't remember what made her think of Greece now, but it seemed like a good idea.

If she timed it well, the night wouldn't last very long. In just a few hours, she would be asleep on the sofa, dreaming about nothing. She wouldn't have to worry about Sean, or feel the ache of Mishti's cold shoulder.

It was exactly what she needed.

THE FIRST TIME she had ever taken pills, Ciara felt great. She was in college, living at the bedsit, trying to not disintegrate after Eoin Brophy's rejection and Teresa's betrayal. She took Mrs. Leary's prescription bottle from the bathroom, where she'd seen it in the medicine cabinet months before. They were sleeping pills—it clearly said so on the label. She couldn't think of one good reason to not take them. All she wanted was to go to sleep. To fall into a deep sleep and to forget about Eoin and Teresa. She was embarrassed by what she felt toward them: resentment and, above all else, malice.

The first day, she took two pills and returned to her room, sinking into the single bed. She'd already pulled the curtains. The room was dark, and she felt cocooned under the covers. She slipped and slid quickly into a kind of deep, unthinking sleep. She'd never experienced anything like it before. When she woke the next morning, everything was exactly the way she'd left it. Mrs. Leary hadn't noticed the missing pills. The sun shone a little brighter, but the edges of her vision were somewhat blurred. Eoin and his rejection seemed a bit further away than it had the previous day. Like it belonged in someone else's story. She wished she'd had these pills when her father left.

Ciara took two more pills from Mrs. Leary's bottle. This time she drank half a can of cider before the first pill. She slept even better that day, all through the afternoon and the evening. One more pill to finish off the cider, and it was enough to pull her down. Deep into a calm and soundless sleep for the night.

By the fourth day, the pills in the bottle were halved. When she reached for it again, she knew Mrs. Leary would notice. She couldn't risk getting caught, even though she'd considered never returning to college.

She had needed the sleep to see things clearly, and now the job was done. It was as though she had awoken on the other side with a more pristine view of the world. She would never forgive Eoin Brophy or Teresa, but forgetting them seemed possible. It was a gift the pills had granted her.

Since then she'd made sure to say what a GP needed to hear to provide her with a small but steady supply of pills. Over time, they didn't do the job as well. She was still chasing the rush of her first time, but it was fading. For the desired effect, she needed more, and she needed alcohol. She didn't know what Parth wanted in exchange for the prescription he'd reluctantly given her, but she was sure he'd think of something. They always did.

For a few days she'd considered sleeping with him, but she didn't want to anymore. The idea of Parth Guha had been attractive. However, like every other man in her life, he too had disappointed her. Besides, if the affair with Sean had taught her anything, it was to not shit where she cooked her children's meals.

After she took the pill, she went upstairs and changed into something more comfortable—a robe she'd brought home from the dry cleaner's that afternoon. It smelled like early-morning air. Then she returned to the kitchen and poured herself a big glass of wine. Before carrying it to the sitting room, she tucked a few more pills into the pocket of her robe and returned the bottle to her handbag.

She hardly even noticed the scattered toys anymore. She pushed some to the floor with her foot and sat on the sofa, spending a few minutes surfing the hundreds of channels on the TV. Her thoughts drifted to Mishti's visit from the afternoon. After days of silence and what had initially felt like a rejection, Mishti had shown up at her door again. Perhaps her video had prompted it. Gerry's early arrival from work had interrupted the opportunity to talk, but Ciara was hopeful again that Mishti might eventually move past this small bump in their road.

Ciara gave up scanning the channels and settled on an American chat show. Ciara didn't recognize the host, and she wasn't listening to a word being said, but she laughed when the audience laughed.

Her head felt a lot lighter, and she held the glass stem tighter. It was time for the second pill, and it tasted even more bitter this time. She placed it on the same spot on her tongue. It was as though the previous one had left her tongue's flesh scorched. Even the wine tasted hot when she took a swig. She needed the wine—it was going to smooth the passage to the other side.

The doorbell rang, and she cursed under her breath. She didn't intend on sharing this experience with anyone else. She popped a third pill before going to the door, just to keep the buzz going.

MANY YEARS AGO, she had waited for the doorbell to ring, but her father was gone three whole days, and he wasn't coming back.

Ciara hadn't seen her mother in a while either. She refused to leave her room, no matter how many stacks of buttered toast Ciara left outside her door.

"Mam, please, I'm sorry for what I said. I didn't mean it. I'm sorry. You have to let me in." She slammed her palms on the door repeatedly. Her mother hadn't made a peep in over a day, not since Ciara blamed her for him leaving. She was considering breaking the door down, using her father's hammer from the shed.

When she finally heard the shuffle of her mother's feet, she was relieved. The door opened. Her mother had a cigarette dangling from the corner of her dry mouth.

"I know you didn't mean it, pet, but it's true. I'm pathetic."

Ciara followed her in, looking around the bedroom in panic. She was expecting to find the room in disarray, but it wasn't. Not any more than usual.

She watched her mother get into bed, then she sat down close beside her.

"We can do this together. Can't we, Mam?"

"Do what?"

"This. I mean, we can get through this. We'll make it."

Her mother reached for her hand and patted it.

"*You* will get through this, Ciara, because you're a strong girl. You don't need him, but I do."

Ciara forced a lump down her dry throat. It seemed to chafe along the way. "He never loved you, Mam. He was with her the whole time you've been married. He said so himself. He told me he's always loved her."

Her mother smiled as she flicked ash from her cigarette onto the floor. "Yes, I know. He wouldn't have married me if it wasn't for you. He wanted you to have a daddy. A real family."

"I hate him, Mam. I hate him for what he's done to you."

Ciara brushed her wet cheeks with her wrists. Her mother was shaking her head.

"Don't hate him, pet. He gave you a good childhood. The best he knew how."

"And what about you? What did he give you?"

Her mother was silent, but it didn't seem like she was thinking of a response. She stared out the window. It was dark and musty in the bedroom but bright outside. The walls needed fresh paint; the carpet had damp patches and coffee stains, just like all her mother's clothes did. The foot of the bed was heaped with clothes and shoes she didn't wear anymore. There were toast crumbs everywhere.

"You'll do better, won't you, pet?"

Ciara nodded.

Her mother crushed the cigarette into a biscuit tin on the bed. "I know you will."

It was the last time she saw her mother smile. She slit her wrists that night. Of all the things, that was what her mother got right.

Chapter 35

September 29
10:37 P.M.

MISHTI SAT UP JUST MINUTES AFTER SHE HEARD THE front door shut. Her back had been turned to Parth when he got out of bed. She'd listened to the rustling of his clothes. He hadn't even bothered to stow his pajamas away somewhere, leaving them strewn on the bedroom floor.

She sat with her legs thrown over the side, trying to think rationally. It was what she did. Rational thinking had steered her life in this direction. She'd told her mother about Neel only because eloping was such an irrational idea.

She couldn't get those photographs out of her mind. When she tried to picture Ciara's face, the only thing she saw were those feet. She hadn't studied her friend's feet before, but now they seemed ugly to her. Too narrow, too pale, tiny square toenails painted in a garish shade of red.

Mishti remembered the desperation she'd seen in Sean's eyes that day he was hiding in Ciara's utility room. Ciara certainly had a way of turning men into strange creatures. *She* was the one who had turned her husband into this. Something unrecognizable.

That day, Ciara had begged Mishti to stay and talk, and she almost did. She had left because she couldn't accept this. This Ciara. But today she had taken Maya to their house again, on the pretext that she didn't want to deprive her daughter of her best friend, but really, she wanted to see Ciara too. Without her, Mishti was alone, not just lonely.

A rage rose inside her as she sat on the bed. It bordered on physical pain in the center of her chest. Her husband refused to even taste the elaborate meal she'd cooked for him, and then he'd slipped away in the middle of the night to take more photographs of Ciara's feet.

Mishti feared confrontation. If she caught them in the act, what would she say? Where would she even go looking for them? She hadn't heard his car backing out of their driveway, so he must have been meeting her somewhere close by.

Before leaving the house, she cracked open Maya's door and looked in. Her daughter was fast asleep. She squinted at the clock on the wall. She was going to give herself twenty minutes, and then she'd hurry back. That was as much time as she needed to see what she knew she had to see with her own eyes.

Over her pajamas, she threw a puffy quilted coat. She walked out of the house and looked down the road. All the lights were turned on in the Dunphy home. When she drew closer, she saw that Gerry's car was gone. The front door was open.

Her mind went there: to the thought of what her husband could be doing in the house. Right there, with Ciara's children asleep in the rooms upstairs.

After all these years, she was just finding out that she didn't know her friend at all.

Mishti charged into the house. She was expecting to find Parth's shoes neatly set by the door. It was what Ciara insisted on, a practice that was second nature to every Indian and had once made Mishti feel at home here.

His shoes weren't there, and neither was he. She sensed the emptiness of the house as soon as she stepped in—the distinct absence of body heat.

"Ciara?" she bellowed, like she was going into battle.

Mishti was so convinced that the house was empty that she nearly turned and walked out. Even when she heard a low groan, she thought it had to be the wind outside.

The second time, the groan was more like a cry. A chill ran down her back and she stepped farther into the foyer. The kitchen door was open, and it spilled out more bright light.

The third groan led her gaze to the spot at the bottom of the stairs.

Ciara was on the floor on her back. Her eyes were shut, and her body was contorting. It looked like she was trying to move but couldn't.

"What happened?" Mishti screeched. She ran in Ciara's direction and fell to her knees.

Some blood was smeared on the side of Ciara's forehead; Mishti saw it now that she was closer. Her arms looked strange, like they could never possibly be straight again.

"Can you open your eyes? Can you move?" Mishti asked, breathing hard, but too afraid to touch her.

There was a tremor in Ciara's eyelids, but they remained shut. She was struggling, and a part of Mishti was crumbling.

"Help. Me. Please. He tried to kill me."

Ciara's words were stunted and barely discernible. Mishti crouched over her, holding her face as close to Ciara's mouth as she could. It took a moment for the words to settle, but she knew what she had heard.

Ciara was severely injured. There was blood. Her limbs were twisted from a fall, and she was most likely concussed.

It was Parth. Mishti knew he'd come to see her. He had tried to kill her, and he had failed.

If she called for an ambulance and took her to the hospital, Ciara could recover. That would change Mishti's life forever. Their family would be torn apart. Maya would lose her father; she would turn into the daughter of an attempted killer. This would make the news; Mishti could see it now. Where would they go? Ciara's followers would make sure that they could never hide. How many years would Parth spend in prison?

Ciara was mumbling again, slowly trying to move her head.

"Ciara . . . Ciara, listen to me." Mishti spoke in whispers, kneeling over her so her curls brushed Ciara's damp face. "You told me you weren't going to do this to me. That you were going to stay away from him."

Her mouth opened wordlessly as Mishti gently turned Ciara's head.

"You are my best friend," Mishti continued.

Ciara took a deep breath, as though she was preparing to speak, but then it sounded like she was underwater, gargling. Mishti flinched and hissed repeatedly, as she would if she was pulling a hot tray out of the oven with no mitts on. She thought she was crying, but she couldn't feel any tears. She twisted Ciara's head farther around, doing it slowly because Ciara didn't have any fight left in her. She didn't need to go all the way—Ciara's breathing was already full of bloody bubbles. She was drowning, and her limbs jerked. Mishti recoiled, crawling away.

When she stood up and made to walk to the front door, her eyes drifted to the kitchen. On the floor, beside Ciara's handbag, was a note. Even in the kitchen, as she picked up the piece of paper, she could hear Ciara's frantic guttural gulps growing shallower. The note was a prescription in her husband's handwriting. Precise and patient, so very unlike him.

She took it with her when she left the house. She clutched it like a winning ticket. A ticket that was going to buy her a trip to India. Perhaps several trips to India. Never again would he touch her when she didn't want him to.

She was going to miss Ciara, which was why she couldn't wait and watch her end.

Chapter 36

September 29
10:13 P.M.

PARTH'S STOMACH RUMBLED SOON AFTER HE GOT IN bed. He regretted rejecting Mishti's offerings at dinner. He was thinking of his mother's kosha mangsho, and it made his mouth water.

Mishti had turned the lights off in their room sometime earlier. Then she'd silently slipped in beside him, but he was still awake. Her breathing had evened out soon after, and the house was quiet. He pushed the duvet off and changed out of his pajamas, the way he sometimes did after she fell asleep. He kept an eye on his wife the whole time, though she had never woken before.

Parth stopped by the kitchen first, checking the fridge for the kosha mangsho. He couldn't find a trace of it anywhere. Not even in the bins. Wherever Mishti had decided to dispose of it was far from the house.

Before he left, he texted Ilona again. She usually met him halfway, but it was still a thirty-minute drive for him. He didn't want to go all the way to the hotel if she wasn't going to turn up.

I need to see you tonight

Eight months ago, when he first started sleeping with her, Ilona seemed so full of promise and admiration. Like most of his other students, she was in awe of him. Her eyes followed him around the classroom; she hung on his every word. He wanted her for the shape of her perfect arse but even more for the sandals he'd first seen her in. Once he'd caught sight of those toes with red polish, and the perfectly dainty heel he wanted to suck on, he could think of little else.

In these past weeks, however, Ilona wasn't as quick to respond to his texts. She'd even stood him up a couple of times. Parth wondered if the fantasy had started to fade now, as he expected it to. The fantasy of banging a professor.

Parth's obsession with Ilona's feet was just a kink. Everybody had one. She was amused by it when she first found out, in a way none of his girlfriends in Calcutta ever had been. It was why he knew he could never go back, why he never dared tell Mishti. Ilona even let him put his cock between the arches of her feet, holding them up together like she was in prayer. These days, she just seemed bored of their games.

Parth stepped out of the house. Instead of waiting in his car as usual for Ilona's response, he decided to go for a walk.

Standing in the Dunphy driveway, he checked his phone again. Ilona hadn't even read his text yet. He stuffed it back in his pocket and stared up at the house. Gerry's car was missing, and the front door was ajar.

The presence of Ciara's Beetle told him she was home, and it seemed strange that she would leave the front door open at this time of the night. He'd been thinking about her lately, about what had transpired between them. Now that he thought about it, maybe she *did* owe him something. He had done her a favor, and she appeared grateful. The sexual tension between them was palpable.

"Ciara?" he called for her, pushing the door and stepping inside.

This house was nearly as quiet as his own, where his wife and daughter were asleep. There were no sounds of children around, the TV was off, and there were no voices in the kitchen. However, all the lights downstairs had been left on—the house was blazing bright.

He called for her again as he walked down the foyer. Through the kitchen door, he saw a nearly-empty bottle of wine. A plastic bottle of pills was beside it. Parth cursed.

He grabbed the pills and was about to storm out of the house, when he looked in the direction of the stairs, and that was when he saw Ciara's heaped figure on the floor.

She was on her side, curled, with her arm bent in a way no human arm should ever be. He couldn't see blood from where he was standing, but he couldn't see her breathing either.

"Shit. Fuck. Shit. Fuck."

Parth rarely cursed aloud, but there was nothing else to say.

He could, he *would,* lose his job if they found out about his bogus prescription. She wasn't a real patient. He'd lose his clients, his reputation, and his license to ever practice again. He would lose his residence permit in Ireland and would have to return to India in disgrace. It was out of the question.

He didn't want to go anywhere near Ciara. He'd already left too much biological evidence on the scene.

She'd had an accident. A bad fall down the stairs, as a result of the pills he'd given her. He wasn't the one who recommended mixing alcohol with the pills. Nonetheless, this was on him.

He could only hope she hadn't told anyone about it.

Before he left the house, he dribbled the remainder of the wine down the sink. It was silly, he knew. They would find alcohol in her system if they checked.

He looked at the bottle of pills still in his hand. Then he thrust it deep into his pocket and headed for the front door.

Chapter 37

September 29
9:18 P.M.

THIS WAS THE SECOND TIME THAT SEAN HAD TAKEN the liberty to present himself at Ciara's door unannounced. But these were dire circumstances.

"I noticed Gerry drive off with the kids. Thought this would be a good time for us to talk." He stood with his feet wide apart, his eyes sunken. He hadn't been sleeping very well.

"Oh, all right, just come in."

Surprised by Ciara's reaction, he stepped in quickly, not wanting her to change her mind.

He noticed a strangely giddy smile on her face as he followed her to the kitchen, and he hoped her mood had changed. That she would be more receptive to him now.

"Lauren knows. Lauren knows everything," he blurted.

"What?" She squinted her eyes.

His eyes were on her as she shuffled through her handbag, like she was desperately looking for something.

"What are you doing, Ciara? What are those?" He saw a bottle of pills in her hand, and then she reached for the wine on the counter.

"Nothing that concerns you."

"Are you mixing wine with those things?"

"Will you please just shut up?"

"Did you even hear what I said? Lauren knows everything. She knows it's you."

"Of course she bloody does. You were here that day when she turned up. Why else would she have come to talk to me?"

"She had her suspicions, but there is no doubt in her mind anymore. I don't think we're going to last, she and I. She hates you. I reckon she would have made her peace with it if it was anybody else."

"But now that she knows it's me, she's never going to get over it. Oh, you're the last person who should be looking at me like that. This can't be new to you." She shook the pill bottle, then put it down on the kitchen island.

"But I don't like the look of it, Ciara. You need to check yourself out in the mirror. Your eyes are like hot-air balloons."

That made her laugh, but Sean didn't feel like laughing. He watched as she poured more wine in a glass.

"You know, you're giving me one of those looks my father used to give me. And all this time I thought this was about Eoin Brophy," she continued, still chuckling.

"What? I don't know who that is."

"Anyway, what did you want to talk about, Sean?"

"Lauren is going to try and take the children away from me. I know she is." He wanted her to acknowledge his situation, at the very least.

Ciara suppressed a yawn.

"I'm sorry. Am I boring you?" He couldn't believe it. His life was falling apart around him, and this woman couldn't care less.

"A little. You're complaining like a child when you're a fully grown adult. You should take responsibility for your actions."

"I *am* taking responsibility for my actions, for fuck's sake, Ciara. I'm here, trying to make you see that this is our chance."

"You're here complaining to me because your girlfriend is on the verge of kicking you the fuck out of a house that doesn't belong to you."

When she saw the surprise on his face, she smiled.

"Oh, come on, Sean, everyone knows it's Lauren's house."

Sean followed her out of the kitchen, while she took sips from the glass. It was like she was gliding over the marble floor on a magic carpet.

"I don't expect anything from Lauren. I don't want her house. I don't *need* that house or her money. Not that she has much. I can go back to the city, open another shop, make music."

"Make music? When was the last time you wrote a song?"

He chose to ignore that. "I just want to make sure I can still see my kids. I'm not losing them over this, Ciara."

She turned the TV off in the sitting room. "And this is exactly the reason why you shouldn't have told Lauren about the affair. She didn't suspect us before you went off on your honesty trip. You wouldn't be in this position if you had kept your mouth shut."

"And if you kept your legs together," he said. He was tapping his knuckles on the mantelpiece.

"Excuse me? What did you just say?"

"You heard what I said, Ciara. If you didn't want to take responsibility for your actions, you shouldn't have started this with me."

"I'm not the one on the verge of losing my family."

"But what if you were?"

"What are you trying to say, Sean? Are you threatening me? What are you going to do? Tell Gerry? Why don't you print it in the papers, so the whole country finds out? The thing is, Sean, none of it will affect me. Gerry will not leave me. He doesn't know how to have a relationship with those kids without me. He needs me to run his house. He needs me to spend his money and make his life look good. I have thousands of people on my side. Literally thousands."

Sean turned his face away. He couldn't look at her. This wasn't the woman he hoped she was. Hoped against hope, despite all the warning signs. "So I'm supposed to walk away from everything good in my life, while you continue to be with your family? Live in this house and have this life?"

"Yes, I suppose so. Or maybe Lauren will take you back. By the sounds of it, she's looked past it before."

"She asked me to marry her," he confessed.

"You're joking."

"I'm not. She asked me to marry her, and that is when I told her about the affair. I couldn't accept it. I couldn't have married her while being disloyal to her. If she asks again, I'll accept in a heartbeat. She knows the truth. I'll do anything to keep my family together."

"I do hope you're not expecting me to throw a jealous fit. I couldn't care less what you do with her. You *should* marry her, if she'll have you."

Ciara drank some more, then sank down on the sofa, teetering on its edge, smiling.

"For fuck's sake, Ciara, this is funny to you?"

She covered her mouth with the back of her hand.

"Or is it those bleeding pills you've been taking?"

She had to use her arms as levers to propel off the sofa. "Gerry is going to be home soon, so I suggest you leave. You wouldn't want him finding you here."

"I don't care what Gerry thinks. Does anyone care what he thinks? I care about my family, and they're going to be taken away from me. Because of you!"

She pushed past him, and he grabbed her hand loosely. She was able to yank it away from him. "This is the last time I'm letting you in my house, Sean. We won't be seeing much of each other after this."

"So this is it, eh?"

"We had fun, didn't we? But right now I'm going upstairs to bed. I was going to have an early night in, and you're spoiling it. You know I don't get much time away from the kids."

She was in the foyer again, and Sean was right there behind her. When she was standing at the bottom of the stairs, he followed her there too. He couldn't make himself leave yet.

"Ciara, you can't leave me hanging like this. Tell me you will be here when I need you."

She had to clutch the banister. It looked like she was finding it hard to take measured steps, missing the mark every time she tried. She looked annoyed when she saw Sean over her shoulder.

"Will you show yourself out? I really need to sleep."

As she dragged herself up the steps slowly, she didn't see him following her.

HE DID THIS, not fully aware of his own actions. It felt to Sean like he'd been taking those pills too. He watched Ciara wobbling, clinging to the banister. She half-crawled up the steps, mumbling under her breath about needing to be in bed.

"I can't leave you in this state," he said.

She turned to him, startled. They were nearing the landing.

"You're still here! I thought I told you to go."

"Ciara, I just said, I'm not leaving you like this."

"If you think I'm going to let you come into my bedroom, you're mistaken. You can forget about tucking me in or anything like that." She was trying to sound firm, but the silly smile on her face unsettled him. This wasn't only the wine, he was certain.

"I'm trying to make sure you're safe in your room for the night," he replied.

She managed to crawl up the last few steps. Then she stood, leaning against the wall with her hips thrust out invitingly. The thought did cross his mind. If he were to strip her down right now, she wouldn't stop him. One last fuck before it all ended. It was the least she could do for him, after everything she'd done to him already.

Things couldn't get any worse than they already were.

Ciara stood in a silky robe. It was a deep maroon, reminding him of Christmas tablecloths. She had no makeup on, and her hair was tied in the usual ponytail. He couldn't tell if she was clothed under-neath it. All he could see were long, pale legs and smooth buttery skin.

He took a few steps toward her and must have startled her, be-cause she straightened quickly. She was blinking like she was trying to wake herself up.

"What are you doing?" she snarled.

"Nothing. I'm not doing anything." He held his hands up. "I just want to make sure you're okay, Ciara. I'm genuinely worried about you. You don't look very well."

She rolled her eyes. "Oh, will you shut up about it already? I got the pills from a doctor. A real medical professional who knows what he's doing. Do you think he would've written me a prescription if he didn't think I was capable of handling it?"

"You're seeing a therapist? I didn't know about this. Shit. Ciara, why didn't you say something?" He took a few more steps, but slower this time. He was trying not to frighten her.

His eyes traveled to where the dressing gown loosened around her cleavage. Her breasts rose and fell. It wouldn't be very different from how it was usually between them, he told himself. If he touched her like that, she'd remember the way he made her feel.

"No, I'm not seeing a therapist, not really. Parth Guha gave me the pills."

He stopped in his tracks. When their eyes met, she stared chal-lengingly back at him. She was trying to hurt him, to make him jeal-ous, he could tell from the way she bit down on her lip like she was enjoying herself.

He didn't want her to, but she stepped away. She was walking backward, in the direction of an open door. It had to be the master bedroom.

"So you see? It's all good. It's all fine. I'm going to sleep now. To-morrow I'll see things more clearly."

"You've been seeing Parth Guha?"

"He's my closest friend's husband. We occasionally have meals to-gether as a family. You don't understand what it's like to have friends."

"You've been sleeping with him?"

"Oh, give it up, Sean."

"It's a question, Ciara. Just fucking answer it. Have you been sleeping with him?"

"And what if I have? What will you do about it? Just leave me alone, Sean. Will you just get out of my house?"

She spun around and made for the bedroom door, but he grabbed her by her arms and yanked her backward, unaware of his own strength. When she shrieked, he realized how forceful his grip was. He released her. Ciara was already falling backward, tripping on something on the carpet. It was a dress, too small for even a child. It could only have belonged to a doll.

Sean didn't want to touch her again. He didn't even help steady her, for fear that she'd flinch or cry for help. She pulled herself together by reaching for the banister. Her eyes were dark, and her eyelids were heavy.

"That was a brilliant performance, Sean. It was exactly what I needed. I'm going to make sure everyone sees these bruises you've left on my arms. Lauren is going to find out what you came here and did to me. You think she'll ever let you near the children again? You shouldn't have touched me."

She'd been fighting him so long, and he suddenly felt exhausted. This wasn't going to work. At first he'd been flattered by Ciara's interest in him. Back in those bookshop years, he had all their attention, and he basked in it equally. The classic beauties, the hippies, the punks, the girls next door. He loved all women. Having the children had made him starkly aware of his own mortality, and his sagging neck wasn't helping. When Ciara set her sights on him, it felt like his last chance. But it was a mistake. She made him weak. Messed with his head. He now found himself in a position where he was losing his family. Things had never been so bad before.

She couldn't have looked any more frightening if she had fangs in her mouth or long curling nails winding across the floor. Her sparkling hair had come undone from her ponytail, and it fell across her face. Her hand was like a claw, trying to grip the banister. Her back was to the steep fall down the stairs. All she needed was one step in the wrong direction.

"That shut you up, didn't it?" she hissed.

He couldn't let Lauren hear this. Not if Ciara was going to tell the story in her own words, show the bruises.

If he had a choice, he wouldn't have picked her. She picked him.

Lauren was right. Of all the women in town, did he have to fall for Ciara Dunphy? It disgusted him that he still wanted her, even when she looked like this.

He took a few steps toward her, like a ram would: with his head tilted down, his horns showing. It was all he needed to do; he didn't even have to touch her. Ciara jerked backward and fell.

Chapter 38

September 29
11:15 P.M.

GERRY WATCHED HIS MOTHER WALKING AROUND THE sitting room. Finn was pressed to her chest. He'd only just stopped bawling and had finally fallen asleep on her shoulder. Liz was too anxious to sit down, worried it would wake him again.

"I'm sorry, Mam. I know this is not how you would have liked to spend your birthday," Gerry said.

Liz eyed him in the mirror above the mantel, simultaneously patting Finn's bottom. She didn't want to interrupt the rhythm that had finally put him to sleep.

"It's not that, Ger. You know I don't care about marking my birthday. It just pains me to see Finn in such a state. He needs his mammy. I don't know if this was such a good idea, bringing them over here for the night."

"It'll be hard the first couple of nights, and then he'll get used to it. Won't he?" He was hopeful. If things were going to change, everyone needed to be prepared, especially the children. He was going to file for divorce. Now that he knew about Sean, he couldn't allow Ciara to raise his children.

He had to make sure he got custody, but he knew she would fight him on it.

"Maybe you should wait until he's a little older. He's not ready to be away from her yet," Liz said. She continued walking in despondent circles, looking worried, even though she was the one complaining to him every time Ciara dropped the kids off at hers.

Bella was already asleep in the spare room upstairs. She wasn't such a concern for either of them. Gerry needed confirmation that Finn would get there eventually. That he would learn to not need Ciara so much.

"You should talk to her," Liz continued. "You ought to remind her that her place is with the children, while they're still little. You can wait a few years, can't you, Ger? You've dealt with her this long."

Gerry couldn't wait. He was ready now. The children would have to catch up.

"I need to make a few phone calls for work. I'll do it in the car," he said, standing up quickly.

"At this time of night?"

"I'll be back soon, Mam."

He left the house in a hurry. As soon as he got in his car, he drove off.

GERRY SAT WITH a cold styrofoam box of curry chips on his lap. The seat in his Audi reclined far back, and he had enough leg space to stretch out and fall asleep if he wanted to. He didn't think he was going to get much sleep tonight, though.

His phone was fixed to its holder on the dashboard. He'd been staring at the screen, barely eating. There were hidden cameras in the kitchen, the bedroom, the master bathroom, the foyer, and the top landing of the stairs. The cameras had caught everything. He watched the recordings, with his mouth open and fingers splayed on his knee. He was glad that he'd taken care to hide the cameras well. It would give him time to take them down before the Guards found them.

He used to enjoy watching Ciara when he wasn't at home. Months ago, he had installed the cameras on a day when she was out of the house. He told himself he was doing it so he could see the children when he was at work, but he only ever watched the recordings to stare at his wife.

Ciara in her leggings, bent over the laundry basket in the bedroom. Ciara trying on new clothes, rearranging outfits in her secret wardrobe. Ciara lifting her arms up in front of the bathroom mirror to fix her ponytail. Her belly button showing on a flat stomach. Her skin-care routine was arduous, and sometimes she recorded it for Instagram. While her followers watched her through her screen, he watched her through his, at an angle she wouldn't have found flattering. He couldn't get enough of it.

Even when he suspected she was sleeping with someone else, he couldn't stop.

She never brought her lover home. He went through hours of footage and microphone recordings, but she never spoke to or about her secret lover inside the house.

It could have been any of the men around the village. A stranger from the city. A childhood friend.

He had considered following her on the days she went to the city, but he decided against that too. He didn't want to know. His best guess was Parth Guha. He never would have guessed Sean O'Grady. Old. Loser. A scumbag.

He had heard it clear as day, coming out of Lauren's mouth. After that, he went back and found the footage of Sean in his house, hiding in the utility room while Lauren made a sudden appearance. Mishti was in on it too. Since then, everything had changed for Gerry. They had made a fool of him.

He wished he had never fallen in love with Ciara. That he didn't enjoy watching her. If it wasn't for how much Finn needed a mother, he might have even ended her himself.

Now she was lying at the bottom of the stairs in an assemblage of broken limbs and blood. His initial shock at what he was watching was soon replaced by a kind of relief. He searched for grief, and all he found was the knowledge that he'd miss the Ciara he first met. The sexy blonde with a wide smile, who used to drum her manicured fingernails on his chest when he'd lie on top of her, nose-to-nose. They used to lie like that all the time, even just to talk. She said she liked the weight of him on her heart. He'd been missing that Ciara for many years already.

This was simpler than fighting over the children in court. None of the three people who visited the house had killed her, not individually at least. She had done it to herself. She'd just needed some help along the way.

Gerry watched Mishti running out of the foyer, with the prescription in her hand. He had a pretty fair idea who had written that note, why it was so precious to her. He wanted Mishti to use it, to make Parth's life uncomfortable.

When she'd stepped out of the door, he switched to the cameras outside. There was one frame where he got a good look at Mishti's face. In her eyes, he saw guilt. She was forever going to carry the burden of Ciara's death on her shoulders. If he'd zoomed in on the faces of Sean and Parth, he would have seen the same look on their faces. He didn't bother. The Guards would call it an unfortunate accident. When the toxicology report showed the alcohol and pills in her system, they might even deem it a suicide. He was going to get a call soon. He needed to think of the right way to break it to the children.

He didn't want to look anymore; he was going to let it go. Let her go.

He deleted each recording. One by one. Then he was going to go home and remove the cameras.

Chapter 39

September 29
10:42 P.M.

LAUREN WAS ASLEEP WHEN SHE FELT THE BED SAG beside her. She woke up when Sean shifted and moved, curling up within himself like a little fetus. She felt the icy coldness of his flesh.

She had spent the day without him, seeking him out in the spaces he usually occupied. He wasn't on the sofa. His dog-eared books were scattered around the house. There were mugs of stale coffee underneath his side of the bed and in the bathroom. In the garden, she found his reading glasses on the grass. The pans he used for omelets and pancakes were clean, stowed away in the press. She never thought she'd miss seeing them lying unwashed in the sink. The children had been asking for him too. She told them he was helping a friend move.

Now she wanted to wrap herself around him. She wanted to allow him to see her cry. They were going to lose everything they'd built together. He had done this to them.

"Lauren, are you awake?"

She was relieved. "I missed you today," she said, turning over toward him. She couldn't be anything other than honest with him.

"I missed you too. Lauren, I'm sorry. I'm sorry for everything."

She sat up, fluffing the pillow behind her. Sean didn't move. She noticed how he had his arms wedged between his legs, like he was desperate for his own warmth.

"What are you sorry for, Sean? You don't seem to think you've done anything wrong."

"I don't want to break up our family. I don't want to lose the kids, or you. This is my home. I don't want to be anywhere else."

"Why did you do it? Why did you pick her?"

"I don't know. She came after me. What the hell was I supposed to do? I'm weak."

"Did you think you really had something with her? That it was going somewhere?"

He remained silent, pressing his eyes tightly closed. In the dark, he resembled a little child sobbing. She wanted to throw her arms around him. They could have sobbed together. "No other woman has ever compared to you, Lauren."

"But you keep trying with others."

He turned, stuffing his face into the pillow. He hugged the bed like it was a warm body. "What's wrong with me? I don't deserve to be forgiven, not after what I've done." He opened his eyes, they were filled with tears.

"You went to see her tonight, didn't you?" She had her arms crossed over her chest. She didn't care that her nails were digging into her flesh. "Answer me, Sean. I need you to be honest with me."

"Yes, I went to her house. I wanted to tell her it's over."

"And is it? What did she say?"

"Nothing. Well, whatever she said amounted to nothing. Yes, it's over."

"I want to look at your fucking face," she said.

Sean made a big show of gathering himself and sitting up. He pulled the pillow along with him, using it as a protective shield over his stomach. She still couldn't see his face in the dark. At least he appeared more like an adult now.

"I don't want you to look at her ever again. I will kill her if you do. I'll kill you."

He rubbed a hand over his face, letting the pillow slip away from him. "Shit. Okay, I'm never going to see her again, Lauren. You have my word. I just want to make it work between us. Can we do that? I'm begging you. This will never happen again."

The only thought in her head was how she couldn't fathom being a single mother to her children. How intensely they would miss their father if they couldn't wake up to him every day. He had missed most of Freya's birth, but he was the only person who had shared in the births of Harry and Willow. He was there for most of their nappy changes. He got out of bed every night the children couldn't sleep. He was a good father, the best he could be, better than hers had been. Perhaps, in a year, she would have rid herself of how he'd betrayed her. The same way she had been able to forget about Roseanne and all the other women who came before and since. She had thought the children had changed him. Now she knew that their births had only put a temporary pause in the nature of their relationship.

Lauren hoped it was Ciara who was going to end the cycle. "Yes, I think we can make it work. I want to."

"Will you marry me?" he asked.

"I don't know. Ask me in a year."

He reached for Lauren, and she met him halfway. She held herself away from him, only allowing him to half-hug her. She wasn't prepared to kiss him just yet. Not while he still smelled of Ciara's home.

For the first time, it was Sean being left to the mercy of a lover's whim. This time it was Lauren who had to do the forgiving. There were going to be no more blackouts, no short circuits in her memory. She was going to remember everything.

September 30

THIS MORNING, EVERYTHING HAD RETURNED TO normal. Lauren woke up feeling grateful that they had made up. The children were happy to see their father. Lauren was glad she wasn't going to have to do this alone. She even allowed herself a cigarette to celebrate.

No matter how much she tried to let go and move on, though, she knew it would be a hard task to forget Ciara. The woman was right there, living in that mansion next door. Just as always, Lauren's eyes were drawn in that direction while she smoked in her garden.

She needed to go see her. She wanted Ciara to be the first person she told that she was going to sell her gran's house. She didn't want to live here anymore.

The Dunphy house looked empty as she walked up the driveway. Ciara had to be home—her car was parked right there. She checked on Willow, asleep on her back, and she breathed in deeply in preparation for what she was going to say. She imagined Ciara finally breaking into a smile, congratulating her on her brilliant idea. They wouldn't have to be neighbors any longer.

Lauren promised herself this was going to be the last time. Her fascination with this house was gone. There was nothing to see here anymore, nothing she wanted. Sean was done too.

This was going to be the last time she ever set foot in the Dunphy house, and then she was going to leave this village.

Acknowledgments

I couldn't have written this book without the early encouragement from my grandfather, *dadun,* who recognized the storyteller in me as a child. He would have been immeasurably proud to have this book in his hands.

I am forever indebted to my agent, Marianne Gunn O'Connor, the original champion of this book. What a woman to have in my corner!

I am especially grateful to my editors Jenny Chen, Harriet Bourton, and Isabel Wall for their vision and meticulous attention. To Katy Loftus and Andra Miller, for seeing potential in this manuscript, and in me. To Michelle Kroes and Jiah Shin at CAA, who are taking this story beyond these pages. To the wonderful people who have helped make this seemingly daunting task of publishing a breeze: Victoria Moynes, Mae Martinez, and the rest of the teams at Viking and Ballantine. You have all been a delight to work with. To Vicki Satlow and the early readers of the manuscript, for rallying me on.

I appreciate all those who read and encouraged my work during my time at UCD: James Ryan, Éilís Ní Dhuibhne, Paul Perry, Anne Enright, Lia Mills, Anne Griffin, Phil Kearney-Byrne, Colm MacDiarmada, Eamon McGuinness, and others.

I am thankful to my parents, Gautam and Debadrita Bose, for their unconditional love through my several unconventional life decisions. To my mother-in-law, Helen O'Shea, for being a good friend and our support system. To my friends, most especially, Marie Dunne, who kept me grounded when I felt untethered.

I am most grateful to my daughter, Ellora Bose O'Shea, my mainstay, who in three short years has energized, inspired, and persuaded me to write in a way nothing has before.

Finally, Richard O'Shea, my husband. His blind faith in me, his love and gentle presence, has made room for this book to exist in our lives.

About the Author

Disha Bose received a master's in creative writing at University College Dublin, where she was mentored by Booker Prize winner Anne Enright. She has been shortlisted for the DNA Short Story Prize, and her poetry and short stories have appeared in *The Incubator Journal, The Galway Review, Cultured Vultures,* and *HeadStuff.* Her travel pieces have appeared in *The Economic Times of India* and *Coldnoon.* Bose was born and raised in India and now lives in Ireland with her husband and their daughter.

dishabose.com
Instagram: @dishabossy
Twitter: @dishabossy

About the Type

This book was set in Minion, a 1990 Adobe Originals typeface by Robert Slimbach. Minion was inspired by classical, old-style type-faces of the late Renaissance, a period of elegant and beautiful type designs. Created primarily for text setting, Minion combines the aesthetic and functional qualities that make text type highly read-able with the versatility of digital technology.

Dirty laundry
MCN FIC Bose   **31659061807901**

Bose, Disha.

DUE DATE   MCN   03/23   27.00

BBR